CW00864791

Somewhere in Ireland

Avenfore

Copyright © 2021 Santiago Ros
Cover illustration © Magdalena Almero Nocea
This is a work of fiction. Any resemblance to actual events or persons, living or dead, is entirely coincidental.
ISBN 13–978-84-09-28622-5
www.avenfore.com

THE SECRET OF AVENFORE

WILLIAM THE KINGFISHER

SANTIAGO ROS

CHAPTER 1

Return to Avenfore

July, 1959

I

A SHRIEK FROM THE TRAIN WAITING ON Platform Three set the butterflies in William Howbbler's stomach fluttering again. 'Are you all right, Will?'

His mother's voice broke his reverie. Prudence Howbbler stood a short distance away with his younger sister, Kristyn, waiting to say their goodbyes. William thought how cool and elegant his mother looked on this hot July day.

'I'm fine, thanks, Mum,' he said smiling at her. Although inside, he knew he really wasn't. At the very least, it was a day of mixed emotions. He would be parted from his family for the first time in his life. But today was also the day he would finally return to Avenfore – the place he'd been longing to go back to for the past ten years – the place that he and his family had mysteriously left when he was four years old.

Another roar erupted from the engine beside them and Kristyn's tiny bottom lip began to tremble. William bent down to give her a goodbye hug.

'Don't be sad, Krissie. And don't worry about me. I'll be fine. You and Mum and Dad'll have a wonderful time in Marburg and I'll be safe in Avenfore.'

'But why can't you come to Germany with us, William?' Kristyn's blue eyes were tearful. 'I don't want you to be all alone without us.'

William smiled. 'I won't be alone, Krissie. I'll have Aunt Edna, Uncle Walter and cousin Elsie to look after me.'

'But I don't want you to live in Avenfore,' Kristyn wailed. 'Why can't you come with us?'

'Hush now, sweetheart, don't upset yourself.' Prudence Howbbler bent to comfort her daughter. 'William will be starting at his new school in St Elm's in September and Daddy and I thought all the travelling to Germany and then back again for the school term would be too unsettling for him. Which is why we asked Aunt Edna and Uncle Walter if William could spend the summer in Avenfore with them.'

His mother was smiling, but William could see the sadness in her large hazel eyes. So like his own, he knew. He was sure Prudence would have preferred to spend the summer with both her children together, but she and Kristyn would be leaving for Germany in a few days' time. There was so much to organise before his father, Arnold Howbbler, started in his new job as Professor of Celtic Studies at the University of Marburg – including a new house to furnish and a new school for Kristyn.

'Mum's right, Krissie,' William said. 'I'll be safe as houses with Aunt Edna and Uncle Walter and, anyhow, we'll all be together again at Christmas.'

Kristyn sniffed loudly, but she looked happier. 'Promise?' she asked, wiping her eyes with her sleeve.

'I promise. And what's more, I'll have a really great Christmas present for you.'

Kristyn threw her arms around William's neck and kissed him. 'Me too,' she cried. 'Mine'll be from Germany and it'll be the bestest Christmas present ever!'

'I'm sure it will, Krissie-wissie,' he said, giving the little girl another hug.

His mother was staring at the large station clock suspended above the platform. 'It's nearly time, Will,' she murmured, 'you should say goodbye to your father.'

William looked over to where Arnold Howbbler was chatting with his uncle, Walter Harckwell, a short, stout, man with a mop of unruly white hair, who was carrying a rather large cuckoo clock haphazardly wrapped in brown paper under his arm. Walter looked around as the stationmaster blew sharply on his whistle urging passengers to board the train.

'Goodness me,' he said, hurrying over to William and Prudence. 'We'd better hurry. Don't want the train to leave without us. I'd never hear the end of it from Edna. Now, where's that porter chappie gone with all our luggage, Pru?' The cuckoo clock bounced up and down precariously in his arms as he spoke and Kristyn giggled as the mechanical cuckoo suddenly popped out of its miniature house with a loud 'Cuckoo'.

William's mother put a hand on Uncle Walter's arm, knowing full well that her brother-in-law always got himself into a tizz if he thought there was even the slightest chance of them being late for anything.

'Come along, Walt,' she said with a smile. 'The porter's over there. Kristyn and I will help you make sure everything gets on the train on time.'

As Prudence led Walter and Kristyn away towards their luggage, Arnold drew William to one side. In contrast to his uncle, William's father was tall and broad-shouldered with short wavy brown hair just like his son's.

'I want you to do something for me when you get to Avenfore, William.'

'Yes, of course, Dad. What is it?'

Arnold didn't answer and, for a brief moment, William thought he saw an anxious look in his father's eyes. It surprised him: his father was a quiet man, but William had never thought of him as anything but brave and confident. He hoped Arnold wasn't worrying unnecessarily about his going to school. How could he? William was going to St Elm's Boys' School, one of the most prestigious schools in the country, situated in Arnold's own home town of Avenfore. Why Arnold himself had gone there: he had been Head Boy in his time and had even taught at St Elm's for a few years when William was a child. And yet William could see concern etched into his father's face.

His father pulled a small sealed envelope out of his pocket and quietly slipped it to William.

'I need you to give this letter to Abelard Greewoof, the Latin master at St Elm's, William. Can you do that for me?'

'Of course, I will, Dad. But isn't Mr Greewoof one of your best friends in Avenfore? Couldn't you just post it to him?'

Arnold Howbbler shook his head vehemently.

'No, no, William, it's very important that you deliver the letter in person.'

To William's amazement, Arnold looked about warily, as if he was checking to see if anyone was watching them. William had never seen his father behave like this: it was all very strange.

Content that they were not being watched, Arnold continued. 'You must give the letter to Abelard as soon as you can. And you must deliver it yourself. Don't give it to anyone else or tell anyone else about it. Promise me you will do this?'

William nodded solemnly.

'Yes, Dad, I promise.'

A look of relief crossed Arnold Howbbler's face and he smiled at William.

'Thank you, Will, I appreciate it. Now, hide the letter away safely in your jacket pocket and make sure no one sees it.'

An impatient hiss emanated from the railway engine and the stationmaster blew a final-boarding whistle. Uncle Walter, now safely ensconced on the train, yelled to William from the carriage window as the train began to gear up to leave the station.

'Will! Come on! You'll miss the train! Hurry up, or you'll be left behind!'

William sprinted along the platform, stopping only to give his mother and Kristyn a last goodbye hug, before leaping onto the train to join his uncle at their carriage window.

'Thank you for coming to fetch him, Walter,' Arnold shouted as the train began its slow chug along the station platform.

'My pleasure, Arnold,' Walter replied, 'I always enjoy a trip to Dublin and I managed to get this!' He patted the badly wrapped cuckoo clock which he was still clutching under his arm.

'I know it will be like home from home with your uncle and aunt, and your cousin Elsie, but don't forget to write to us often, sweetheart,' Prudence called to William.

'Telephone us, if there's an emergency, Will,' Arnold added, 'but don't forget to tell the operator to reverse the charges.'

'I will, Mum, Dad, don't worry,' William replied over the shriek of the engine's whistle as it built up momentum and began to pull its way slowly along the platform.

Then he waved from the carriage window until the train had left the station and his family were no more than tiny dots on the distant horizon.

II

William continued to stare out of the window as the train chugged its way from Dublin city. Uncle Walter sat opposite him. Lulled by the warmth of the early evening sunlight streaming through the carriage window and the chug-chug of the train, he soon dozed off, his arms wrapped around the clock and his head lolling gently over it as though he was whispering some pleasant secret to it.

The grey of the city with its rows of houses and shops had been replaced by the lush, green landscapes of the countryside and the evening sun was fading before William looked up from his book and glanced at his wristwatch. Two hours had passed. They should be at their destination soon.

The sight of the watch brought a grin to William's face. It was brand new – a bang up-to-date 1959 model – his father had bought it for him for his fourteenth birthday only a few days previously. Even Uncle Walter, who knew all about clocks, was impressed.

William remembered the pride and affection in his father's face when he gave him the watch, but also a spark of concern: the same concern he had seen earlier in the railway station when Arnold had given him the letter for Mr Greewoof.

The letter! William patted his jacket to be sure. The letter was still there. He wondered again about it, but his attention was drawn by a peculiar sight outside the carriage window as the train slowed for its approach to the railway station. A strange figure in a helmet and dark glasses riding an old-fashioned motorcycle with a sidecar was hurtling along the country road which ran parallel to the railway track. The figure was comical and frightening at the same time and William was not certain if he should laugh or be somewhat anxious. But he had no time to think further about it as the train entered the station and screeched to a halt beside the platform.

William hastily shoved his book back into his satchel. Uncle Walter was still snoozing, so he tapped him gently on the shoulder.

His uncle awoke with a start. 'Eh… What? Are we there?' he burst out as he adjusted his tie and the collar of his jacket, 'I'd almost dropped off, you know.' Then looking out of the window, he exclaimed, 'By gum! We're in Drunfarnam!'

Uncle Walter took out a comb and started to tidy his hair. William watched him, fighting back a laugh.

'Elsie and Edna are meeting us at the station,' Uncle Walter continued, 'they're going to be really pleased to see you again. They've been making plans all week.'

Sure enough, Aunt Edna and Elsie were waiting for them when William and Uncle Walter stepped off the train. Aunt Edna hadn't changed a bit. A few years younger, shorter and plumper than her brother, Arnold, she was as cheerful and welcoming as William remembered. His cousin, Elsie, on the other hand, he hardly recognised. A few months older than William, she looked all grown-up, with her luxurious light-brown hair cut in a fashionable bob, large, bright eyes, and a mischievous grin. She was also as tall as him, and William was tall for his age.

'My, Will, but you've grown since we last saw you. You're more and more like your father,' Aunt Edna murmured as she hugged him.

'It's great to see you, Will,' Elsie said, and she too gave him a hug.

It was windy outside the station and Aunt Edna kept a hand on her hat as she led them across the street to where she had parked their van. As they went, William noticed a figure coming out of the station door behind them. It was the motorcyclist he had seen from the train. The man was wearing a grey knee-length gabardine, his old-fashioned motorcycle helmet and dark glasses. He lingered at the front of the railway station and, for some odd reason, William couldn't help feeling that he was watching them furtively from the other side of the street. Then he laughed to himself. How silly of him! His father's strange caution must be rubbing off on him – he was seeing shadows around every corner.

Aunt Edna had stopped in front of a shiny dark-green Morris Minor van with a smart, cream-coloured convertible canvas roof at the back and was rummaging in her bag for the keys. 'Ah, here they are,' she exclaimed, as Elsie and William climbed into the back of the van, and Uncle Walter plonked himself in the front passenger seat, his arms protectively around the cuckoo clock on his lap.

The sun was dropping below the horizon as they left Drunfarnam. By the time they arrived in Avenfore, night had fallen, and the streets were deserted. William took the chance to peek out of the window in the canvas for his first glimpse of Avenfore in so many years. As he did so, he noticed a motorcycle and sidecar with no lights, half-hidden in the dark, stopped by the side of the road on the way into the village. *Strange*, William thought, it looks just like one I saw back in Drunfarnam. Perhaps the motorcyclist lives here in Avenfore? But then he saw the signpost for Fern Lane up ahead and the excitement of seeing his aunt's house and his old home once again banished all thoughts of strangers and motorcycles from his mind.

III

Fern Lane, where the Harckwells lived, was a quiet cul-de-sac. A wall at the end of the street separated it from the woods, and the area in between abounded with the ferns which gave the street its name. The lane had four houses on one side and five on the other. The Harckwell's house was the last on the right.

But before it had been the Harckwell's house, it had been William's home. He and his parents had lived in this house for the first four years of his life. Of course, it had been his father's family home first – Arnold and Edna had grown up in that house. When Arnold moved his family to Dublin, Aunt Edna, Uncle Walter and Elsie had moved into the house from their flat over Uncle Walter's antique shop in the village square.

Aunt Edna had opened the front door and switched on the lights. Elsie grabbed William's hand. 'Come on up and see your bedroom!' she said, dragging him up the stairs.

When they got to the bedroom door, Elsie made him close his eyes. Then she opened the door and led him inside. 'Okay, you can open them now,' she said proudly.

William opened his eyes. 'It looks fantastic! And so cosy, too!'

'It's your old room but we've done it up a bit for you, of course. New curtains. Mum sewed them herself. We've put on a new mattress, which is *so* comfy,' she added, letting herself fall onto the bed. But she was up again immediately to switch on the lamp on the bedside table. 'The lamp is *art déco*. I chose it myself from Dad's shop. It was half-hidden among all the antiques. It looks so much better here.'

'It's perfect, Elsie. Really, I don't know what to say.'

He heard footsteps on the stairs outside and then Aunt Edna burst into the room. 'Ah, here you both are,' she said. 'I've been looking for you. Come on, Elsie, let William settle in. You've got all day tomorrow to talk. But if you're hungry, pet, there are some sandwiches for you in the kitchen.'

Elsie rolled her eyes behind her mother's back as she followed her out of the room.

'If you want those sandwiches,' she whispered with a grin, 'you'd better get to the kitchen quickly. Otherwise Dad'll assume they're for him and they'll be gone.'

William lay on the bed and stared up at the ceiling, allowing the memories of his childhood flood back into his mind. Most of them were of happy times playing with his cousin, Elsie. However, some memories were more curious and puzzling. What he did remember was that when he had turned four, something happened to make his father insist the family leave Avenfore and move to Dublin. His mother had always told him it was because his father wanted to study for a doctorate in history at Trinity College Dublin. But there was always something niggling at the back of William's mind – a memory of something darker and more shadowy than all the other memories of Avenfore and the same look of concern on Arnold's face as he had seen in the train station that afternoon.

Whatever the reason for leaving the village, his parents had made a life for the family in Dublin and William's little sister, Kristyn, had been born there. William, however, had always missed Avenfore. Even if all he remembered about the place was that he'd been happy in it.

What had always struck William as odd was that his father had himself returned frequently to Avenfore to attend meetings of the Night Bird Society – a local birdwatching club based in Drunfarnam and which held regular meetings at Ravenwood Castle. Unfortunately for William, Arnold had always insisted on attending the meetings alone. Each year William would plead with his father to be allowed to accompany him, but to his surprise and frustration, his father had always refused and would give no reason for his refusal.

William had also not understood why he had not been allowed to attend his father's old school, St Elm's. After all, it was one of the best schools in the country and both his parents wanted the best education for him. But his pleadings in this respect had equally been rebuffed by his father for many years. There was a long waiting list for places, Arnold had said, and William's name was way down the list. William was sure with his father's connections to the school that he could have tried to have his son's name moved nearer to the top of the list, but to his disappointment, Arnold had told him there was nothing to be done and he would simply have to wait his turn.

Therefore, William's joy and excitement had been boundless only a few weeks beforehand when his father had told him that he had been offered and had accepted a place at St Elm's for William for the coming autumn term. He had been bewildered and delighted in equal measure when Arnold also told him that he and Prudence had thought it a good idea that he stay with his aunt and uncle in Avenfore for the summer months to allow him to settle in there before the new school term began.

Of course, William couldn't help feeling that it would have been even better if Arnold, Prudence and Kristyn had come to Avenfore with him, but the professorship in Marburg was an academic prize his father had worked hard for and could not turn down. His thoughts were suddenly interrupted by a low growl from his stomach which told him he was hungry. Ravenous, in fact.

He jumped off the bed and made his way downstairs to the kitchen, where – thankfully – the sandwiches were still laid out on the table just as Aunt Edna had promised. As he sat down to eat, William had to admit that he did indeed feel at home: in fact, more at home than ever.

CHAPTER 2

Best Friends

I

EXT DAY, WILLIAM WAS UP LONG before Elsie and Aunt Edna. Uncle Walter, as was his habit, had been up before dawn and was already in his shop. Elsie had promised she would show him around the village that morning, but when William awoke, he decided to explore on his own for a while. Leaving notes for Elsie and Aunt Edna, he went out without having breakfast in his eagerness to see if the village was still as he remembered it.

It was a cool, but pleasant, morning and William wandered around the streets exploring every inch of the village. Avenfore was not that big: barely a few hundred inhabitants, and of those, most lived scattered out in the countryside.

All the shops, including Uncle Walter's antique shop, faced onto the village square, which was shaped more like a flat-topped triangle, and into which all roads leading to and from Avenfore converged. In the middle of the square was a small, neatly-planted garden, with an ancient eight-foot high stone Celtic cross at its centre. William made his way over to it. The cross was covered with intricate patterns and carvings of odd-shaped humans and animals and he searched it until he found what he was looking for: his favourite carving – a falcon with a curved beak and a large, all-seeing eye. He traced the contours of the carving with his finger watching the tiny quartz crystals in the grey granite sparkle in the morning sunshine as he did so.

Leaving the square, William strolled down a narrow laneway until he reached a jetty reaching out over the river Inni, where a number of boats were moored. From there, he headed along the Drunfarnam road past a large church with a bell tower and a clock and a huge, old oak tree beside it. After the hustle and bustle of the city, it seemed strange not to meet anybody as he walked. The only sound was that of the rooks cawing as they flew among the beech trees and the younger oaks which lined the riverbank.

As the church bells began to chime eight o'clock, William decided it was time he should be getting back – Elsie would be up and waiting for him by now. As he walked back the way he had come, a rather oddly-dressed figure in the distance caught his eye. It was the strange man he had seen at Drunfarnam railway station the previous evening – he was still wearing the grey gabardine and black trousers. The man drew nearer, and William gave a slight shudder. The man was decidedly odd in appearance, with piercing eyes that looked out from a pale face marked by a small scar on the left-hand side of his chin. His hair was rather peculiar too: without his helmet, he had a mane of hair, like some medieval monk.

To William's surprise, the man appeared to be heading directly for him. As he neared, William tried to hurry past him, but to his alarm, the stranger blocked his path.

'Pleez,' the man said, twisting his face into a sinister smile, 'vat is ze time?'

'Eh, eight o'clock,' William said, indicated towards the church clock across the way from where they were standing. However, the stranger didn't look at the clock. Instead, he stood there staring at William in a rather sinister way.

'Excuse me,' William said, feeling increasingly uneasy. 'I've got to go.'

Again, the man blocked his path, but, to William's relief, he heard someone whistling a song from behind. Turning around, he saw a tall, auburn-haired boy with a post bag slung over his shoulder wheeling his bicycle along the footpath towards them.

'Hello,' William said, running up to the post boy. 'I don't suppose you have any post for the Harckwell's, do you?'

The youth looked at William earnestly. 'Er, well ... I may do.' He began to rummage in his post bag. 'I'll just have a look.'

'Thanks,' William said, as he turned around to check what the monk-motorcyclist was doing. To his surprise – and relief – the strange man was gone.

'You're William Howbbler, aren't you?' the post boy said.

'Yes,' William said. 'How do you know who I am?'

The older boy held out his hand. 'Chris Durffan,' he said. 'I'm a friend of your cousin Elsie.'

William grinned and shook Chris's hand. 'Great to meet you, Chris. But aren't you too young to be a postman?'

Chris laughed. 'My dad's the postman. I just help him out during the school holidays.'

'Do you go to St Elm's?' William asked eagerly.

'Yes, but I'll be in the class above you. Anyway, we'd best be going. Elsie asked me to keep an eye out for you. She is meeting us at Mr Harckwell's shop.'

II

Uncle Walter's antique shop was on the corner of one of the streets running off the main square. It was fine old two-storey building, with an arched side entrance, where Aunt Edna usually parked the van. When William and Chris arrived, it was still closed, but Uncle Walter was clearly expecting them as he opened the shop door before William had a chance to knock.

'There you are, boys,' he said. 'The girls are on their way. Look, I'm about to get to work on the cuckoo clock I got in Dublin. It just needs a good clean, some adjusting and a bit of oil. Do you know, it's an authentic Black Forest cuckoo clock? I'll soon have it ready to add to in my collection.'

William's thoughts flipped back to the encounter with the strange man with the heavy accent on the riverbank.

'The Black Forest? That's a part of Germany, isn't it?' he said.

'Indeed, it is,' replied Walter, as he picked up a rag dipped in a mixture of wax and turpentine and began to polish the clock.

Just then the shop door opened and in came Elsie, accompanied by a pretty girl William didn't recognise.

'Morning, Dad. Morning, William. Eh, morning, Chris,' Elsie said. 'William, do you remember my best friend?'

William looked awkwardly at the girl, who smiled at him and fiddled with her cardigan. For the second time that morning, Chris Durffan came to his rescue.

'Of course he's not going to remember her, Elsie,' Chris said. 'This is my sister Bridget Durffan,' he explained to William.

Bridget scowled at her brother and put out her hand. 'Welcome to Avenfore, William, I'm very pleased you're here.'

William stepped forward and put out his own hand, accidentally knocking against a tin clockwork figure in the shape of a drummer boy on a nearby shelf as he did so. The sudden burst of loud tin drumming made him jump, which set the girls off giggling and William blushing.

Elsie linked his arm and grinned at him. 'Come along. We're going to show you around the village.' She glanced over slyly at Chris 'Do you want to come along too, Chris?'

William saw Chris redden slightly as he answered Elsie.

'Thanks, but I can't just now. I've still got a parcel to deliver to Miss Molly.'

'Oh.' William couldn't help noticing the disappointment in his cousin's voice. But before she could protest, Chris was already out the door of Uncle Walter's shop and back on his bike.

'Welcome to Avenfore, William,' he called as he rode off, 'good to meet you.'

Flanked by the two girls, William crossed the street from the antique shop towards the garden in the middle of the square.

Once there, Elsie climbed onto the stone pedestal of the Celtic high cross. 'So, this is the bird's eye view,' she said and gestured around the square dramatically. 'This is the main square in the village. And that's the way to Drunfarnam, the next biggest town to Avenfore,' she said, pointing in the direction of the church. 'You can also get there by boat along the river Inni. It takes longer by road because it detours right round the mountain. To the west you go to Drishlean, which is a tiny village that is much further than Drunfarnam.' Elsie was like a compass, her arms whirling around the cardinal points. 'The river Inni flows through Ravenwood Forest, with Ravenwood Castle in the middle of it. The castle is right beside the lake, and on the other side of it is Dronfore Mountain. According to the legends, it's where the druids used to live.'

'St Elm's Boys' School is on the road to Drunfarnam,' Bridget added. 'Past the church, about two hundred yards from St Clementine's Girls' School, which is where me and Elsie go to school.'

Elise jumped down from the cross pedestal. 'Anyway, Avenfore's tiny. In a couple of days, it'll be like you never left.'

'I hope so,' said William, 'I'm looking forward to knowing where everything is. It's not that I don't remember it. Just not clearly enough and some things look quite different when you're four.'

The girls laughed and sat down on the bench in the small garden in front of the high cross.

'I like sitting here,' Elsie said. 'You get to see everyone passing by.'

At that moment, a tall, dark-haired man dressed in a long, black purple-lined cloak crossed the street to the square garden. His face was serious and elegant, but reflected a certain bitterness, William thought. Or maybe he was just plain grumpy? And what was with the cloak? It made him look like something out of an old Victorian detective novel. The man walked straight by them, his cloak brushing against Elsie as he swept past. He didn't seem to notice them at all.

'Who is that?' William asked, as the man strode off in the direction of the church.

'That's Bryon Mullween,' Elsie said. 'The owner of Ravenwood Castle. I don't like him. He's a bit creepy.'

'He's awfully gloomy,' Bridget agreed.

'I always get the feeling he's hiding something,' Elsie added. 'And we're not the only ones in the village to think so.'

'Does he live alone at Ravenwood Castle?' William asked.

'Almost. When his father died, all the staff left except for Ernest Wiglann, his father's faithful old caretaker and the Dreephys, Mary and Elwood. She's the cook and her husband is the gardener. I certainly can't imagine anyone wanting to work for such a sour-looking man. Hardly anyone in the village likes him.'

Personally, William thought Byron Mullween and Ravenwood Castle were rather intriguing, but the look on Elsie's face made it clear he wasn't going to get any further information from her about them at this point in time.

Having sat for long enough, the three left the high cross garden to explore the rest of the village. Elsie showed William the library and Malconary's sweet shop and café. The village hall was located at the start of the Drishlean road, while the village park at the back of the hall led onto the forest road out towards the old Hollypoint water pump, Bridget explained.

'Maybe we could go for a bike ride later this afternoon? I'll ask Chris to come too.' Bridget added.

'That's sounds great,' William said. He smiled at Bridget and now it was her turn to blush.

'Meet us outside Dad's shop at half past two, so,' Elsie said.

Bridget left, waving goodbye to William as she went. Grinning broadly, Elsie linked arms with her cousin and pulled him in the direction of Fern Lane and home.

CHAPTER 3

The Lake

I

THE CHURCH CLOCK HAD JUST STRUCK the half hour as William and Elsie arrived at Uncle Walter's antique shop as arranged. William had borrowed Aunt Edna's bicycle, which she hardly used now she had the new van. He hadn't ridden for a long time and was a bit unsure of himself at first.

Bridget and Chris were already outside the shop waiting for them and all four set off in the direction of the church and the Drunfarnam road.

First up was St Clementine Girls' School which both Elsie and Bridget attended. The school was situated next to Avenfore church and was a rather stately building with huge gardens and a six-foot high iron gate. William listened with fascination as Chris explained that both St Elm's and St Clementine's had been built by Fergus Mullween of Ravenwood Castle, the current owner's grandfather, to ensure that the boys and girls in the area would not have to leave home to study. Fergus had also funded a great part of the building of the new church in Avenfore in 1888 after the old one at Hollypoint had burnt down. All in all, William thought St Clementine's looked like a good place to go to school and judging from the way Elsie and Bridget talked about it, they were very happy there.

Nor far past the girls' school William saw a track that seemed to be little used.

'Where does that lead to?' he asked, pointing to it.

'It goes through Blackwood Forest and then off in several directions,' Elsie explained as they cycled on. 'But it's all too easy to get lost and hardly anyone uses it.'

St Elm's Boys' School lay a few hundred yards further out on the opposite side of the road overlooking the river Inni and was the last building on this side of the village.

Chris got off his bike and announced, 'William, your new school.'

The entrance to the building was not quite as regal as that of St Clementine's. A somewhat deteriorated wrought-iron arch bearing the school's name spanned the two solid stone pillars on either side of the iron gate. The school building lay at the other end of a large well-tended garden, which was divided by a long driveway, bordered by beeches, chestnuts and centuries-old oaks, that led up to the main door

'It's magnificent!' William cried, 'and far bigger than I'd imagined. Can we go in and look at it close up?'

Chris hesitated. 'We're not really supposed to,' he said. 'Mr Normental, the caretaker will read the Riot Act if he finds us,' – Chris checked his wristwatch – 'but I think I saw him heading into Avenfore for his lunch earlier, so we should be able to get in without being seen. But we'll have to be quick about it.'

Bridget was looking rather uneasy. 'Do we really have to go in?' she asked.

'Oh, come on, Bridget; don't be a scaredy-cat, please come in with me,' Elsie pleaded, hopping from one foot to the next with curiosity.

Bridget sighed. 'Oh, all right,' she said, and Elsie threw her a bright smile.

The four ventured into the garden almost as far as the main doors and crouched behind a fountain adorned with marble cherubim in the front courtyard of the school. The main doorway boasted an elegant, gently arched portico. The high chimney stacks rising from the roof also caught the eye. The classrooms and refectories were on the ground floor, and the first and second floors housed the boarders.

'We'd better leave,' said Bridget, looking worried, 'I feel I'm being watched, and I don't like it. There,' she said, gesturing towards one of the second-floor windows. 'Somebody's looking at us out of that window.' They all looked up to where Bridget had pointed, but the curtains were swiftly drawn, and they couldn't see who it was.

'Oh no, that must be Mr Normental!' Chris said. 'Let's hope he didn't recognise us.'

'No, I don't think so,' his sister protested. 'I think it was a woman.'

'Don't be silly, Bridge,' Chris replied. 'Now let's get out of here.'

He took off towards the gate with the rest following him at a fast pace.

As they got back on their bicycles, Elsie gave a sigh of relief. 'Well, let's go to the lake, shall we?'

'But that will take ages, Els,' Bridget grumbled. 'We'll have to go back into the village and all around. It's just so far.'

'Not really,' her brother said. 'I know a secret path into the forest near here which goes near Ravenwood Castle and then on to the lake.'

Elsie smiled at Chris, 'Let's do that, so,' she said, ignoring the sulky look on Bridget's face as they set off along the path to the lake which ran alongside the boys' school in the direction of the river.

II

After a while, Chris stopped. 'From here on, we'll have to walk.' Leaving the bikes against a tree, the four of them set off along another narrow pathway. Even Elsie and Bridget were intrigued – they didn't know of the existence of this path and they'd never been in this part of the forest before.

Minutes later, Chris stopped again. Twenty yards or so to the right they could make out an area of particularly thick overgrowth that made a natural barrier. Chris headed towards it and gestured to them to follow. They followed the natural barrier for a while, Bridget hanging on tightly to Elsie's arm.

In a clearing where there was more ivy than bushes, Chris paused and looked around him, studying the undergrowth. 'I'm certain it's this way,' he said, tugging up some of the ivy. 'Ah, here it is!'

Hidden among the plants was an iron gate which, by the look of it, had not been used for ages. Chris pulled away the last ivy creepers and tried to open it. He could hardly budge it an inch, so he called to William to help. Together they managed to pull it open.

'This is the secret entrance to Ravenwood,' Chris explained. 'Hardly anyone knows of its existence, not even Mr Mullween. I'd appreciate it if you wouldn't mention it to anyone else'.

'And how did you come to know about it, Chris?' asked Elsie.

'Some years back, when I used to go fishing with Dad, we once saw Elwood Dreephy, the gardener, coming out of here.'

'It's obviously not used very much,' said Bridget, who was still holding on to Elsie.

Before going through, Chris urged them not to make noise. On the other side of the gate, they made their way through the trees to the top of a mound from where the castle could be seen below them.

Ravenwood Castle was in a magnificent setting. It faced south and was only a hundred yards from Lake Dronfore. A path through the garden led down to a mooring point, a reminder of its aristocratic past. William was fascinated by it all, even though it was nothing like he'd imagined.

'The garden seems rather abandoned, don't you think?' he murmured at last.

'I guess it's too much work for just one gardener. Even so, I like it the way it is,' replied Chris.

Elsie whispered, 'Frankly, I can't see how anyone would want to stay there.'

'Not much choice,' said Bridget. 'It's not as if there are many other places to board in the village.'

William was puzzled. 'Stay there? I thought Mr Mullween lived there alone?' he asked.

'Not entirely,' Chris explained, 'Byron Mullween gets some money in rent from St Elm's and St Clem's, but that wouldn't be enough to pay for the upkeep of the castle, so Ravenwood is a guesthouse these days. It might not look like it, but the inside is very tasteful and welcoming.'

Elsie threw Chris a look which clearly said she didn't believe anything to do with Byron Mullween could look tasteful or welcoming.

'I'd love to see inside the castle.' William said eagerly.

'I don't think they'd let you in,' said Bridget, sounding rather relieved that they wouldn't.

William looked so disappointed that Elsie took pity on him.

'Actually, Will, I just remembered,' said Elsie, 'Mr Mullween called on Dad the other day to ask him to go and service a grandfather clock he has. I think Dad's due to go over there next week.'

'That's great, Elsie, thanks. I'll ask Uncle Walter if I can go too. It would be a wonderful opportunity to get to know the castle better.' Delighted with the idea, he added, 'Shall we go to the lake now?'

'Follow me!' Chris cried, and the three others followed him down the narrow pathway which ran through the forest that led to the lake.

Even though it was close to Avenfore, Lake Dronfore, which lay at the foot of Dronfore Mountain, was surrounded by an ancient forest that made it almost inaccessible. The few existing paths were rough and hardly any of the villagers went there, except for those, like Chris's father, who were keen fishermen.

They reached a clearing near the lake and William and ran to the shore. He gazed at the lake for a few long moments, never imagining it could be so vast. Its waters were teeming with birds: there were herons stalking the still shallows at the edge of the lake, seeking out their prey, and graceful swans sailing along with their cygnets in tow.

Elsie and Bridget perched themselves on some large rocks at the edge of the forest and chatted, while Chris joined William at the shore. 'Quite something, isn't it?' he said.

William was so absorbed and lost for words that he simply nodded. Chris pointed at a thick clump of forest and rock which rose up out of the lake a way out from the shoreline to their left.

'That's one of the largest islands on the lake. It's called the Isle of Lesciern. It has curious feature: although it's an island, you can actually walk to it.'

William didn't quite follow this, but he didn't question Chris further. He felt like an explorer coming across uncharted land.

'It's incredible how this place hasn't changed for hundreds of years.'

'I guess you're right,' Chris replied, 'but when you live here you don't see it like that. It just seems normal.' Pointing along the lake edge to their left, he said, 'You see that area overgrown with reeds and lilies? That's the source of the river Inni. As you can see, all those rushes make it impossible to get here by boat from the village.'

'So, no boats at all can get into the lake?' William said.

'The only boats on the lake are those at the Ravenwood pier and the mooring belonging to Mr Greewoof, the Latin teacher at St Elm's.'

'Mr Greewoof,' mused William. That name rang a bell.

'Do you know Mr Greewoof?' asked Chris.

William shook his head. Then he remembered the letter his father had slipped him at the station and which was still in the pocket of the jacket he had been wearing the day before. He'd completely forgotten about it, but now some questions were starting to nag at him. Why had his dad asked him to tell nobody about it? What could it mean? William was starting to get interested in Mr Greewoof.

'You say he teaches Latin at St Elm's?'

'That's right,' Chris explained, 'he's also an expert in botany, and he's passionate about old books.'

'So, where does he live, then?' William asked, trying not to sound too interested.

Chris pointed further up the shoreline to their left. 'Look, over there, in those trees. Can you see a thatched roof?' William had to look very closely to make out what Chris was trying to show him. A little distance along the shore and among the trees, he could just discern a brownish patch of something poking out from among the trees. 'That's the roof of his house. Abelard Greewoof is a kind chap. I'm sure he'd lend us his boat if we asked.'

By now, Elsie and Bridget had joined them.

'It's probably time we were heading back,' Elsie said.

'You're probably right. Come on, Will, let's go.'

They turned to leave, but at that moment, something caught William's eye over towards the Ravenwood end of the lake.

'Look,' he said. 'Over there.'

'What?' Elsie asked. 'What is it?'

'There, on the lake! There seems to be a boat with two people in it.'

'It's a boat coming to the Ravenwood mooring point,' said Chris.

'Ooh, I don't like this,' Bridget wailed. 'What if they see us?'

'Bridget's right,' William said, and crouched down behind one of the large rocks which littered the shoreline.

The others did the same and they all watched in silence as the boat finally reached the mooring point and one of its occupants jumped out to tie it up. The other followed and between them they hoisted a heavy sack out of the boat, put it into a wheelbarrow and set off towards the castle. The four friends looked at each other in amazement when they saw that the sack was covered in red stains that looked horribly like blood. Beside William, Bridget gulped in terror. The two figures took the sack to the servants' entrance, which led to the cellars of the castle.

'I don't know about you lot, but I'm getting out of here,' squeaked Bridget, and she set off crawling down the mound.

'Wait, I'm coming with you,' Elsie hissed. As she got up she accidentally stood on a dry branch, which broke with a loud snap.

Elsie threw herself down again behind the nearest rock and held her breath, not daring to move a muscle. The sound alarmed the ravens in the trees behind them and they flew off cawing. All four froze, worried that the sound had given them away.

The two figures at the castle stopped in their tracks, alarmed by the ravens and looked towards the shoreline where William and the others were hiding. Bridget, who was nearest the forest and out of sight, fled in fright. The other three kept still, low behind the rocks on the shoreline. They could see a strange light glinting from the left side of the face of one of the individuals as he looked in their direction. They couldn't be sure if they'd been spotted, but when the two men went back to their task, the three of them slipped away from their hiding places and sprinted off after Bridget.

Hastily pushing the gate closed, they tore back to where they'd left their bicycles. Fighting to get her breath back, Bridget started to speak, 'Do you think what we saw was normal?' Still panting she went on, 'I've had more than enough for today. I'd like to get back to the village, if you don't mind.' They all agreed that after all that had happened it was the most sensible thing to do.

Elsie shook out her dress before getting on her bicycle and then said, 'It was Byron Mullween and his caretaker. I know because Ernest's got a glass eye. I always thought Mr Mullween was a shady fellow,' she continued, 'but I never thought him capable of, well … *that.*'

William noticed that Elsie and Bridget were both staring at Chris, as though waiting for some explanation.

'Don't stare at me like that!' Chris said. 'Right now, I can't account for what we saw, but I'm convinced it can't be anything like what you two are thinking.'

'Well, until you come up with a reasonable explanation, I'll continue to believe that that sack had a body in it' said Elsie, visibly angry.

Chris threw up his hands. 'Are you crazy, Elsie? You can't believe that.'

William could find no explanation himself for what he'd just seen. Then a thought occurred to him. 'It might not have been a human body they were carrying,' he suggested, 'maybe they'd been hunting?'

'Eh, no, it's not the seas—' Chris began, then suddenly seemed to change his mind. 'Actually, you know, you might be right, William. It must be some game they were carrying.'

William had the feeling Chris was deliberately holding something back, but it was clear Elsie and Bridget were happy with that explanation, although Bridget still wanted to return to the village as quickly as possible.

'Do you think they saw us?' asked Elsie.

'I hope not,' said Chris with a worried look. He was obviously feeling guilty about taking them there. 'You must all promise that you'll never say a word about the secret entrance.'

'Don't worry, Chris,' William reassured him, 'we won't say anything to anybody.'

'Thanks, William,' Chris replied.

'Well, at least I now know why it's called Ravenwood!' declared Elsie trying to lighten the mood, 'I don't know what frightened me more, what I saw or all those ghastly ravens.'

'It's all rather funny,' said William. 'This morning when I got up early and walked around the village I thought Avenfore was the most peaceful place on earth.'

To his embarrassment, Bridget took his hands in hers and gave them a squeeze. 'I'm so sorry, William,' she said softly, 'you've been really unlucky that this has happened on your first day here. Nothing out of the normal ever happens in Avenfore. From now on we're going to have a great time, I promise.'

CHAPTER 4

The Latin Master

I

As HIS FATHER HAD INSTRUCTED, WILLIAM had not mentioned the letter addressed to Abelard Greewoof to anyone. Following his trip to Dronfore Lake, he had spent a long evening trying to figure out how he would be able to arrange a visit to Mr Greewoof without having to explain why he needed to go to see him. As luck would have it, the very next day Aunt Edna announced that she planned to visit Mr Greewoof as he had promised her some flowers from his garden and she wondered if Elsie and William would like to join her. Mr Greewoof supplied Aunt Edna with some of the best seeds for her kitchen garden, Elsie explained to William.

All three walked together to get the van from the garage next to Uncle Walter's shop. Aunt Edna popped inside for a moment to let Uncle Walter know where they were going, while William and Elsie waited outside. Elsie peered in the shop window and waved to her father, who waved back. William waved too, but as he did so, he saw something which made him start. The strange man in the grey gabardine was in the shop with his uncle! Panicked, William jerked to one side out of sight of the window, bumping into Elsie and making her trip.

'What's got into you?' grumbled Elsie getting her balance back, 'have you gone mad?'

William tried to think up a quick answer and not look like an idiot in front of his cousin: after all, maybe the strange grey-gabardined man was only a tourist.

'We shouldn't be distracting your dad,' was the best he could come up with, 'can't you see he's with a customer?'

'Sure I can,' retorted Elsie, 'but there's no need to push, is there?'

William was saved from any further argument by the arrival of Aunt Edna who led the way to the garage. He hoped he had seen the last of the odd stranger. Truth be told: the man gave him the creeps.

To get to Abelard Greewoof's house they first took the Dronfore Lake road and once outside the village immediately took the first turning off to the right.

William was eager to meet Mr Greewoof. He was also very curious to know the contents of the letter his father had given him, which was safely stowed in his jacket pocket.

As she drove, Aunt Edna chatted away as usual, and William was able to glean further information about Abelard Greewoof.

'As a boy, Abelard was a great friend of James Mullween,' Aunt Edna explained, hardly pausing to take a breath, 'that's Byron Mullween's father. They went to St Elm's together. Abelard left the village after graduating and travelled around Europe. He learned quite a few languages. He even spent two years in the monastery of San Millán de Yuso – that's in Spain – where he studied restoration and conservation of old books. After that, he went to Rome, where he worked restoring books in the Vatican library, no less. Finally, before returning to Avenfore and taking up the post of Latin master at St Elm's, he spent four years teaching Latin at the University of Edinburgh.'

Aunt Edna slowed down almost to a halt as they reached the fork in the road that led down to Abelard's house. The track swung round to the left and ran almost to the foot of the mountain. A narrow lane off to the right took them to the house. Outside the house there was an inscription in Latin carved into the trunk of an old oak tree: UT SEMENTEM FECERIS ITA METES. William, who was good at Latin, translated it aloud: 'As you sow so shall you reap.'

'Is that what it means, William?' asked Elsie. But before he could reply, an odd man in green trousers and braces, a dark red shirt and Wellington boots suddenly appeared from the side of house. A luxurious mane of white hair trailed down his back in long wisps from under his green felt hat. William couldn't help thinking that Mr Greewoof looked extremely like an extra large version of an elf, or even a leprechaun.

William stared: Mr Greewoof was nothing like he'd imagined. Seeing him there, nobody would have taken him for a respected Latin teacher at a school like St Elm's. Elsie had to give William a nudge to stop him gaping and to get him out of the van.

Aunt Edna greeted Mr Greewoof with a cheery wave.

'My dear Abelard,' she said, 'you haven't been to the village for some time, so I've brought you some of that apple pie that I know you love.'

Mr Greewoof held the pie up to his nose and breathed in the sweet aroma of baked apple and cloves. 'How kind of you, Edna, you needn't have, but I do thank you,' he said with a smile. 'You're right, I don't go into the village much these days. I spend most of my time in the garden. You have to take advantage of the good weather and get things growing.'

'As you can see,' Aunt Edna continued, 'I've brought Elsie and William along. William is Arnold's son.'

Mr Greewoof took off his hat and, with a mischievous twinkle in his eye, he made a low bow to Elsie.

'Good day to you, Elsie, you've grown into such a pretty young lady since I last saw you.'

Elsie grinned. 'Thank you, Mr Greewoof,' she replied, with a mock curtsey, 'it's a pleasure to see you again too.'

Turning to William, Abelard shook his hand, 'It's lovely to meet you, William. You must be tired of hearing how much you take after your father, but it's the truth!'

'I'm delighted to meet you, Mr Greewoof,' replied William politely, 'but I don't think my dad and I are so alike: not that I'd mind if we were, of course.'

William noticed that a sombre, earnest look briefly crossed the Latin master's face.

'I expect we shall find out soon enough,' he murmured.

Then Aunt Edna explained that William was going to be living with them and studying at St Elm's.

'Well done, William! I look forward to having you as a student. If you're as good as your father was, St Elm's is just the place for you.' Abelard Greewoof beamed as he ushered them all round towards the back of the house towards the garden. 'Let's get started in the garden, shall we?' he continued, 'it's such a lovely day it would be a shame to waste it.' To William's surprise, he winked at him, speaking in a voice too low for Aunt Edna and Elsie to hear. 'I'm pleased you've come to visit me, William. Something tells me we have quite a lot to talk about.'

Mr Greewoof handed Elsie some secateurs and Aunt Edna a basket so that they could pick all the flowers they liked, and off they went together happily.

Once William was alone with Mr Greewoof, he immediately produced the letter his father had given him from his pocket. Abelard took it without a word and moved a few yards away to read it. William watched, intrigued, dying to know what the letter contained. As he read, Abelard Greewoof kept glancing towards the forest. Then he took out a cigarette lighter and burnt the letter. William looked on helplessly. There was nothing he could do. The letter had been addressed to Mr Greewoof and he was free to do with it as he saw fit. But the episode only served to heighten his curiosity. What on earth could his father have written to make the Latin teacher destroy it?

Carrying on as if nothing had happened, Mr Greewoof sat down, pulled off his Wellington boots and put on his shoes. 'Come with me, William,' he said, 'I want to show you something.'

The old wooden steps creaked beneath them as William and Abelard Greewoof climbed the stairs to the very top of the house. The attic room was spacious with a single window that didn't let in enough light to reach right into all the corners. There were books and papers everywhere: they filled the shelves around the room to overflowing; they covered what appeared to be the only furniture – a table and two chairs – and even more were scattered in piles of varying heights and sizes across every inch of the floor. William had never seen so many books and papers together in his life.

'I suppose your aunt will have told you something about my hectic lifestyle. As you see, I've accumulated a lot during the course of my life.' Once again, there was a mischievous twinkle in Mr Greewoof's eye as he spoke. 'Maybe too much; and sooner or later, I'll have to start getting rid of some of it.' William could only nod his head in mute agreement.

Mr Greewoof now made his way towards the only other object in the room: a telescope mounted on a tripod pointing out the window towards the forest and beckoned to William to follow him. William crossed to the window and peered out. The view from the window took in the pier at Ravenwood and a bit of the castle. He could also see the cross on the church spire jutting up among the tall trees. Mr Greewoof swung the telescope around 45 degrees to the right, took off his glasses and looked into the eyepiece. It took him a few minutes to focus it, then he turned and smiled at William in a conspiratorial way. 'There he is! Take a look for yourself, William.'

William carefully put his eye to the eyepiece to make sure he didn't jog it. He had to focus it to his own eye, but what he finally saw caused him to step back in alarm. 'What the devil!' Hidden among the bushes and wearing a crash helmet was the man in the grey gabardine, with a pair of binoculars trained on Mr Greewoof's house.

'He calls himself Gregor Watengroe,' Mr Greewoof explained softly, 'but his real name is Jaeger Knrumbad. He's German and was a member of the SS. At the end of the war he assumed a new identity and now passes himself off as an antique dealer. He arrived here a week ago and is staying at Ravenwood Castle. You're not what he came for at first; the person who sent him had other plans. But, unfortunately, when he learnt you were coming – as did the whole county thanks, unfortunately, to dear Edna – he changed his plans.' The teacher took out a hip flask and offered it to William. 'Tea with lemon balm and honey. I always carry it around with me in summer. A swig of tea does wonders after a bad shock.'

William shook his head. 'Thank you, but I don't feel like anything right now.'

Abelard gave him a kind look. 'Of course, you are concerned,' he continued, 'so would I if I was being followed, and especially not knowing why and to what purpose.'

The Latin master stood up and peered through the telescope, checking that Gregor was still there.

'All your questions will be answered in due time. But we can't talk here. Not now. All I can say for the moment is that the letter may well change many things in your life. We'll meet again in a few days' time and things will be clearer. But not a word to anyone about this conversation. From now on, we must tread cautiously. Keep your eyes peeled and keep away from Gregor. Whatever you do, don't talk to him or even approach him. Now he's sure who you are, he's more dangerous than ever. He's going to trail you everywhere, but don't worry. I'll sort things out soon enough.'

Mr Greewoof picked up a dusty, rather tattered-looking, leather-bound book from the top of a particularly tall pile of books close to the telescope. William watched in puzzlement as the Latin master pulled a pen out of his pocket and drew a quick sketch on the last page of the book before handing it to him.

'Thursday afternoon, we'll meet at three o'clock at the old church. The area around the church has been made into a bird sanctuary. It's a protected area, and nobody goes there. You'll find it easily enough; the turnoff is a short distance before the water pump at Hollypoint. Keep going past the no-entry sign at the edge of the forest and you'll get to the church. I've sketched a map for just in case. Now remember, you're to come alone and do everything you can to shake Gregor off.'

William cradled the book in his hand. 'You can count on me, Mr Greewoof. I won't be followed,' he said. He wished they could meet sooner so that he could learn what was going on, but he didn't think it would be wise to push the matter.

'Oh, and you can keep the book as a souvenir of our first meeting,' Abelard Greewoof said as he showed William downstairs and out into the garden where Aunt Edna and Elsie were tying the flowers they had collected into bunches.

'Thank you so much, Mr Greewoof, the flowers are beautiful,' Elsie exclaimed.

'Yes, thanks indeed, my dear Abelard,' chirped Aunt Edna. 'You've been so kind. By the way, those amaranths are extraordinarily beautiful for the season. I don't know how you do it.'

Abelard Greewoof gave a broad grin and winked again at William. 'Well, Edna,' he replied, 'you know me; an old druid has his secrets.'

II

William couldn't sleep that night. For a long while, he sat by the window and looked at the night sky. It was one of those summer nights when the sky was ablaze with stars.

Still restless despite the late hour, he picked up the tattered book Mr Greewoof had given him and examined it more closely.

The first thing that struck him was the faded gilt figure of a falcon on the front cover. It reminded him of the falcon carving on the Avenfore High Cross in the village square. Below it was the name of the publisher: NBS Press, Avenfore. William had never heard of a publishing company in Avenfore before.

On the inside page of the book was a colour illustration which showed a group of twelve Knights in full armour standing at the top of a rocky outcrop. The Knights were wearing white mantles with red crosses emblazoned across their chests and their swords were raised in battle, each sword with a strange cross symbol – like a cross with a shamrock leaf at the end of each arm. William immediately recognised them for what they were: Knights Templar, members of the famous order of warrior-monks who had led the Crusades in the Middle Ages.

William stared at the picture for some time, admiring its vibrant colours and the ferocity and grim determination on the faces of the twelve Knights and Saladin's Mameluke warriors. Its title was as intriguing as the frontispiece: the *Chronicle of the Noble Order of the Alliance*. Pulling the bedsheets tightly around him, William settled in to read.

CHAPTER 5

The Order of the Alliance

I

THE *CHRONICLE* BEGAN IN 1311 WHEN a group of Knights Templar, fleeing from France and other parts of Europe, arrived on the coast of Clogherhead in Ireland. With them they had brought everything they had been able to save as they fled: relics, gold, and, most important of all, their most treasured possessions: their books.

One book in particular was of immense value: it was known as the *Book of the Knights Templar Errant* and it contained the only written record of three centuries of the secrets and wisdom of their Order. It also contained details of the location of the relics, gold and treasures that were the source of the Order's great wealth and power and which was hidden in places all over Europe and the Middle East as far as the Holy City of Jerusalem. Everything was written in code, using symbols and pictograms that only the Brothers of the Order understood.

The Knights' mission was of the utmost importance: to keep the *Book of the Knights Templar Errant* safely out of the hands of their persecutors: the agents and allies of the French King, Philip the Fair, who, out of jealousy and greed, had vowed to destroy the Order and seize its treasures. All Templars, including those already in Ireland, had already been arrested and imprisoned. Only this small group of Knights remained to ensure that everything was safely hidden from those who would use them to do harm.

Once ashore they hid the bulk of the heavy gold and treasure from the ship in a secret location near the beach. They only kept a limited amount of gold and a few relics to bring with them. And, of course, the *Book of the Knights Templar Errant*.

Leaving Clogherhead, they bought horses and, where necessary, people's silence. Under cover of darkness, they journeyed inland in search of a safe place to hide. They travelled for days, crossing mountains and forests, hunted at every turn by those wishing to claim a reward for their capture.

After an arduous journey, the Knights Templar arrived at a lake surrounded by thick forests, and protected by dense vegetation, where they camped for several days. One day when they were hunting, something occurred that aroused their curiosity and alarm. On the other side of the lake, they saw some deer walking on the water. They dispatched three of their members to investigate.

Making their way around the lake, the three unravelled the mystery. A spit of land barely three inches under the surface of the lake ran from the shore out to an island. From a distance, this peculiar feature could not be appreciated, and created the illusion that one could walk on water.

The three Knights crossed over to the island just as the deer had done. Their companions on the other side could hardly believe it when they saw the men walking on the water and began to believe that the island had magical powers. It was only when the three Knights returned that they learned the truth.

Here William gave a gasp and looked up from the book.

The island was exactly like the isle of Lesciern: the island Chris had pointed out to him when they were by the lakeshore a few days ago! How strange that a similar island should be in this book. And how exciting!

II

The Knights Templar could hardly have imagined a more perfect place than the island for them to settle. But they soon discovered that the island was not uninhabited. At its centre, they discovered an ancient stone megalith which – although it was over seven feet tall – was dwarfed by the ring of larger oak trees surrounding it. To the Knight's astonishment, an elderly hermit, almost as ancient as the megalith itself, appeared all of a sudden as if from nowhere. The hermit stretched out his arms and spoke to them:

'Welcome, dear Brothers, welcome to my home. I am Elm, and I am the last guardian of this blessed Isle of Lesciern.'

William gave a start. 'It *is* Lesciern,' he said to himself out loud. Anxious to know more, he continued reading:

The Knights did not know what they should do, but the old hermit beckoned to them to follow him. He led the astonished Knights to a secret entrance behind the megalith down into a large underground cavern beneath the great stone. There, in the centre of the cavern which was decorated by ancient carvings and paint-ings, burned a cheerful fire scented with the sweet smell of sapling wood and aromatic herbs. Elm smiled at the Knights and gestured towards the fire.

'You are safe here, dear Brothers. Please sit and rest yourselves. I have waited many years for your arrival and we have much to talk about.'

Over many days and nights and many conversations, the monk explained that he was the last in a long and ancient order of monks whose origins stretched back to the druid-priests of the Celts who had worshipped the trees and stones of the island and the sacred waters of the lake. Many centuries ago, the order had converted to Christianity. But they still preserved and adhered to old ways of the Celtic church and the lore of the ancient druids.

The Knights and the monk immediately struck up a friendship, since they had much in common. They offered him a golden cross from their rescued treasure in thanks for his hospitality and kindness, but the old man shook his head.

'What need have I of gold?' he said, pointing around him. 'Everything I need is here.' Then he tapped his head and said, 'And here. But there is something you can do for me. You can help me to pass on what must be passed on.'

The Knights nodded. They understood what the old monk meant.

For many weeks thereafter, the old hermit and the Knights shared their experiences, their wisdom and their secrets and the Knights wrote everything down in the *Book of the Knights Templar Errant*. Among all the valuable secrets that they shared with the hermit was a very special one, perhaps the most valuable secret of all: the place where the Holy Grail was hidden.

Not long after the Knights' arrival the old hermit-monk died. With great sadness, they buried him on Lesciern and marked the spot around his grave with a great circle of stones within the circle of mighty oaks as befitted the last Druidic guardian of the island. They built their first church on the site where Elm's stone cell had stood at the edge of the forest.

Now the Knights were alone on Lesciern. There they survived for many years with few problems. The large lake and the forests afforded abundant hunting and fishing. Most importantly, they were safe from their enemies and the terrible fates which had befallen their Brothers in France and across Europe. The treasure of the Knights Templar remained hidden, as they had no need of it on their beautiful and secluded home.

However, with time, the Knights realised that if they remained completely isolated, they too would die out like the druid-monks and their knowledge and secrets would die with them. Hearing their arch-enemy, Philip the Fair, was long dead, they journeyed away from Lesciern and sought out other places in the mountains and valleys around the island where they could settle and cultivate the land. They sought out nearby villages and communities where they could find people to join them. They built a new settlement on the river Inni and called it Avenfore.

Good Lord, William thought to himself. *Avenfore! Is this really true? Was this village – his village – really founded by the Knights Templar?* If it was, then it was even older and more exciting than he had first thought, he eagerly turned to the next chapter.

III

In 1327 the Knights founded a new Order to protect Avenfore, the island and their legacy. They chose twelve of their ablest warriors as Knights, with twelve others to train as their Squires. From now on the brotherhood of the Order would comprise of these twelve Knights and twelve Squires. They wanted it to be secret so that it would not draw attention to itself, therefore, the members of the Order swore an oath of loyalty and silence. Now to be a member, you had to be a direct descendant of an existing member.

From that moment the Isle of Lesciern was reserved exclusively for Brothers of the Order, who met there to appoint new Brothers. The huge stone slab megalith on Lesciern would serve as the symbolic pillar for their newly-founded brotherhood, which was to be known as the Order of the Alliance.

For the next two centuries, the community established by the Order of the Alliance thrived, protected by the forest and by their anonymity. The island of Lesciern remained their great secret, not only because it served as a refuge when needed, but also because it was where they kept their most precious of treasures: the *Book of the Knights Templar Errant*.

But in the sixteenth century, something happened which would shatter the peace of Lesciern and the Order of the Alliance throughout centuries to come. The *Book of the Knights Templar Errant* was stolen. The thief was a Squire called Corneille the Grey. This betrayal by one of their own was a bitter blow to the Order and Brothers were dispatched throughout Ireland and far across Europe to search for the missing book. But although they searched for many years, the *Book of the Knights Templar Errant* had vanished completely and could not be found.

Of some comfort to the Order was that the only cipher for the Book was still in their possession. Without this cipher, the Book could not be decoded and read. Luckily for them, Corneille had not been able to steal the cipher also.

'That was a piece of luck,' William said to himself. He was still amazed that so many exciting and interesting things appeared to have happened in his village so many centuries ago.

'I wonder where the book is now?' he whispered. 'That is, if it even exists. Maybe it's just a story?'

He yawned and glanced at the alarm clock. *Was that the time?!* He had been reading for hours! He had been so engrossed in the book, he hadn't noticed the time passing. Putting it away, he turned off the light and lay in the darkness, his head filled with knights and battles and missing books, until he finally drifted into sleep.

CHAPTER 6

Triple Trouble

I

T HE SUN WAS HIGH IN THE sky when William came down to breakfast the next morning. Nobody was in the house: Aunt Edna was in the garden tending her vegetables, Uncle Walter was in his shop, and Elsie had gone out leaving him a note saying that he could find her later in the library.

After making himself some breakfast, William set out for the library. He was surprised not to see Gregor Watengroe as he walked along the street, although he was sure he was hidden somewhere, spying on him as Mr Greewoof had warned he would. His uncle waved to him as he passed by the antique shop and William remembered that he had a favour to ask him. Entering the shop, he stood by the window so that he could keep an eye on the square in case Gregor was about.

'Good afternoon, William,' Uncle Walter greeted him with a chuckle, 'I hope you slept well.' It must have been obvious from his appearance that he'd only just got up.

'Yes, thanks, Uncle Walter. By the way, Elsie said you would be going to Ravenwood Castle to fix the clock some day and I'd love to go with you if I may.' As he spoke, William searched the square for any sign of Gregor, but he was still nowhere to be seen.

Uncle Walter threw up his hands and exclaimed, 'Heavens above! The grandfather clock at Ravenwood! It's tomorrow! I'd completely forgotten. Just as well you reminded me, William. If you want to come with me, mind you, you'll have to be here at ten minutes past nine tomorrow morning, and not a minute later.'

William was thrilled that his uncle was letting him go with him to Ravenwood; he was really curious to see the inside of the castle, even more so after what Chris had told him.

As Uncle Walter ambled off towards the back of the shop to search for his tools, William spotted Gregor Watengroe on the opposite side of the square, pretending to read a newspaper. Leaving the shop, William walked towards him, noting that, as he neared him, Gregor raised the newspaper to hide his face. William strolled right past him, as if he had no idea who he was, and headed in the direction of the library.

II

William had never been inside Avenfore library before. It was a modest sub-library, the main library for the area being located in the neighbouring town of Drunfarnam. According to the brass nameplate on her desk, the sub-librarian's name was Miss Veronica Aguevals. William looked at her curiously as she handed him a new membership form to complete. She was a rather severe-looking woman. With her prim and proper appearance, thin-rimmed glasses, perfectly-outlined lips, and her blonde hair worn up in a stiff bun and held in place with lacquer. There was something cold and unforgiving about her, William thought. However, she returned William's greeting in a friendly manner and gave him a gracious smile as he filled out his name on his new library card.

'My dear William Howbbler, you may now enjoy our wonderful library; I hope you find a book to your liking. If you need anything in particular, please let me know and I will do all I can to accommodate your request.' William thanked her, surprised at her friendliness.

Elsie and Bridget were sitting at the back of the library and they beckoned William over to join them.

'You seem to have made a good impression on Miss Aguevals,' Elsie whispered into his ear, 'she's not usually as friendly as that. It's not easy to get a smile out of her and she never says a word more than the bare minimum. Normally, it's as if everyone upsets her.'

Bridget gave Elsie a little kick under the table to silence her. Veronica Aguevals was staring at them over the rim of her glasses. Then, clearly unable to contain her excitement any longer, Bridget whispered to William, 'We're preparing a play for the Falcon Fair. It's a festival that's held every summer in Avenfore and it's sponsored by the Night Bird Society. There are various competitions throughout the day and we're going to go in for the short play competition. It's the most important one and it's held in the village hall. Chris has written the script and now we're looking for ideas for costumes.' She paused for a moment and then looked at William with a shy smile. 'Chris has included you in the script. We wanted it to be a surprise.' Bridget looked at Elsie and they both giggled as quietly as they could.

William was taken aback. 'I'll have to think about it; I've never acted before, not even in a school play.'

'But you can't say no,' Bridget whispered in alarm, 'Chris wrote the script with you in mind.'

Elsie was glaring at him. 'Anyway,' she hissed, 'we'll be in costume and made up, so who's to recognise you? We've loads of time to rehearse too. It's going to be great fun.'

William had no choice: he realised he'd been well and truly set up. Pleased with their victory, the girls each kissed him on his cheek at the same time, which made him rather uncomfortable. He wondered what his part in the play was going to be and how Chris had managed to come up with the script in such a short time. But before he could ask about his role, the main door burst open and three unruly, rather troublesome-looking boys entered the library.

With their light ash-brown hair, blue eyes and prominent noses, the three were almost identical to each other and William surmised that they must be brothers. What they most definitely were not was well-behaved. Rather than being quiet, they appeared to be trying to make as much noise as possible. William wondered that Miss Aguevals, the librarian, had not taken them to task over this until he realised that she was no longer at her desk.

Turning to Elsie and Bridget he noticed the smiles had disappeared from their faces and their heads were lowered over their books. Barely moving her lips, Bridget murmured, 'Don't look at them, William, please. Just pretend you're reading.'

Seeing how upset the girls were, William did as Bridget asked, shifting closer towards her as if he was reading her book since he hadn't got one himself. There was a tense awkward silence as they pretended to concentrate on their reading. Even with his head down, William sensed the gaze of the three brothers on them. He felt uncomfortable and thought it was ridiculous that they should be acting like that for fear of these three boys.

Elsie, who seemed to have sensed that William was struggling to control himself, muttered, 'Please William, don't look at them. Pretend they're not there.' But William had had enough of this farce. Raising his head, he met their eyes. The three of them were standing near the librarian's desk staring at him defiantly.

One of the boys – the ringleader, William thought – sauntered towards them.

'Hi, girls,' he smirked at Bridget and Elsie, 'I see you've got yourselves a new little friend. Aren't you going to introduce him to us?' The two girls remained motionless, acting as if they hadn't heard him. William, however, stared back at him, angry at the way he'd spoken. The boy leaned forward, his hands on the table in front of William, in a provocative gesture. 'Didn't any of you hear me, then?'

Elsie grabbed William's wrist to stop him standing up. He looked furiously at the youth, who gave him another annoying smirk. They tried to outstare each other for a few tense moments, when, all of a sudden, the other boy screwed up his face and groaned in pain. The librarian, Miss Aguevals, had crept up behind him and was giving his ear a good sharp twist as she marched him to the library door.

'Tom Aguevals, I'm not going to put up with this behaviour either in the library or outside it,' she warned. 'Have I made myself clear? Now off home with you this instant. Pat, Jack, you too.' Miss Aguevals gestured at the other two boys who were looking every bit as terrified as Tom, 'I shall deal with you all later!'

Tom Aguevals ran off holding his ear, his two brothers close behind him. To William and the girls' surprise, Veronica Aguevals came over to their table and smiled at them sweetly. 'I must apologise for my nephews' appalling behaviour,' she said, 'If they bother you again, please let me know and I assure you, I'll take harsher measures.' After seeing the look of pain on Tom's face, William couldn't even begin to imagine how much harsher the measures might be.

'Boy, that must have hurt,' Elsie muttered, as Miss Aguevals returned to her desk.

'They're her nephews?' William said.

Bridget nodded, smiling at the incredulous look on William's face. 'Her brother's children,' she whispered. 'Their parents are in the United States and the triplets were born there.'

'What are they doing here, then?' William asked.

'You mean other than causing trouble and generally making a nuisance of themselves?' Elsie retorted.

'They go to St Elm's,' Bridget explained.

'There's no chance they'll be in my class at St Elm's, is there?'

'Don't worry, they're a year older than us.'

Calm returned to the library, and William suddenly wondered where Chris was.

'We're meeting him at twelve o'clock in Malconary's,' Elsie said, 'to talk about the play and have an ice cream.'

'I bet that's where those three like to hang out,' said William.

Bridget hastened to reassure him, 'They won't dare approach when they see Chris,' she said with pride in her voice. 'At the beginning of last school year, he gave them a good hiding. Two of them went for him one day after school, but he took them both on. They've steered clear of him since then.'

Elsie picked up her books and stood up. 'Let's go,' she said rather loudly, eliciting a sharp glare from Miss Aguevals, 'it's almost twelve and Chris will be waiting!'

III

Malconary's coffee shop was at the other end of the village square to the library. As they walked along, William cast a look around but failed to spot Gregor Watengroe, although his motorcycle and side-car was parked in full view, so he wasn't far off. Seeing the sidecar gave William an idea how to prevent Gregor from following him to his rendezvous with Mr Greewoof. He would need Chris's help and had no choice but to trust him to be discreet. But even though he'd only known Chris a short while, he felt sure he could count on him.

At the entrance to Malconary's, Elsie and Bridget met the Arinduff sisters, Gladis and Arline, coming out of the shop and stopped to chat to them. William was pleased, it would give him an opportunity to have a word alone with Chris.

He got straight to the point as soon as he sat down. 'I've got a problem, Chris, and I need you to help me out if you can. If you agree, I'm afraid you'll have to go along with what I say no questions asked. It's all rather complicated to explain.'

Chris didn't bat an eyelid. 'Go ahead. What do you want me to do?'

William pointed discreetly out the window across the square to where Gregor Watengroe's sidecar was parked. 'You see that sidecar? I need you to pour water into the petrol tank. I'll be here at two o'clock tomorrow and I'll leave my bike in the centre of the square. Then I'll set off walking down Chestnut Close towards the jetty.'

'Sorry to butt in, but it's such a narrow alley way that hardly anyone goes down it.'

'Which is precisely why I've chosen it,' replied William, 'He'll have to follow me on foot. Don't worry, Chris, I've thought this through. When I get into the alley, I'll start to run fast and then I'll double back via High Street. It won't take me more than a few minutes to get to the jetty and back. That's all the time you'll have to do the job.'

Chris had been listening attentively. 'No problem, William, I'll have it done in under a minute. You can count on me.'

'Not a word about this to anyone, please.'

'Trust me, William,' Chris replied, 'Mum's the word. Oh!'

William stared as Chris grabbed the menu from its holder on the table and began to study it as though his life depended on it. He looked up to see Elsie making her way towards them with a suspicious look on her face. 'What are you two up to?' she asked, as she and Bridget sat down beside them.

William grinned at Chris, whose face was now bright red. 'Do you fancy a vanilla cone?'

CHAPTER 7

Ravenwood Castle

$\mathcal{A}$ T SIXTEEN MINUTES PAST NINE THE following day, William dashed off to his uncle's shop. Walter, dead on time, was waiting for him at the door, his tool bag packed and ready. Aunt Edna was in the garage starting the van. 'Good morning Uncle Walter!'

His uncle looked pointedly at his pocket watch and said, 'Six minutes late. Punctuality does not seem to be one of your strong points. Not to worry. We still have three to spare. From here to the castle it takes exactly eleven minutes.' William found it amusing that his uncle was such a stickler for punctuality, although maybe it wasn't so surprising given all the hours he devoted to clocks.

The elegant entrance to the castle was flanked by stone statues, which the ivy had almost completely smothered. Aunt Edna dropped them off at the main door and said that she'd be back to fetch them in a couple of hours.

Mr Dreephy came out to meet them. 'Mr Mullween has asked me to convey his apologies. A rather pressing matter cropped up early this morning and he has had to go to Dublin,' he explained, as William and Uncle Walter followed him inside up the stone steps to the door and entered the castle.

The spacious entrance hall was graced with symmetrical flights of white oak stairs that rose on each side to meet on the upstairs landing. Two huge oil paintings, on either side of a low lancet doorway, dominated the arch-shaped hollow under the landing: one was a landscape, showing a rather bleak view of the castle with Lesciern and the lake in the background; the other was a portrait of a dark, rather brooding-looking man in a starchy Victorian suit, who bore a striking resemblance to Bryon Mullween, the man in the cloak that William had seen in the village square some days previously.

Crossing to the painting, William read the shield on the large gilt picture frame: THE RT. HON. FERGUS MULLWEEN, MP, 1882. As far as William could recall, Fergus Mullween, was Byron's grandfather who had built Ravenwood Castle and both St Elm's and St Clem's schools. He glanced up at the solemn figure in the painting. From this angle it looked as though Fergus Mullween was staring down at him in a rather formidable and disapproving manner. No wonder Byron Mullween looks grumpy, William thought, it must run in the family.

William realised all of a sudden that he was alone in the entrance hall. Uncle Walter and Elwood Dreephy had gone on without him and were nowhere to be seen. Walking to the centre of the hall, he looked about him for any clue as to which direction they may have gone, but, to his dismay, the entrance hall boasted a profusion of doors to choose from. Other than the lancet door beneath the staircases, there were two other doors at the bottom of each flight of stairs. Up on the landing were a further two doors, leading to – well, goodness knows where.

William paused. He had no idea which of the five doors led to the room where his uncle was. Neither did he wish to take pot luck. All he could do was follow his intuition. He opted for the door on the right, because it was the nearest. Gently easing it open, he called:

'Uncle Walter?'

He waited a few seconds and on hearing no reply, he went over to the door on the left and called again:

'Uncle Walter!'

Again, there was no reply. He decided against going up to the first floor, thinking that the bedrooms would be there. He tried the small lancet door, but it was locked, so he tried the only remaining option: the door to his left. He opened it cautiously and entered a long corridor. It took him to the servants' area, and the kitchen, where Mary Dreephy was working. She guessed he had lost his way and pointed him in the direction of the library on the first floor where Uncle Walter was working on the grandfather clock.

On his way to the library, the sound of a familiarly unpleasant voice stopped William in his tracks.

'Ah …! Mr Dreephy, zere you are,' the voice said from somewhere further down the corridor.

William froze in horror. He could still see the expressionless face of the voice's strange owner, with his weird haircut and the cold piercing eyes. But what on earth was Gregor Watengroe doing here?

His heart thumping so loud, he was afraid Gregor would hear it, William crept carefully further along until he could see Gregor at the other end of the corridor, talking to Mr Dreephy. As far as William could make out, the German was asking about the mooring jetty at the back of the castle.

'It's private,' he heard Mr Dreephy snap, 'not for the use of guests.' With that the gardener stalked off – thankfully away from William – in the direction of the kitchens. However, Gregor Watengroe, it seemed, was not prepared to take no for an answer quite so easily. He followed Elwood Dreephy along the corridor, still pestering him about the jetty, until they were both out of William's sight and earshot.

William gave a long sigh of relief and, checking the corridor to make sure the coast was clear, he bolted for the library where he was sure Uncle Walter was waiting for him.

When William reached the library, his uncle wasn't there. Then he remembered that Uncle Walter usually checked all the clocks in the house, and not just the grandfather clock, on his annual inspection. So he sat down in the library to wait.

Mrs Dreephy had left a tea tray on one of the library side tables and William munched on some tasty shortbread biscuits and examined the collection of old books while he waited for his uncle to return. One book in particular caught his attention. It was a small volume entitled *Plants and their Secrets*, and the author was none other than Abelard Greewoof.

Just then a burst of organ music floated through the library from somewhere outside. It sounded like one of William's favourites: Bach's *Cantata BWV 645*. He wondered for a brief moment if Gregor Watengroe was playing the organ, but quickly decided that it couldn't be him. There was a brightness and sweetness about the playing that William was sure Gregor did not possess.

William left the library and followed the music. It led him into a charming music room adjoining the library. The door was ajar and peeping through he saw a magnificent piano at one end, dominating the room. Seated at the piano was a girl, about the same age as himself, he guessed, with long, dark-brown hair tied in a pony-tail with a brightly-coloured band. Engrossed in her music, she did not notice William slip quietly into the room. He stood there, fascinated by the way in which she was able to coax an extraordinary sound out of the instrument.

The piece ended, and William found himself spontaneously applauding. The girl wheeled around in surprise. Now that she was facing him, William could see that she was beautiful; not in the same pretty way as his cousin, Elsie, or Bridget, but in a more striking, almost alarming way, with strong features and the brightest green eyes William had ever seen.

'I'm sorry to startle you,' he said, 'but I heard you playing, and I just had to come and listen. You play brilliantly.'

'It's very kind of you to say so.' She held out her hand to William. 'I'm Amaranta Bonclane. It's a pleasure to meet you …?'

'William Howbbler,' William said as he shook her hand. 'I'm here with my uncle, Mr Harckwell; he's repairing the castle clocks.'

The girl smiled – quite a dazzling smile, William noticed.

'Why, yes, I met Mr Harckwell earlier, coming out of the library. He seems very nice.'

'He is,' said William, then paused, unsure of what to say next. Eventually, he managed: 'So, are you a guest here?'

'No, I live here.'

It was William's turn to be surprised. 'Really, I thought Mr Mullween lived here alone?'

Amaranta nodded. 'Yes, he did, but Ernest Wiglann is my uncle and so Mr Mullween is kindly allowing me to live here because I'm starting school in August. I have a place at St Clem's.'

'Oh,' William said, 'me too! I mean, I'm starting school in August. Not at St Clem's obviously. At St Elm's.'

Aramanta laughed, a bright, musical laugh that made William smile.

'We can be newbies together then,' she said.

Somehow William liked the sound of that.

At that moment, Elwood Dreephy appeared at the door of the music room, wearing the same droll expression on his face as earlier. William couldn't help wondering if it was the only one he had.

'I came to tell you your uncle has finished,' Mr Dreephy said, 'and your aunt has arrived to collect you both. They are waiting for you at the main door.'

William turned to say his goodbyes. 'It was very nice meeting you, Amaranta,' he said, shaking her hand once again.

'Likewise,' Amaranta replied cheerfully, 'and I hope we meet again soon, William Howbbler.'

As he turned to follow Mr Dreephy towards the entrance hall, William hoped so too.

CHAPTER 8

The Night Bird Society

I

O N Thursday, William couldn't wait for the afternoon to come after spending half the night turning over questions in his mind that he trusted Mr Greewoof would answer. *Why was Gregor following him? What had the letter said? Was that why he was being followed? Was his dad mixed up in this business? Why was all this happening to him?*

At two o'clock on the dot, William left his bike in the middle of the square and walked off towards the jetty. As he expected, Gregor Watengroe followed him on foot. As arranged, Chris set about putting water into the tank and then hid in the park to check everything went to plan.

A few minutes later William was back in the square and pedalling off towards Drunfarnam. Gregor followed some distance behind on his sidecar, careful not to lose sight of his quarry.

William cycled along the Drunfarnam road past the two schools and Ravenwood Bridge, which led to Ravenwood Castle. There was no traffic on the road and glancing back, he saw his pursuer still following. William began to feel disheartened. Why hadn't the engine seized up? He couldn't work out why it was still going. Things weren't going as planned and he was now a long way out of the village. His only hope was that the engine would seize up soon. Gregor was closing the distance on him and his legs began to ache as he pedalled as hard as he could.

The road now curved around through the trees hiding William from view and Gregor now accelerated until he was right behind him. William pedalled even harder, not wasting a second even to glance behind, but, to his horror, Gregor drew level with him and put out a gloved hand to grab William's saddle. As he did so, there was a short, sharp explosion and then a spluttering sound and to William's immense relief, the motorcycle jolted to a halt: the water had finally got into the carburettor. Gregor cursed and shook his fist, trying to work out what had gone wrong with his vehicle. William turned his bike around as quickly as he could in the direction of Avenfore, and with a broad grin of satisfaction, he sped past the furious, sweating Gregor who was still wrestling to get his motor-bike going.

William was jubilant as he cycled back through the village and set off along the Dronfore road. He was so proud that his plan had worked that his legs no longer ached. From time to time, he threw a cautionary backward glance, but Gregor was nowhere to be seen. Just before Hollypoint, he took the turning off to the right, exactly as Mr Greewoof had told him. A little way along the track, he saw a rather weather-beaten sign atop a decaying wooden post which read:

Bird Sanctuary. Protected Area.

No Entry!

By Order, Night Bird Society

Beneath the writing was the symbol of a falcon, which looked very familiar to William: it was identical to the falcon on the Knights Templar book Mr Greewoof had given him. He remembered the name of the publisher on the book: NBS. Could that be 'Night Bird Society'? But William had no idea why a birdwatching society would want to publish a book about the Knights Templar.

William leaned his bike against the post and walked the few yards to an old rusty gate. Birches, ashes, oaks and alders had all grown up in what had once been the old churchyard. Nature, it seemed, had needed no help from man to reclaim her lost territory.

Some fifty yards down the churchyard path stood the remains of the church itself. Although curious, William decided to wait where he was for Mr Greewoof. He checked his wristwatch and saw that it was three o'clock. A few seconds later, he had sensed that some-body was behind him and swivelled round to see who it was. 'Mr Greewoof!' he exclaimed, 'I didn't see you coming.'

'I'm sorry, I didn't mean to scare you, William', said Mr Greewoof, 'I arrived early as I wanted to observe a pair of flycatchers that have started nesting again in the church. They've come back this season after many years without appearing.'

Mr Greewoof had come out of the church. He had a pair of binoculars around his neck and was carrying a kerosene storm lantern. In his beige gabardine coat with its enormous hood, he looked as if he was wearing a monk's cowl. William was slightly disconcerted at the Latin master's strange attire, but was pleased to see him nevertheless. Mr Greewoof asked him to follow him.

'This is a wonderful place for birds,' the Latin master whispered. 'Nobody disturbs them, and they can nest in the shelter of the church walls that are still standing. Oh, and I see you managed to shake off Gregor,' he murmured. 'Well done! Now come this way.'

Cautiously, so as not to disturb the birds, they entered the church and made their way towards the back, winding their way through the stones and the brushwood that were strewn around inside the crumbling walls. William somehow recalled hearing that the fire that had burned down the church had occurred one night about forty years ago, and although its cause remained a mystery, most of the villagers put it down to a bolt of lightning. Since then it had been at the mercy of the elements. Protected by the walls, the lush vegetation had thrived; ivy had wrapped itself around the columns, ferns hung from the beautiful capitals, the branches of oak trees had pushed through the window openings. Birds had built their nests in the walls, the abacuses and the gargoyles. William began to see why Mr Greewoof liked the place, it was like a strange, carefully abandoned garden.

At the end of the nave they reached what had once been the sacristy, the only part to have entirely escaped the fire. Mr Greewoof took out his lighter and lit the lantern he was carrying. At the back of the sacristy, William saw an elaborately carved narrow stone arch jutting out of the wall. Handing the lantern to William, Mr Greewoof rummaged in the pockets of his gabardine and took out an old iron key.

'Now you'll see why I've brought you here,' said Abelard Greewoof. He pushed hard against the part of the wall enclosed by the arch. William jumped as the wall made a low, grinding noise and began to revolve to reveal a narrow dark corridor, at the end of which stood a solid oak door the same shape as the arch.

Mr Greewoof asked William to shine the light so that he could find the keyhole, then he inserted the key, turned it three times and pushed open the heavy door. It was almost pitch-black inside. Instructing William to stay where he was, he rummaged in his pockets again, took out his silver lighter and lit one of the old-fashioned torches that was fixed to the walls on either side of the door. Carrying the torch, Mr Greewoof disappeared into the blackness. As William watched from the doorway, one by one, the warm glow of oil lamps began to fill the room until it was bathed in light. Then Abelard beckoned to William to enter.

'Welcome,' he said, 'to the secret chamber of the Night Bird Society!'

II

The chamber was almost rectangular in shape, with a stone floor and high ceiling. A tiny skylight at the top should have allowed some light through but was blocked on the outside by thick vegetation. The first thing William noticed was a large, cherry wood lectern at the far end of the room. At its centre, was an elaborate carving of a falcon, similar to that he had seen on the sign and the cover of the book Mr Greewoof had given him some days ago. Behind the lectern, the entire wall from floor to ceiling was covered by a magnificent tapestry, depicting a medieval battle between the Knights Templar and Saladin's Mameluke army. William gasped in surprise. The tapestry was an exact replica of the frontispiece illustration he had seen in the Knights Templar book.

'Ah, I see you recognise the picture, young Howbbler?'

William nodded, unable to speak. Bewildered, William looked around him. Apart from the lectern, the room was sparsely furnished. In one corner stood a heavy writing bureau. In the middle of the chamber were two ornate oak armchairs, the armrests of which were carved with more falcons. There was a strange, but not unpleasant, smell of fat and wax from the lamps illuminating the chamber, and William was suddenly struck by an overall sense of déjà vu. He felt his legs turn to jelly and he quickly sat in one of the armchairs.

The teacher sat in the chair opposite William. He took off his glasses and wiped them slowly. All the doubts and questions that had been haunting William since the day before came flooding back. He looked at Mr Greewoof, impatient for him to begin.

The teacher finished wiping his glasses and looked over at William. 'You are here today, William Howbbler,' he began, 'because everything in this chamber is part of a great secret: a secret which your father wishes you to share. It was here that your father himself learned the secret and it was I who had the honour of revealing it to him. Today you too will learn many things that are known only to a privileged few, but, before I go on, you must be warned that nothing that you hear is ever to be repeated to anyone else.'

Abelard Greewoof stood up and took a minute glass phial containing a green potion out of his pocket. Showing it to William, he placed it on the bureau in the corner. 'For your peace of mind, you should know that if, after hearing what I have to say, you don't wish to go on, you can wipe everything from your memory with a sip of this potion and it will all appear as a dream.

'As I said, only a certain few have inherited that right. It has been passed down over the centuries from father to son. But it is not enough to have inherited the right – one must also show that one is ready to assume the commitments and responsibilities that it entails. Once you know the great secret, your life will never be the same again. If you are *not* convinced of going through with it, you have only to drink the potion.'

William stared at the phial on the bureau, torn between an immense curiosity to know more about this great secret and fear. It was all so sudden. He, William, part of an ancient secret? And his father, who had been keeping this secret all this time. Had this something to do with why they left Avenfore so unexpectedly ten years ago? He had to admit to himself that he was anxious of what lay ahead. Unsure of what to do, he looked about the chamber. In the flickering light, his eye was drawn towards the tapestry behind the lectern and the faces of the Crusader Knights confronted, as they were, by overwhelming odds.

He turned his gaze back to the Latin master, who was watching him curiously. 'Thank you, Mr Greewoof,' William said, 'I won't be needing the potion. Please tell me what my father wants me know.'

CHAPTER 9

The Wicked Crow

I

'DID YOU READ THE BOOK I gave you, William?' Mr Greewoof's eyes twinkled as he continued to stare at William.

'Yes, Mr Greewoof, I did.'

'Excellent! With a mind as curious as yours, I had no doubt you would. And so, I must ask you: what did you think of it?'

'It's a wonderful story, Mr Greewoof. I really enjoyed it.'

'What if I were to tell you that the *Chronicle of the Most Noble Order of the Alliance* was not a storybook, but a *history* book? The *true* history of Avenfore. What would you say to that?'

William realised he was now staring at Mr Greewoof with his mouth open. He could hardly believe what he was hearing. The Order of the Alliance was real? The story of the Knights Templar was *real?*

Abelard Greewoof sat back in his chair and began:

'Many years ago, an evil man was born here in Ireland, the son of a Transylvanian nobleman and his Irish wife. In his youth, he set his sights on a political career, when his father died, however, the young man inherited an immense fortune. He therefore abandoned his seat to devote his time to his real calling: witchcraft and black magic. This despicable character's name is Ignatius Nosmorum, although, he has always been known as the Wicked Crow on account of his tall, thin frame, dark eyes and his peculiar habit of always wearing black.

'The Wicked Crow is also a collector – of things, of people, and of books. One day he gained possession of the most important legacy of the Alliance: the *Book of the Knights Templar Errant*, which having been lost for over five centuries could hardly have fallen into worse hands. Of course, Ignatius wasn't aware of its real importance at the beginning. But, one day, he discovered that the book was far more valuable than he had thought.

'Upon learning of the book's significance, Ignatius took the book to an expert in classical languages in Dublin to see if he could decipher it. As you know from the *Chronicle of the Noble Order of the Alliance*, the *Book of the Knights Templar Errant* is written in a complicated cryptographic language. As luck would have it, the expert turned out to be a good friend of mine, who, the moment he opened the book, realised just how unique and extraordinary a document it was.

'This friend asked the Wicked Crow if he would leave the book with him for a few days to examine it more thoroughly. Ignatius Nosmorum refused to let him keep it. The moment he left, my friend called me to tell me what he had seen. I immediately set off for Dublin, convinced that he'd seen the *Book of the Knights Templar Errant*. Since its disappearance in the sixteenth century nobody had set eyes on it – there have been rumours and false leads, of course, but always to no end. To recover it has been amongst one of the most important missions of the Order of the Alliance since its founding.'

William, who had been very quiet so far, could not resist asking something that had been going around and around in his head, 'So the Order of the Alliance still exists?'

Abelard Greewoof smiled mysteriously.

'Indeed, it does, young Howbbler, and your father and I are members of it.'

William stared at Mr Greewoof in amazement. It suddenly dawned on him that the birdwatching club his father belonged to and the Order of the Alliance were one and the same. 'Wow!' was all he managed to say.

Mr Greewoof chortled. 'Indeed, young Master Howbbler! Now, let me show you something.'

Abelard Greewoof pulled an old-fashioned looking key from one of the many pockets of his gabardine. He walked to the writing bureau in the corner of the chamber and unlocked one of the drawers, withdrawing from it an old, time-worn leather cylindrical case. Beckoning William over to the bureau, the Latin master undid the leather cords that secured the top of the case and with immense care took out a rolled-up parchment and gently spread it out in front of them.

William gasped in astonishment: the parchment was filled with symbols, hieroglyphs and Latin annotations. With its borders of red and gold and lapis lazuli blue, it was a thing of beauty in itself. He could have looked at it forever.

'It's beautiful, isn't it?' Mr Greewoof said softly, his eyes reflecting bright in the dim torchlight shining on them from above the bureau.

'This parchment contains the code to decipher the *Book of the Knights Templar Errant*. Without the code, it cannot be read or understood. The book is not just a record of where the treasures were hidden, it also tells all the secrets of the Order and the ancient lore of Lesciern and the druid-monks. Above all, there is a secret that the book holds which makes it so important to us: the exact place where the Holy Grail was hidden.'

Mr Greewoof looked at William solemnly before adding. 'You cannot talk about this with anyone, even if it is one of ours. Have you understood this young Howbbler?' William nodded.

Mr Greewoof carefully rolled up the parchment and returned it to its sheath, which he then locked away again in the writing bureau. His face was solemn as he returned to his chair.

II

Silence had fallen and William sat anxious for the teacher to continue his story. He waited a few minutes before asking. 'So, what happened next, Mr Greewoof? Did you get the book from the Wicked Crow in the end?'

'No, William, we did not,' sighed the Latin master. 'The book is still missing, and we are none the wiser as to its whereabouts.'

'But this Wicked Crow must have it then?'

'That's the thing, young Howbbler. We don't know.' He looked over at William who was trying hard to conceal his impatience. Clearly, he wasn't trying hard enough as Mr Greewoof gave a wan smile and continued.

'Firstly, I must tell you about Aaron Seblean. Aaron was one of us, a gallant Knight of the Order. He worked at the main library in Drunfarnam. Imagine Mr Seblean's surprise when, about a year ago, and years after he had consulted my friend in Dublin, Ignatius Nosmorum appeared in Drunfarnam library asking to access its rare book collection in the hope it would help him decipher the contents of his book.

'That day he was accompanied by his sidekick, Gregor Watengroe, and, in his hand, he carried the *Book of the Knights Templar Errant*. Ignatius went up to the counter and asked to consult some old books. Mr Seblean saw the book in his hand and immediately recognised it from my friend's description which I had passed on to him. He couldn't believe his good fortune at having such a god-sent opportunity to recover the most precious legacy of the Alliance.

'Mr Seblean then put his plan into action. First, he made a show of helping Ignatius by showing him some ancient books, which Mr Seblean knew full well would not help the Wicked Crow in any way but would keep him occupied. As Ignatius pored over the books, Mr Seblean locked the doors and then called the police to say that a couple of individuals were trying to make off with a highly valuable book. When the police arrived, Mr Seblean asked them to wait at the desk while he checked the library records to make sure there had been no confusion.

'Mr Seblean then informed Ignatius and Gregor that they too had to leave the library on account of an unforeseen occurrence. He also advised them that they had to leave their book in the library until the necessary checks had been made. Barely containing his rage, Ignatius Nosmorum threatened Mr Seblean with his walking stick – an evil-looking weapon with the sharp ebony head of a crow at its tip – but with the police standing by the desk, he was forced to rein in his fury. With a curse, he handed over the book to Mr Seblean saying that he'd better have everything sorted out when he came back the next day.

'Mr Seblean then telephoned me to ask me to meet him in Drunfarnam, where he would give me the book. We arranged to meet in the bookshop called The Falcon's Nest, which was our usual meeting place. The whole building belongs to the birdwatchers' club or, as you now know, to the Order of the Alliance. I waited there until quite late, along with Mr Valcott O'Neill, who runs the shop and is, of course, one of our Brothers. Alas, neither Aaron Seblean nor the book appeared that night.

'The next day we looked everywhere for Mr Seblean, but to no avail. For a week we searched high and low for some clue as to where he was or, at least, to what had happened. All we found was his jacket, floating in the Inni River near Drunfarnam.

'In the jacket pocket we found a note that we haven't been able to decipher. We assume it contains a clue as to the whereabouts of the book, but we don't know that. It's a riddle we haven't been able to solve and it may have no bearing on the book whatsoever, for all we know. But I'm convinced Ignatius was behind his disappearance.

'When Gregor came back to Avenfore a week ago, it was a great surprise, but, ironically, a cause for celebration too. We thought that maybe Ignatius didn't have the book, after all, and had sent Gregor

to search for it. Or perhaps he has the book and he's sent Gregor
to look for the cipher parchment. But we can't be sure; it's all guess-
work. Or then, again ...' here Mr Greewoof paused momentarily
and looked at William gravely, 'it is possible that Gregor is here for
other motives.'

'What other motives?' William asked.

'I don't wish to alarm you, dear boy. As I say, it's all conjecture,
and the only thing that's certain is that Gregor appears to have
changed his plans when he learnt you were coming. But since you
arrived at the station, he's been following you, and we believe he is
waiting for the chance to kidnap you.'

Despite Mr Greewoof's assurances, William felt completely
alarmed. 'Kidnap me? But why? Why would Gregor Watengroe
want to kidnap *me*?'

Abelard Greewoof looked gravely at William for a moment, and
at last said. 'Because of your father.'

William paled. 'My father? But what has this got to do with him?'

'Everything, I'm afraid. You see, it was your father who alerted
Ignatius Nosmorum to the significance of the book.'

'No!'

William felt himself grow hot and angry. Mr Greewoof was
wrong. Even though he had only just found out about the Order,
he knew his father. Arnold Howbbler was not the sort of man to
betray a trust in that way; he was quite sure of that.

'You're wrong, Mr Greewoof; my father is no traitor.'

Mr Greewoof smiled and patted William's shoulder gently.

'Easy, young Howbbler, please remain calm. Although, I must
say, your loyalty to your father does you every credit. Of course,
you are right; your father is no traitor to the Order or anyone else
for that matter, but, nevertheless, he was responsible for Ignatius
becoming aware of the *Book of the Knights Templar Errant* and the
powerful secrets contained within it waiting to be unlocked.'

William looked at the Latin master miserably. He simply couldn't imagine his father doing anything as wicked or as foolish as having anything to do with a man like Ignatius Nosmorum.

'Please, Mr Greewoof, please tell me what happened. I need to know.'

'Of course, you do, dear boy,' said Abelard Greewoof. 'You see, it was your father who discovered the existence of the *Book of the Knights Templar Errant* after all these centuries of being lost. Many in the Order believed that the Book was just a legend, or that it had been destroyed many centuries ago. But not your father. He always held that it still existed, and it was this conviction that spurred him on to track it down. He spent many years studying the *Chronicle of the Most Noble Order of the Alliance* and the diaries and accounts the Knights had written of their decades-long searches following the disappearance of Corneille the Grey and the book for clues as to where it might be.

'The Order of the Alliance owes a great debt to your father. He never gave in, even after countless failures and disappointments, always uncovering a new clue that refreshed his hopes. Finally, about ten years ago, he found proof, not only of its existence, but that it was in the possession of Ignatius Nosmorum, who at the time was a complete stranger to your father and to the Alliance.

'It appeared that part of Ignatius's inheritance included a large mansion on the outskirts of Drunfarnam. Like Ignatius, his grandfather had been an avid collector of rare manuscripts, art and antiques and it was likely that it was he who had found it and brought it back to Ireland. After so many centuries, it was tantalising for your father to know that the book, so precious to the Order of the Alliance, was now so close to home.

'After so many frustrations and lost opportunities Arnold simply could not bear the thought of the Alliance having to do without this treasure. Neither could he bear the idea of its remaining in the hands of such a despicable individual. He was ready to do anything to regain it. Unfortunately, he told no one of his plans. He was prepared to act alone, unwilling to involve or endanger the other Knights in his desperate mission.'

Mr Greewoof paused for a moment.

'Or perhaps, he was unwilling to risk that reason might prevail and he would be talked out of what he intended to do?'

William felt the question, rhetorical though it might be, hanging uncomfortably in mid-air. The Latin master continued his tale. 'The next morning, before it was light, your father broke into the Nosmorum mansion. He had the book in his hands when Ignatius and one of his henchmen discovered him there. Although outnumbered, Arnold fought against them, but was unfortunate to receive a blow on the head from Ignatius's walking stick with the crow's head tip and the book was wrenched from his hands.'

Mr Greewoof paused again and looked directly at William.

'And that was the moment when Ignatius realised that the book was of great value to somebody and he was determined to ascertain who and why.'

William felt his heart sink.

'You see, William,' he said softly, 'sometimes, despite our best intentions, life does not always go to plan. Do you agree?'

'Yes, Mr Greewoof,' William said. His mind was racing with all sorts of conflicting ideas.

'Do you want me to go on?'

William thought for a moment. Part of him didn't want to hear any more, but another part of him knew he needed to hear the whole story. After a moment, he looked up at Mr Greewoof and nodded.

Mr Greewoof smiled at him. 'Good. So, let us continue. Stunned by the blow, your father was unable to prevent Ignatius pulling back the balaclava he was wearing to look at his face. Luckily, he managed to push the evil man aside and flee from the mansion. Ignatius roared at his dogs to chase your father, but they were fast asleep in the garden, having eaten drugged meat your father had given them earlier and he escaped safely back to Avenfore.

'For some time, your father lay low and we heard no more from this malignant character. However, one day a few weeks later, Ignatius spotted your father coming out of the Falcon's Nest Bookshop in Drunfarnam and recognised him. After that Ignatius began making inquiries to identify your father and it was about that time that we believe he encountered someone in Avenfore' – now it was Mr Greewoof's turn to look upset – 'who was willing to act as his accomplice and give him the information that he needed to discover where your father lived.'

William was stunned. Someone in Avenfore had betrayed his father? He could hardly believe it?

'But who?' he cried. 'Who in Avenfore would do such a thing?

'That is the one thing, despite our best efforts over the past ten years, which we have been unable to find out. We do suspect, however, that whoever the spy is, they have been working with Gregor Watengroe. That man appears to know far too much information about your comings and goings than can be good for him. Or for you, for that matter.'

William was puzzled. 'But why would Gregor be interested in me? That's what I don't understand, Mr Greewoof? You said he wanted to kidnap me earlier, but why? Why would he, or Ignatius, want to kidnap me? Is there something else you aren't telling me?'

'Has your father ever told you why he took you and your mother away from Avenfore to Dublin?' Mr Greewoof asked.

William shook his head. His father had always refused to discuss the matter and had become irritated on the few occasions William had tried to press him on it.

Mr Greewoof gave him a sad smile. 'I didn't think he had, William, and for good reason. Arnold loves you, and your mother and Kristyn. Even if he could tell you, he would not have wanted any of you to live with the fear and suspicion which has haunted him in the ten years since we first encountered Ignatius Nosmorum. You see, the reason we suspect Gregor may be planning to kidnap you, is because this would not be the first time Ignatius or one of his cronies has attempted to do so.'

William was astonished. 'What do you mean? When? Where?'

'Here. In Avenfore.'

William was even more astounded. 'Here? But I don't remember … surely I would remember if someone had tried to kidnap me?'

'There is no reason why you should remember, William. You were very young at the time, barely four years of age.

'You were playing in the front garden, as you often did, when a car pulled up opposite your house in Fern Lane and Ignatius Nosmorum got out. He took a piece a paper from the inside pocket of his black coat, read it and walked across the road towards the garden gate. He stopped to check that there was nobody else around. Then he quickly entered the garden, his eyes fixed on you playing happily in the garden, unaware of his presence.'

William felt his throat go dry. He had no idea he had ever been in such danger and it wasn't a pleasant feeling. 'But how did I escape? Did my Dad turn up to save me? I don't remember.'

'Not your father,' Mr Greewoof explained, 'but fortunately for you, there was another member of the Order nearby. He tackled Ignatius before he could get to you and, taken by surprise, the evil man ran off back to his car and sped away from the village. You went on playing in the garden, blissfully ignorant of what was going on just yards away from you. As he fled, Ignatius dropped the piece of paper showing the map and directions to your house. We know that it was made by his Avenfore spy. Unfortunately, his handwriting is all we know about him, even to this day.'

'I … I …' William was lost for words.

'Your father has never told you about these events because they involve Order business and he swore an oath of silence. But the idea that your life was in danger led him to take the decision to move away from Avenfore. The Order helped to find him a safe place to live in the city. Given what had happened, it seemed best to keep you all well away from the activities of the Alliance until we discovered who Ignatius's spy was. Unluckily, that is something that still eludes us.'

'So that's why Dad didn't want me to go to St Elm's before?' Now William understood.

'Yes, that was one unfortunate side-effect of the whole dreadful business. For a long while, Arnold thought it best that you not attend St Elm's in case it put you in danger.'

'Then why did he change his mind?'

'Following Aaron Seblean's disappearance, your father contacted me to discuss a substitute Knight. Believing that you were ready to become a member of the Alliance, I put your name forward, and the other Knights signalled their approval. Your father resisted at first, but we talked him round. Actually, it wasn't that difficult to persuade him in the end: he knew you were ready for the challenge, whatever it might bring.'

William had no idea that a person could feel as proud – and grateful – as he did now. His heart felt full to bursting.

'Thank you for putting me forward, Mr Greewoof,' he said. 'And thank you, Dad,' he whispered to himself.

III

Mr Greewoof stood up and walked over to the writing desk. He picked up the phial with the forgetfulness potion and with a smile he uncorked the phial and downed its contents. William looked at him in disbelief.

The Latin master began to laugh. 'Umm! This herbal liqueur is quite delicious!' he said, chortling at the shocked look on William's face. 'Surely you didn't believe it could make you forget what you'd heard? I was certain you'd accept. An intelligent and curious chap like you would never pass up the chance to learn about new and secret things revealed only to a chosen few.'

Now William was laughing too. Then a thought struck him, and he stopped.

'Mr Greewoof,' he said excitedly, 'I think I know who Ignatius's accomplice in Avenfore might be.'

Now Abelard looked surprised. 'Really? Who?'

'Byron Mullween,' William announced triumphantly. 'And possibly even his caretaker too, Mr Wiglann?'

Mr Greewoof frowned. 'But what makes you think that, young Howbbler?'

'Well, firstly, Gregor Watengroe is staying at Ravenwood Castle. And, secondly, we saw Byron Mullween and another person – I think it was his caretaker – carrying a heavy, bloodied sack into the basement of the castle only the day before yesterday. They were definitely up to no good.'

A flicker of a smile crossed Abelard Greewoof's face. It then turned into a grin and finally, he was laughing heartily.

'Oh, goodness me, dear boy, Ravenwood Castle is the only guesthouse in Avenfore, and Gregor is a guest. And that wasn't blood you saw; it was only paint. Byron often comes to my house with Ernest Wiglann and takes vegetables from my garden. I myself lent them the sack so that they could take some potatoes back to Ravenwood. I even helped them to load it onto the boat.'

William, although slightly embarrassed, held his ground.

'But how can you be so sure they are not spies, Mr Greewoof?'

'Because I have known Byron Mullween all his life, he may be a troubled man, but he is not an evil one. And as for Ernest Wiglann …'

The Latin master was staring directly at William.

'When Ignatius Nosmorum was challenged by a brother of our Order in your front garden all those years ago, he lashed out at his adversary with that cruel walking-stick he always carries. Our brother tried to ward off the blow, but the sharp beak of the crow's head tip smashed into his eye. So, now you know why Ernest Wiglann has a glass eye.'

William stared. He was at a loss as to what to say. He said the only thing he could say.

'I'm sorry, Mr Greewoof, I'm truly sorry.'

'No matter, dear boy, you weren't to know. No harm done.' He looked at his watch. 'It's very late and I'm afraid we must be on our way. There are still many secrets for you to learn if you are to be a Knight of the Order, but they will have to wait until another day. I expect your Aunt Edna will be expecting you back for some delicious tea right about now.'

As Abelard went about the room extinguishing all but one of the torches, William mentioned his father's letter and how curious he was to know its contents. Abelard muttered to himself as he searched through his pockets

'Ah, the letter! Now where did I put it? It must be here some-where in these pockets.'

William looked at him incredulously. Surely, he couldn't have forgotten that he'd burnt it? For a moment, he wondered if the potion the teacher had just drunk was doing its trick after all. But then Abelard drew out the letter and handed it to William.

'How the ...?' stammered William. 'It can't be the letter!' He turned it over in his hands, unable to believe what he was seeing, but there it was as intact as ever. 'But I saw you burn it with my own eyes.' He looked askance at Mr Greewoof, who was wearing a mischievous grin.

'What the eye sees, the mind believes,' said the teacher. 'We Knights of the Alliance still conserve some of the old druid magic.'

'Can I open it?' William asked.

'Of course, I gave it to you for that purpose.'

William eagerly opened the letter and saw that it was indeed his father's handwriting. He read aloud: 'THE LITTLE FALCON MUST

FLEDGE ITS WINGS.' He looked back at Mr Greewoof, not believing that was all it said.

Abelard merely smiled. But when he spoke, his voice was serious. 'Now that you have assented to becoming a Knight of the Order of the Alliance, you must pledge to keep the secret. You are never to speak of the Order to anyone, nor of anything related to it. The discretion of the brethren is vital to its survival. Evil is always lurking, waiting for its moment to strike.'

CHAPTER 10

Encounters

I

THE NEXT MORNING ELSIE CAME INTO William's room bright and early. 'Get up, lazybones,' she said, 'we've got to register the play today and it's market day, so we're going looking for props. You're coming with us, because Chris has to help his dad this morning. Bridget's waiting downstairs.'

'Don't be so cruel,' William groaned, still half-asleep. Truth was, the excitement of his meeting with Abelard Greewoof and the astonishing revelations about the Order of the Alliance, had kept him awake well into small hours of the morning and he had fallen asleep only a short time before dawn had broken. But he couldn't tell Elsie that, even if he had wanted to: firstly, because he was sworn to secrecy about the Order, and, secondly, from the look on Elsie's face, she was in no mood to listen to any excuses.

'Don't be such a baby,' she snapped, although she laughed when he sat up in bed and threw his pillow at her. 'Hurry up and get dressed,' she said. 'Bridget and I are waiting.'

The delicious aroma of Aunt Edna's freshly-baked fruit scones filled the kitchen as William entered the room and made him realise that he was really very hungry.

'Hello,' said Bridget, who looked very pretty in a pale-green summer dress.

Elsie was in a hurry. 'Let's go, folks,' she said, picking up a large brown envelope from the kitchen table and stuffing it into the straw shopping basket she was carrying on her arm. 'There's so much to do and we're already late.' William was about to protest that he hadn't had any breakfast, but she was already ushering him and Bridget towards the door.

Fortunately, Aunt Edna came to his rescue. 'I'm not sending any nephew of mine out on an empty stomach,' she declared. 'You girls go ahead and William can join you after he's eaten.'

'Thanks, Aunt Edna,' William said as Elsie and Bridget left, with Elsie's dire warning ringing in his ears, that if he didn't show up within the next twenty minutes or so, she would come back herself to fetch him.

'You're welcome,' said his aunt. 'Elsie is such a dear girl, but I'm afraid she has inherited her father's impatience.'

William smiled to himself as he tucked into scones and jam and a large cup of hot tea.

About ten minutes later, Elsie made good on her promise to come fetch him if he dilly-dallied.

'There you are,' she said, stomping into the kitchen. 'What's all the delay? I've left Bridget holding our place in the queue to register the play for the Falcon Fair and she's upset about being left on her own. I've promised her we'll be back immediately.' From the determined look on his cousin's face, William decided it was best not to argue with her. Reluctantly he left his half-eaten breakfast and set off with Elsie for the village hall where the registration for the play competition was taking place.

Bridget was not happy when they arrived. The reason was clear: the Aguevals triplets Pat, Tom and Jack had also prepared a play and were waiting to register it in the queue behind her. From the miserable look on Bridget's face, the triplets were being their usual unpleasant selves. Or at least two of them were. The third triplet, Jack Aguevals, was staring at Bridget with a rather strange, pathetic look on his face.

William felt a pang of guilt. It was his fault that poor Bridget had had to stand in the line alone. He smiled at her as he and Elsie joined the queue and was relieved to see she cheered up a little and returned his smile.

As they waited, Tom Aguevals sidled up to Elsie and whispered, 'You ain't gonna win, you know.' Then all three brothers started to giggle in a stupid childish manner. Elsie frowned, but didn't turn around, pretending she'd heard nothing.

Tom persisted. 'This year it's us who's gonna win.' Again, the silly laughter and, again, Elsie held herself in. 'The first prize will be ours,' went on Tom in a mocking voice. Elsie was furious. She took half a step backwards and let her heel come down on Tom's foot, lifting her other foot as she did so that Tom got the full force of her weight. The silly grin was wiped from his face.

'Aaargh!! Hey, what's up with you? Why don't you look where you put your feet?' he shouted, grabbing his foot in pain.

'Oh, I'm so sorry. I hadn't the faintest idea there was anyone behind us,' said Elsie sweetly, as Bridget and William tried not to laugh out loud.

But Tom was in no laughing mood. He glared nastily at Elsie and said, 'You'll be sorry you did that, Elsie Harckwell.'

'Yeah,' his brother, Pat, chimed in, 'you'll be very, very sorry. And your rotten friends, too.'

Elsie turned, hands on hips, and glared back at Tom Aguevals. 'You're pathetic,' she said. 'You don't frighten me.' William had to admire his cousin's feistiness, even if he wasn't convinced of the wisdom of inflaming the argument with the triplets.

Luckily, at that moment, he and the girls reached the top of the queue and Bridget exclaimed, 'It's our turn!'

II

Friday mornings meant market day in Avenfore. Stallholders came from all over the county to sell fruit and vegetables, flowers, clothes and second-hand objects and it was the perfect place to look for some of the props and costume accessories for the play. As usual, Elsie had come prepared. She handed them each a list of the things to look out for. Then she and Bridget set off together to scour the market place for the various items, leaving William to wander about on his own.

As he strolled amongst the market stalls, he kept an eye out in the first instance for Gregor Watengroe, but, to his relief, there was no sign of the spy. Thinking about Gregor brought William back to the trillions of questions whizzing about in his head since yesterday's meeting with Mr Greewoof. He was hoping they could meet again soon, but he would just have to wait until the Latin master contacted him again.

He glanced down at the list Elsie had given him. The first item on the list was:

An elf hat (or something that looks like it) red/green /blue?

William groaned inwardly. How on earth would he know what an elf hat looked like? This was not going to be easy. He would have to ask for help.

He spotted the girls over by a bric-a-brac stall and was about to join them when he noticed something odd. Jack Aguevals was standing a little way away watching the two girls, with that same soppy look on his face as earlier. William glanced about quickly for the other two triplets, afraid they were hiding somewhere close by to play a nasty trick on Elsie and Bridget, but they were nowhere to be seen. Just at that moment, Jack Aguevals noticed William. He turned suddenly and ran off through the market stalls. William followed, but the market was busy at that time of the morning and he lost him in the crowd of marketgoers.

William was so furious at the thought that the Aguevals would try to follow Elsie and Bridget that he didn't notice someone else approach him until they spoke.

'Hello, William, it's lovely to see you again.'

It was Amaranta Bonclane, the girl he had met at Ravenwood Castle a few days earlier. William knew it was impolite, but he couldn't help staring at her. In jeans and a crisp white cotton blouse, with a bold floral pattern, she looked even more strikingly green-eyed and dark-haired than before.

'It's nice to see you too, Amaranta. You look … uh … very summery.'

'Thank you,' she said with a smile, 'so do you.'

There was an awkward pause while William struggled to think what to say next. He wasn't usually this tongue-tied and it puzzled him.

'Well,' Amaranta said at last, 'I'll let you get on with your shopping.'

'Shopping?'

'The list?' She gestured towards Elsie's list. He'd completely forgotten about it.

'Oh, this list. It's not shopping. Well, it is, but not the usual kind of shopping. I mean … eh … it's shopping for the play.'

'The play?'

'Yes. I'm in a play. For the Falcon Fair competition.'

'Really? How exciting! What's it about?'

William stared at her dumbfounded for a moment. 'I don't know,' he admitted finally.

Amaranta giggled. 'That sounds really funny. How can you be in a play and not know what it's about?'

William grinned. 'Because Chris has only finished writing it for the registration today and we've not had the first read-through yet. That's this afternoon, I believe, or so Elsie tells me.'

'Elsie?'

'My cousin, Elsie Harckwell. She's in the play too. And her friend, Bridget Durffan – Bridget's Chris's sister.'

'It sounds fun.'

'I suppose so.'

Amaranta laughed. 'You don't seem very enthusiastic. Don't you want to be in it?'

William smiled. He was beginning to feel more confident now. Talking to Amaranta was actually pretty easy. He shook his head.

'Honestly? Not really. But don't tell Elsie that. She's rather insistent.'

She laughed again. 'Elsie sounds great. I'd love to meet her.'

'Meet who?' William jumped at the sound of Elsie's voice, as she and Bridget appeared behind him. They were each carrying a number of items in their baskets – their shopping trip had obviously been more successful than his.

'Hello,' said Elsie staring at Amaranta curiously. 'Who's this? Aren't you going to introduce us, William?'

'Er … yes, of course. Amaranta, this is my cousin Elsie Harckwell and her best friend, Bridget Durffan. Elsie, Bridget, this is Amaranta Bonclane, Mr Wiglann's niece. Amaranta's starting at St Clem's in the new term.'

'Oh, how wonderful,' said Elsie. 'What year will you be in?'

'Third,' Amaranta replied.

'You'll be our class then,' Elsie explained. 'Well, it's lovely to meet you, isn't it, Bridget?'

'Yes, lovely,' she mumbled. But she had a rather odd expression on her face.

'So, where are you living?' Elsie said brightly.

'With my uncle. At Ravenwood Castle.'

A look of horror crossed Elsie's face. 'At Ravenwood? Oh, you poor thing. How awful for you.'

'Actually, I quite like it there.'

'But, Mr Mullween,' Elsie retorted, 'I mean, he's the grumpiest man in Ireland. How can you bear it?'

'Well, he can be quite gloomy sometimes, I must admit,' Amaranta said, 'but he's been very kind to me so far.'

Elsie did not look convinced. 'It must be dreadful for you in that dark, gloomy place all on your own,' said Elsie, 'don't you think so, Bridget?'

Bridget didn't answer and William couldn't help noticing that she looked thoroughly miserable, although he had absolutely no idea why. Suddenly he felt somewhat outnumbered and wished Chris was here with him.

'Well, I must be going,' Amaranta said, 'it was great to meet you all. And best of luck with the play.'

'Of course,' Elsie said, 'the play! Why don't you join us?'

'No!!'

Bridget blushed crimson-red as they all turned to look at her. Even she seemed surprised at the sharpness of her tone.

'I mean, there's no part for her … you. There are only three characters in the play.'

'Maybe Chris could write another part especially for Amaranta,' said William, trying to be helpful. It clearly didn't help, because Bridget now looked as though she was going to burst into tears.

'But we've registered it already with just the three of us,' she whimpered.

'Bridget's right,' Elsie said, 'we have registered it for the competition with just the three parts.'

'Oh, that's no problem at all,' Amaranta replied, with a disarming smile. 'I really wouldn't want to act in the play. I'm not as brave as you and Bridget; I'd be far too scared. But I'd love to help out backstage. If you'll have me.'

Elsie beamed happily. 'Great, that's settled then,' she declared. 'First rehearsal is this afternoon at two o'clock at my house.'

CHAPTER 11

Odyssey in the Greenwood

I

IMMEDIATELY AFTER THEIR TRIP TO THE market and a hurried lunch, Elsie marshalled William upstairs to help her get everything ready before the others arrived for the rehearsal. They cleared out the attic and made it into a cosy place where they could rehearse undisturbed, with large cushions, an old sofa to sit on and a wooden box that served as a table. They found some curtains in a large wicker basket full of second-hand clothes and material that Aunt Edna and her friends had donated for costumes, and decorated one of the walls to give it the appearance of a stage with its backdrop. Elsie also brought her record player up to the attic so they could listen to music if they wanted.

The others arrived shortly before two o'clock and William introduced Amaranta to Chris. Although Bridget still appeared to be a little sulky, Chris was clearly pleased to have someone to help out behind the scenes. The three girls and William sat down on the cushions and waited for Chris to start. He pulled a bundle of papers out of his satchel and looked at them all nervously.

'This is the script,' he said, 'I've been working hard on it for a few weeks, and, well, I'm happy with it. See what you think.'

'I'm sure it will be great,' Elsie said, beaming encouragement at him. Chris sat down on the sofa looking quite pleased with himself. The others listened with rapt attention as he began to read:

'Our tale begins deep in an imaginary forest and tells the story of a fairy called Yss, who could only live during the hours of night. Her mission was to rescue elves and day fairies who were caught by the night. The moment night fell, Yss would come out into the dark forest.

'One night as she did her customary rounds of the forest she discovered Aorr, a day- elf, who had been caught by nightfall before he could get back to his home. She found him huddled up in the hollow of a tree trunk where he had sheltered to await the first light of day. They spent the whole night playing and laughing, oblivious to all else. As the hours slipped by, they realised that they had found more than just friendship; they had fallen in love.

'As the first shafts of sunlight pierced the sky, their situation became all too painfully clear. Yss had to disappear before the sun was up, or she would die. Aorr desolately clung to her hand looking into her delicate tear-stained green eyes. Yss placed her white cheek next to his face in a gesture of love and sadness. Aorr let go of her hand and ran off weeping through the forest, not daring to look back.

'Distraught he wandered aimlessly as the rain began to pour down on him. He slipped and fell into a deep mire and lay there, weeping sorrowfully until finally the rain ceased. As he lay face up in the mud his gaze lit on the rainbow that followed the storm. And it was then that he remembered the nymph, Obrixele, who appeared and disappeared with the rainbow. But if an elf was able to see her before she faded away, then their wish would be granted. Aorr was rather sceptical, but what had he to lose?

'Aorr ran through the forest in search of the magical nymph. He weaved among the trees and vaulted over the rocks and tree stumps. He shinned up a tall tree to locate the centre of the rainbow. He had to think of his wish before the rainbow disappeared, and with it Obrixele. Yet so exhausted and breathless was he that, when the nymph asked him to utter his desire, Aorr could not find his breath.

'Obrixele looked at him from an ever-greater distance as the colours of the rainbow lost their hue. Aorr, his hands on his knees struggled to find his voice as he saw his chance was slipping away, for Obrixele was only visible once in the life of an elf. He would never see her again in a rainbow. Making one last huge effort, he gasped out his wish in an almost inaudible voice, and raised his head towards the nymph, but saw only the sky.

'Defeated, he fell to his knees and wept in despair. When suddenly the gentlest of voices murmured, "Your wish has been granted." To his astonishment, there before him was Yss, smiling and happy. Beside her, floated Obrixele, playing a harp as the rainbow finally disappeared, and, with it, forever, the nymph. Aorr and Yss kissed. Then, hand in hand, they ran off through the forest together.'

Chris finished reading and looked up. 'So,' he said anxiously, 'do you like it? If you don't, I can make changes.'

'Oh, no, Chris,' Elsie said, 'it's perfect. You don't need to change a word!'

'It's wonderful, Chris,' said Bridget proudly.

'It really is great,' said Amaranta.

William, on the other hand, was feeling uncomfortable. Thoughts of the elf hat on Elsie's shopping list rattled around his head and he was beginning to wonder exactly what he let himself in for when he agreed to be in the play. 'Eh … it's very well written Chris, but … er … isn't it a bit childish?' he said.

'Well, of course, but it's just for fun Will,' snapped Elsie. 'And there will be lots of children in the audience anyway.'

'I suppose … but I'm not too sure about the kissing bit at the end?'

'Oh, yes, well …' Chris said. 'I can take that out, if you like.'

'No!' All three girls spoke in unison.

'The play is just right as it is,' Elsie said, 'and everything's staying in. So, come on, let's get started; we've got lots to do and less than a fortnight before the competition.'

They spent the rest of the afternoon rehearsing. Bridget was cast as the fairy, Yss, with Elsie playing Obrixele. Much to William's dismay, he discovered that Chris had given himself the part of the narrator, which meant he wouldn't actually have to appear on the stage: his voice would only be heard from the wings. Despite all his objections, William was given the part of the elf, Aorr.

'Chris is too shy, William, he'd never be able to do it and it wouldn't be fair to make him,' Elsie insisted.

Amaranta nodded in agreement. 'I think you'd be perfect for Aorr.'

But Bridget's argument won the day: 'I'm not kissing my brother in a play,' she snapped, 'and that's that.'

After the reading, the girls began to rummage through the wicker basket for costumes. Elsie put a record on the record player and her and Bridget giggled as they wrapped themselves in lengths of gauzy fabric and danced and messed about on the makeshift stage in time to the music. Amaranta sat on one of the big cushions watching them, although William noticed a distant expression on her face. He was just wondering what might be going through her head when Chris's voice interrupted his thoughts.

'Girls are fascinating, don't you think?' Chris whispered to William. 'There's something mysterious about them that I can't quite explain. They're like music. Beautiful and captivating. Don't you agree?'

William stared at him, open-mouthed and speechless. He had no idea what Chris was talking about.

II

There was no further sign from Abelard Greewoof for most of the next week, but William didn't have much time to fret about the Latin master's absence. They were rehearsing every chance they got and he had to learn his lines for the play in the evenings.

William was amazed at how quickly and how well Amaranta fit in with the group of friends. Even Bridget became less sullen towards her after a few days of rehearsals. Mind you, it was difficult not to like Amaranta: she was cheerful and enthusiastic and seemed to see the positive in everything and everyone. But every now and then, William thought he could see a hint of sadness in her face. It only showed up when she thought no one was looking and disappeared again when someone caught her eye to be replaced by a bright and brilliant smile. William had no idea what could be making Amaranta so sad at times, but he was glad Elsie had invited her to join them for the play.

By the following Wednesday, William still hadn't heard from Mr Greewoof and his patience had worn thin. There was still so much he didn't know, like when he was he going to actually become part of the Order and what that entailed. He was also very keen to learn more about the other members. So, despite the warning not to be out and about alone, he decided to cycle out to the teacher's house the next morning. After all, there had been no sign of Gregor Watengroe around Avenfore for days and, besides, there was no one to ask to come with him: Chris had to help his father deliver the post most mornings during the school holidays and the girls were too busy making the backdrop and costumes for the play. William had offered to help, but Elsie had declined, telling him he was far too clumsy, although William had a sneaking suspicion that his cousin just wanted him out of the way so they could talk freely about things he wasn't meant to hear.

Thursday morning was sunny and bright and William listened to the birds chirping, and the buzz of crickets in the long grasses along the side of the road as he cycled out of the village towards Abelard's house.

As he passed the old water pump at Hollypoint, he heard a commotion in the forest on the side of the road near the church. Looking up, he saw a flock of rooks wheeling wildly about the blue summer sky above the tree tops. The birds were cawing raucously and making a terrible din, but, above it all, William could hear loud voices and coarse laughter coming from the edge of the forest itself.

Suddenly, one of the birds shrieked and fell from the sky. He felt the anger rise in him. He knew he recognised those voices.

Brimming with rage, William flung his bicycle onto the side of the road and stormed along the forest track towards the ruined church. When he reached the wooden signpost, he saw that he had been right: the Aguevals triplets were in the forest trying to hit birds with their catapults.

'Hey,' William shouted, 'what are you doing?'

Surprised by his sudden appearance, the three youths turned to look at him.

'Oh, look who's here boys,' said Tom. 'Are you going to join us? We were just practising our aiming skills.'

William noticed that Jack Aguevals looked embarrassed, but Pat loaded his catapult and released another stone in the direction of the tree tops. He and Tom laughed nastily as the rooks once again shrieked and wheeled into the air.

'Stop it,' William cried, 'How can you be so cruel?? This is a bird sanctuary! Stop it, stop it now!'

'Come to save the ickle-bitty birdies, have we?' Pat said in a mocking tone.

'You want us to stop?' Tom said, taking a few menacing steps towards William, 'and who's going to stop us, then? You?'

'Yeah,' sneered Pat. 'Who's gonna stop us, Howbbler? You and whose army?'

'This one,' said a gruff voice behind William.

William turned in surprise to see Ernest Wiglann standing behind him. Without saying another word, Mr Wiglann walked over to the bird sanctuary signpost, took hold of it with both hands and wrenched it out of the ground. Although not that big, Ernest was very strong indeed. With the sign in his hands he marched towards the brothers who had been standing stock-still since they had seen him heave it out of the ground. Ernest raised the sign towards them and glared. The triplets dropped their catapults and scarpered: Jack first, followed by Pat and then Tom, hot on his heels. Ernest's glass eye had unnerved them even more than his brute force.

Ernest picked up the catapults and with a slight wry smile put the sign firmly back in its place. William stared in disbelief. It seemed Mr Wiglann could smile after all! And to think that only a week ago, he had believed he was a murderer.

'Mr Greewoof says you wasn't to be out alone,' Ernest said at last. He wasn't smiling any longer.

'I know, but I just wanted to talk to Mr Greewoof', William said.

'He ain't home,' Earnest said in a cutting tone. 'Get in the van and I'll bring you back.'

'Thanks, but I've got my bike with me,' William explained.

'It'll fit in the back of the van,' was all Mr Wiglann said.

Ernest Wiglann's van was parked on the side of the road facing in the direction of Avenfore. William climbed into the passenger seat as Ernest opened the back doors and propped his bike up against the side of the van, wedging it tightly so it couldn't fall. William couldn't help noticing a large, long burlap sack tied tightly at the top with rope on the floor of the van. Ernest saw him looking at the sack and grunted.

'Potatoes. From Mr Greewoof's garden. Need replanting.'

As they set off for the village, William heard a very strange noise coming from the back of the van. It took him a few moments to realise what it was.

'Mr Wiglann,' he said, 'not to sound crazy, but I think your potatoes are snoring.'

Ernest Wiglann remained as straight-faced as ever. 'The rest'll do 'em good,' he said. 'they've a long journey ahead of 'em.'

'Oh,' said William anxiously, 'where are they going?'

'Like I said,' Mr Wiglann replied, 'they needs replanting. Somewhere foreign,' he added.

'Far away?'

'Maybe', said Mr Wiglann. He scowled darkly. 'Far away enough so's they can't hurt you or anyone else. Far enough so's their evil boss won't find 'em in a month of Sundays.'

William imagined Gregor Watengroe waking up on a ship in a few days' time and finding himself stuck in a potato sack somewhere in the middle of the ocean with nowhere to go. *With any luck, he'll be seasick as well*, William thought and laughed out loud.

Mr Wiglann glared at him. 'It's no laughing matter,' he growled. 'The Wicked Crow won't stop at nothing to get what he wants, even if it means boys like you gets hurt. You gotta do what Mr Greewoof tells you to do from now on and don't be gallivanting about on your own. Do you hear me?'

It was the longest speech William had ever heard from Mr Wiglann and it shocked him. All he could do was nod his agreement and they returned to Avenfore in silence.

CHAPTER 12

Blackwood Forest

I

BY THE FOLLOWING TUESDAY MR GREEWOOF still hadn't contacted William, and he accepted Chris's offer to join him on his postal delivery round that day. It was a grey, misty morning, which threatened rain, but William had been cooped up in the house rehearsing for too long and he jumped at the chance to accompany Chris around Avenfore as he delivered post. Chris knew everyone in the village and stopped to talk to most of them, so, despite the early start, it was mid-morning before they were finished. Last stop was Ravenwood Castle, where they chatted with Amaranta and Mrs Dreephy for a while before making their way back along the road leading from Ravenwood towards the village.

As they reached the bridge overlooking the river Inni, Chris came to an abrupt halt.

'Darn it,' he said, pulling a sheet of paper out of his pocket, 'I forgot to give Mr Dreephy the telegraph. I'll have to go back.' He turned his bicycle and set off towards Ravenwood Castle. 'Wait for me,' he shouted to William, 'I'll catch you up in a minute or two.'

William stayed on the bridge for a short time watching the flow of water beneath him. Then he cycled slowly towards the junction where the Ravenwood Castle road met the main Drunfarnam road leading out of Avenfore and waited for Chris to return.

As he waited, a sleek black car appeared along the road travelling from the direction of Drunfarnam. William watched it with fascination. It was a distinctive, top-of-the-range, latest model Cadillac de Ville: shiny black, with chrome trim, its huge sharp tailfins jutting out from its sides like large black wings.

The car was travelling at speed and as it passed William, he only managed to catch a glimpse of the silhouette of the driver. But it was enough to prompt a memory from somewhere deep inside him and he formed an image of a man in his mind: sleek black hair, a pale, expressionless face, marked eyebrows and cold, black eyes that bore into you.

With a sickening jolt, William realised that he had seen that man before. It was Ignatius Nosmorum. But he could hardly believe what he had just seen. What was Ignatius doing in Avenfore?

He watched the Cadillac turn off to the left down a narrow lane immediately before St Clem's Girls' School. William's mind was racing. He should wait for Chris and go straight home. But something inside him wouldn't let him go. This might be the only chance to follow Ignatius and find out where he went or who he met with in Avenfore. He felt queasy at the thought of what Ignatius might do if he caught him, but the little voice told him it was a risk worth taking. 'Nothing ventured, nothing gained,' he said to himself and he got back on his bike and pedalled off in pursuit of the car.

At the entrance to the lane where the Cadillac had turned off the main road, William saw a stone half-hidden amongst the grass that said BLACKWOOD FOREST. That gave him pause for thought. He had heard Elise and Bridget talking about the place. It was a lonely, eerie lane, leading to a lonely, eerie forest surrounded by marshy bog lands, which people did their best to avoid. Even so he was determined to go on. What could be worse than Ignatius Nosmorum?

William caught a glimpse of the Cadillac in the distance through the trees and pushed on after it. The deeper he went into the forest the dimmer the light became. He began to feel a bit anxious, but he couldn't give up now. His senses now sharpened, he pedalled on determinedly. Before he knew it, he was in the heart of the forest. A thick mist had sprung up and he had no choice but to stop. Visibility was down to barely a few feet and he couldn't even see the path he had been cycling on. Caught out by the sudden change in the weather, William got off his bike and looked around him.

A disturbing calm engulfed the forest. There were no birds singing or crickets chirruping. All William could hear was the sound of raindrops hitting the leaves of the trees above him in small, sharp crackles and spits. Beneath the canopy of trees, the thick, damp mist swirled around him and made it difficult to see where he was going. Even more worrying, there was absolutely no sign of Ignatius or his Cadillac.

Not knowing what to do, William decided it was best not to move any further until the rain and mist had died down. In this silence, any sound he made could give him away. For a moment, he wondered if he was dreaming, that all of this couldn't be real. He found a place to shelter by the trunk of a huge oak and crouched there, not daring to move a muscle. He couldn't help thinking that he probably deserved the trouble he was in for not following Abelard Greewoof's advice.

His heartbeat quickened as he heard the rustle of footsteps nearby. He swallowed hard and pushed himself up against the trunk. There could be no doubt: somebody was coming up behind him. He wanted to run away, but fear kept him rooted to the spot. He had never been so afraid in his life. Suddenly, the footsteps ceased, and he knew for sure that whoever it was had stopped on the other side of the trunk. William held his breath, praying he would not be discovered. He could do nothing else: fear had petrified him.

For a few moments nothing happened, which was even more disconcerting. Gently, he let his breath out, trying not to make any noise. A hand shot round the tree and covered his mouth. Terrified, he bit hard into it and leapt up to see who was there.

It was Ernest Wiglann, nursing his injured hand and silently grimacing in pain.

Dismayed, William was about to say how sorry he was, when Ernest gestured to him to keep quiet. Then he indicated to William to follow him and not to make a sound. A rather shamefaced William did as he was told. This was the second time Mr Wiglann had got him out of a very tight situation, and his only thanks had been a nasty bite.

They went across the meadows towards the church and into the graveyard, leaving the misty forest behind them. William wanted to say thank you, to say sorry for being such a terrible fool, but before he could get a word out, Ernest said flatly, 'Now go home. I'll bring your bike later.'

Then he turned and disappeared back into the dark forest.

II

Rattled by the morning's events, William was hardly able to eat any lunch, even though his aunt had cooked his favourite stew. That afternoon, he had a surprise visitor: Abelard Greewoof himself, offering to take William birdwatching for an hour or so. Elsie wanted to come along too, but, luckily, she had already made plans to meet Bridget and the Arinduff twins in Malconary's.

William and Mr Greewoof drove along the Drishlean road in silence for a time. Finally, William plucked up enough courage to speak.

'I'm sorry, Mr Greewoof,' he said. 'Both you and Mr Wiglann told me not to go off on my own and I disobeyed you. I'm really, really sorry for doing that.'

For a long while, Mr Greewoof didn't answer. Then, all of a sudden, he pulled the car onto the side of the road, stopped the engine and turned to William.

'I must say, young Howbbler, it was terribly foolish of you to do what you did. Ignatius Nosmorum is an evil, dangerous man and you put yourself and others in serious danger by following him alone as you did.'

Stung by the teacher's words, William felt himself turn beetroot-red with embarrassment and guilt. He should have waited for Chris and alerted Mr Wiglann. Instead, he had been selfish, arrogant and stupid, putting himself and Mr Wiglann in danger.

'You were lucky this time, William,' Mr Greewoof continued, as if he could read William's thoughts, 'but you cannot rely on Ernest Wiglann to rescue you every time from whatever foolish scrape you've gotten yourself into. If you are to be a member of our Order, you must also realise that your actions will have consequences beyond yourself. Do you understand me?'

William nodded miserably. Then a thought struck him. Maybe his father and Mr Greewoof would change their minds and not allow him become a Knight of the Order after this. He looked up at the Latin master, almost sick with fear.

'William,' said Mr Greewoof, 'you have to promise that you won't do anything foolish like that again. If you do, everything will be all right.'

Relief flooded through William and he nodded nervously. 'I promise, Mr Greewoof. Truly, I promise.'

'Well, then,' Abelard Greewoof continued, 'let's get down to business. When we got rid of Gregor Watengroe, we guessed that Ignatius would come along sooner or later to ascertain what had happened. Even so, we're pretty certain that it's not his only reason for coming here. Whatever his plans are though, we're ready to thwart them. However, one good thing has come out of your recent escapade.'

'What's that?' William said.

'Nosmorum clearly doesn't know who you are or what you look like for the time being.'

'What if his accomplice tells him where to find me?'

Mr Greewoof pulled out his silver hip-flask and took a sip of cordial. 'I don't think Ignatius would be so foolish as to go into Fern Lane. But we'll be ready, just on the off-chance. Clearly, Ignatius is going to meet up with his accomplice. As you can guess, this is a golden opportunity for us to find out once and for all who the rascal is. Ignatius doesn't know we're on the alert, so we have a slight edge on him. But he's a cunning one; he won't be easy to keep track of.'

Abelard Greewoof glanced at his pocket-watch before going on. 'There's something very important you need to know about Ignatius Nosmorum. He's not like other men. It wouldn't be at all wise to underestimate him. His obsessive greed has made him an evil person, and an extremely cunning one too. He is extraordinarily persuasive and seductive. With his cold, inscrutable look he can hypnotise people into doing his will.'

William felt the hairs on the back of his neck stand up as he listened to what Mr Greewoof was saying. 'Here, smell this,' the Latin master said, drawing a glass bottle from his jacket pocket, which he passed to William. Opening the bottle, William sniffed and then quickly pulled away from its pungent scent, screwing up his face as he did.

'Nosmorum uses this exotic perfume he discovered in India to enhance his powers of seduction. The oil comes from a bush that goes under the name of *pogostemon cablin*, but it's better known as patchouli. As you've just seen for yourself, it has an intense and a rather far-reaching aroma. This evil man uses it to mask the scent of a powerful poison which he uses to kill his victims. He carries the poison in his walking stick: the sharp beak of its crow's head handle functions as a funnel to spray a venomous mist at his victims. Anyone who breathes in the full dose is dead within minutes. He used it in Scotland against our Mr Malblenar, who was fortunate to dodge it in time. Remember, William, if you ever find yourself face to face with him, you must protect yourself against his cane. As Ernest knows to his regret, it's not just poisonous, it can deliver a nasty blow, too.'

Abelard put the bottle back in his pocket and wound down the window to get rid of the overpowering smell of patchouli that had filled the van. 'As you know Ignatius inherited a mansion near to Drunfarnam, but he has seldom been there in the past ten years or so. And we have now discovered, through our own sources, that he has also acquired lands on the outskirts of the town currently occupied by some derelict warehouses and an old abandoned fairground. No one ever goes there and we believe he may intend to use it as some sort of headquarters for his criminal gang. Even more worrying is that he appears to be moving into the Drunfarnam mansion.'

'He wants to be close to Avenfore!' William cried.

'Yes, we believe so. Ever since the disappearance of Mr Seblean, he's been showing rather too much interest in the village and the Night Bird Society for our liking.'

William sat horror-struck. The idea that Ignatius may be focussing all his evil intent on Avenfore was a sobering thought.

'We believe,' Mr Greewoof went on, 'that Ignatius has not been able to find whatever it is he has been searching for since your father tried to steal the book from him over ten years ago. However, it is essential that he does not find what he is looking for. He has already shown us that he uses his wealth and power to do evil. There is no telling what evil deeds he would carry out with the immeasurable power and wealth which the *Book of the Knights Errant* would bestow upon him. So, you see, it is vital that we do not allow this treacherous and dangerous individual to ever get his hands on either the book or its cipher.'

Mr Greewoof fell silent. William had never seen him look so serious. Finally, the Latin master wound up the window and turned on the car engine. 'I'd best be taking you back home, young Howbbler,' he said.

The weather changed again as they drove back to Avenfore in silence. The sound of the raindrops pelting against the windscreen of the car, reminded him of the raindrops hitting the leaves of the trees in Blackwood Forest as the Wicked Crow and his black Cadillac vanished into the mists ahead of him. He couldn't help the shiver of fear that ran down his spine at the thought.

CHAPTER 13

Flame of our Ancestors

I

ILLIAM FOUND HIMSELF WITH LITTLE TIME to fret about the Wicked Crow after his meeting with Mr Greewoof. The Falcon Fair play competition was on Friday and Elsie and Chris had scheduled rehearsals all day for the next two days. When they weren't rehearsing, William was frantically learning his lines and trying not to be nervous about acting in front of the entire village. If he were honest, he was a pretty excited about it too. Also, he was looking forward to seeing his father, Arnold, who was due to arrive in Avenfore to attend the Annual General Meeting of the Night Bird Society which would also take place that weekend.

On Thursday evening, Elsie finally relented and gave them all the following morning off to enjoy the start of the Falcon Fair, while, at the same time, issuing dire warnings about not being late for the dress rehearsal on Friday afternoon.

Friday dawned, warm and bright, and William was buzzing with excitement as he and Elsie joined Chris, Bridget and Amaranta down by the riverbank opposite the church to watch the arrival of the local brass band from Drunfarnam. They'd played at every Falcon Fair for decades, Elsie explained, as Amaranta whooped with delight at the sight of the noisy convoy of rowing boats appeared upstream, each laden with uniformed musicians busy tuning their brass instruments, which gleamed in the early morning sunlight.

'Follow me,' Elsie cried suddenly, and William found himself running with the others to the village jetty to watch as the musicians stepped on to the jetty and the chaos of booming oompahs, trumpet calls and shrill clarinet shrieks erupted into the waltzing rhythms and infectious melody of Johan Strauss II's 'The Blue Danube'. Everyone cheered as the parish priest, Father Proherney, declared the 1959 Falcon Fair officially open.

William made his way with the others back towards the village square. The usual Friday market had spruced itself up in honour of the occasion, with brightly coloured bunting running along and between the market stalls. Thick ropes of bunting were also wound around the garden railings in the middle of the square providing a vivid splash of colour against the sparkling grey granite of the Celtic cross at its centre.

Everywhere he looked there was something interesting to do or see. There was a colourful kite exhibition and competition later that morning; there were mouth-watering displays of cakes, breads, biscuits and jams – all entries for the Falcon Fair baking competitions; there were egg-and-spoon, three-legged and sack races; a donkey derby, a lucky dip barrel full of mysterious prizes, a coconut shy and all manner of spin-the-bottle and penny-throwing contests. All the competitions had trophies and cash prizes, which served to give them an added attraction.

William was trying to decide what to try first when Ernest Wiglann pulled up in front of Uncle Walter's antique shop in his van and beckoned William over to him.

'Get in,' he said, giving him his usual blank look. 'Mr Greewoof wants to see you.'

'Oh ...' William looked over at the others who were laughing and giggling at the penny-throwing stall and couldn't help feeling disappointed; he'd been looking forward to his morning at the Fair.

'All right, Mr Wiglann,' he said reluctantly, 'but I'll need to tell Chris where I'm going, otherwise they'll be wondering where I am.'

He thought it would be best to tell Chris – Elsie would ask too many questions about where he was going and why. And he was finding it hard to come up with a good excuse to miss the Falcon Fair.

'Mr Greewoof's asked me to help him with something for the Fair later,' was the best he could think of in the end.

Luckily, Chris asked no questions. 'Don't worry,' he said, 'the Fair's on again tomorrow and there'll be lots to see then. But make sure you're back for the dress rehearsal,' he warned, 'we're starting at three o'clock sharp. Otherwise ....' he nodded over to where Elsie was standing. William grinned and promised him he wouldn't be late. Then he hurried off before any of the girls noticed he was gone.

As he got into the passenger seat of Mr Wiglann's van, William noticed that the older man's left hand was bandaged. He winced at the thought of how hard he'd bitten down on it in Blackwood Forest when he thought Mr Wiglann was Ignatius Nosmorum. It must have really hurt.

A wave of embarrassment swept over William. He could never repay all that Mr Wiglann had done for him and the man had got no thanks for any of it.

The van turned left outside the village along the Hollypoint road and William guessed they were going towards the old church. He was right. Mr Wiglann pulled to a halt opposite the NO ENTRY sign. 'He's in there,' he said, indicating towards the ruined church.

William glanced over at him. As usual, Ernest Wiglann's face was emotionless, inscrutable. It was impossible to know what he was thinking.

'Thanks again, Mr Wiglann. For everything,' said William softly as he got out of the van.

Mr Wiglann gave a strange, low snort and revved the engine of the van loudly.

'Come on, boy, don't keep Mr Greewoof waiting,' was all he said.

II

Abelard Greewoof was waiting for William in the old sacristy.

'Unfortunately, we weren't able to ascertain where the Wicked Crow went,' he told William mournfully. 'We lost his scent in the woods and knew no more until he left the village. Obviously, we suspect that he was with his accomplice, making new plans now that he knows that Gregor is out of the picture. Ignatius must be pretty exasperated by Watengroe's disappearance, and that makes him a greater danger than ever, especially now that he's living almost on our doorstep.'

'Do you reckon he's got the *Book of the Knights Templar Errant,* then?' William asked, breaking the silence.

Mr Greewoof shook his head. 'I really don't know, William, I'm afraid, but I think it's something the Alliance must make their top priority to find out. Along with discovering the identity of Nosmorum's accomplice. Yes, it would all be much easier, if we knew who his accomplice in Avenfore was. The fact that we don't is quite a worry.

'But, first things first,' he declared rather loudly as he strolled over the lectern in front of the Knights Templar tapestry and started to gently leaf through a book that lay open on it. When he found the page he was looking for, he beckoned William over to the lectern.

'As you know, today is the start of the Falcon Fair, the annual summer festival held in Avenfore every year on the last weekend but one in July, which is organised and sponsored by the Night Bird Society. Tonight, after the play competition, disguised as the Annual General Meeting of the Night Bird Society, the Knights all come together at Ravenwood Castle for the yearly meeting of the Order of the Alliance. After a year apart, there's a lot to talk about, as you can imagine. Members travel to the meeting from all over Ireland and abroad. It is a fine opportunity to be together and to discuss in depth all matters relating to the Order. We also take the opportunity to invest new fellow members when this is necessary. As usual, your father will be there. He's never missed a meeting since he went to live in the city. And I hardly think this year will be different, especially since this year' – here Mr Greewoof paused, his eyes gleaming softly in the flickering light of the torches – 'you will be made a Knight Postulant of the Order. Tomorrow the two Knight Postulants, the twelve Squires and the nine Knights will spend the evening together in the castle in order to get to know each other better. At dusk, we will go over to the island of Lesciern, where you and the other candidate will take your vows before being proclaimed members of the Order.'

William couldn't help himself. 'The other candidate?' he cried, 'there's someone else being made a Knight … eh, postulate, too?'

Mr Greewoof's eyes twinkled with merriment. 'Postulant, dear boy, from the Latin verb *postulare* – 'to ask', as I am sure you well know. A knight-in-training, if you will. Yes, this year, there are two of you. To replace our missing brothers, poor Mr Seblean and Mr Benjamin Greether, who is also, sadly, no longer with us.'

'So Mr Wiglann knows that I'm to be made a Knight?'

'Not only Ernest, but all the brethren are obliged to know.'

Now William was curious to know who else in Avenfore might be a member of the Order. He quickly ran through all the people he'd met since arriving, but he was certain that none of them could be members of the Alliance.

Mr Greewoof continued. 'You will be the youngest Knight Postulant of the brotherhood. As you are still underage, during your first years, you will only be able to participate in certain missions. Indeed, your first years in the Order will be a period of apprenticeship, for there is much to learn. However, you are entitled, like any other brother, to put forward suggestions and proposals.'

William couldn't manage any words and simply nodded, it was all so unreal, so exciting. Tomorrow he would officially be part of the Order.

'Now to business.' He indicated towards the book on the falcon lectern before them. Like the cipher manuscript, the book was written on vellum, with brightly coloured illustrations and rich gilt edging and William was afraid to touch it, it looked so ancient.

'Take care with that manuscript,' murmured Mr Greewoof. 'Even though it's only a copy, it's still almost three hundred years old.' He pointed towards some Latin text in the middle of the page: 'You have to learn this oath by heart before your investiture ceremony on Saturday.' He grinned and patted William on the shoulder. 'But I am sure that will be no problem for an accomplished Latin scholar like yourself,' he said as he settled himself back down in one of the armchairs, produced a newspaper from his jacket pocket and began to read.

William didn't share Mr Greewoof's confidence that learning the oath would be an easy task. The text was complicated and the handwritten script was difficult to read. Not to mention the fact that his head was already full of lines he had memorised for the play. But he guessed that was all part of the challenge.

He stared at the first line of the manuscript in wonder:

FLAMMA ACCENSA OLIM MAIORIBUS NOSTRIS EADEM HODIE ACCEN-DEMUS – the flame our ancestors ignited one day is the same as the one we will ignite today.

How many Knights down the centuries had learned and spoken this oath also? And soon he would speak it too, in front of his father and Mr Greewoof and all the other members of the Order. His heart swelled with pride, as he began to learn, determined that when the time came to speak the oath, he would be word-perfect.

CHAPTER 14

The Falcon Fair

I

O F ALL THE EVENTS HELD ON the first day of the Falcon Fair, by far the most eagerly awaited was the short play competition. It was so popular that William was alarmed to see there was already a long line of people queuing for seats outside the hall as he and the others arrived a full hour before the start to put on their costumes and make-up.

As sponsors of the competition, the Night Bird Society was very visible. The front of the village hall was decked out in white pennants which bore the silhouette of a falcon perched on a stone. Similar pennants with the Society's logo lined the street on both sides. At the entrance to the building hung two large flags. Each bore the image of a theatre mask: one smiling, the other downcast.

The stage was located at the farthest end of the hall from the entrance. It stood high above the floor, the actual stage area hidden from view behind a thick dark red velvet curtain trimmed with golden braid. Beneath it, neat rows of wooden chairs for the audience spread out to fill the hall right to the front door where William and Chris were standing. Chris had been relaxed until then, but at the sight of so many chairs, his nerves started to show.

'There's nothing to worry about,' William said. 'It's only a competition and the worst that can happen is that we don't win. We'll have fun anyway, won't we?'

Chris nodded, but he didn't look convinced.

The other participants in the play competition began to arrive at the hall shortly after William and his friends. There were six plays in the competition: two by St Elm's and St Clem's pupils who lived in Drunfarnam, one entered by students who lived near Drishlean and the three Avenfore plays: Chris's play, the Aguevals' play and one entered by Elsie and Bridget's friends, the Arinduff sisters and their friend, Marie Ballygarin. Other than William and Amaranta, they all knew each other and the backstage area of the hall was soon filled with laughing and so many introductions that William's head began to spin. He glanced over at Amaranta who only had time to throw him a quick smile before Elsie dragged her off to introduce to her another of the Drishlean girls who would be in her class at St Clem's.

'Have you chosen an order number yet, William?' Mr Mestfinn, the music teacher from St Elm's who was in charge of the event, bustled over to where William was standing.

'Eh …'

'I'll do it, Mr Mestfinn.' Bridget scurried over to the table by the front door where the large cloth bag with the numbered balls was located. At that moment, the Aguevals triplets rushed in and almost knocked her over.

'Ouch,' Bridget cried, 'why don't you look where you—' she stopped having just realized who it was.

Pat Aguevals turned and gave her a nasty look. William saw Chris stiffen with anger and he quickly put a restraining hand on his shoulder. Then Jack Aguevals stepped forward.

'I'm really sorry, Bridget,' he said to everyone's surprise, including his brothers'. 'We were in a hurry and didn't see you there. Are you all right?'

'Yes, I'm fine … thanks,' she said after a moment, visibly taken aback by the unexpected apology. Bridget turned away quickly to pull one of the numbered balls from the bag.

'Number three,' she said to Chris, whose face darkened.

'Darn it,' he said, 'I was hoping it was number six. I wanted us to go last. We should find out who has six. Maybe they'd swap with us.'

'That's the number we drew,' snapped Bridget in a tone that brooked no argument, 'and whether you like it or not we're third on stage.'

With fifteen minutes to go before the competition was due to start, William peeked out into the hall to see if his father had arrived. There was hardly an empty seat left and the audience members were chatting noisily to each other. Mr and Mrs Dreephy were there, together with Mr Wiglann. Aunt Edna and Uncle Walter were already there in a row of seats about mid-way down the hall. They waved happily at William, who waved back. Arnold Howbbler wasn't there yet. But there were a few empty seats beside Aunt Edna, one of which he knew they had reserved for his father.

'William!' He jumped as Elsie came up behind him. 'What are you doing there? Amaranta's looking for you, you need to get your make-up done.'

William groaned. 'Oh, Els, I hate the stuff. Do I have to?'

The dress rehearsal the previous evening had been a bit of a nightmare for William, with Amaranta insisting on painting his face with what he considered to be a particularly disgusting shade of green.

'I mean … green. Why green?' he had complained.

'Because you're an elf,' she retorted, as if it was the most obvious thing in the world. The thing is, William couldn't remember ever hearing or reading that elves were green, but like Elsie, when Amaranta got an idea in her head, she wasn't likely to change her mind and so he was stuck with a green face. Didn't mean he had to like it, though.

Judging by the look on her face, Elsie was every bit as unsympathetic as Amaranta.

'Come on,' she said. 'Hurry up. The competition's about to start.'

Ten minutes later, William, Elsie and the others took their seats, reserved for the participants at the side of the hall, and waited with the rest of the audience in anticipation for the competition to begin. Arnold's chair beside Aunt Edna was still empty and William began to worry that his father wouldn't make it to the hall on time. He was surprised how much the thought of that upset him. He hadn't realised how keen he was for his father to see him acting in this play with his cousin and all his friends at Avenfore. Especially now that he was to become a member of the Order and the Night Bird Society.

Then Mr Mestfinn drew across the blackout curtains, the lights in the hall went out and the stage curtains drew slowly back to reveal Father Proherney standing on stage in a spotlight. He smiled down at the audience as he spoke.

'Before we begin,' he said, 'on behalf of the people of Avenfore, I would like to give our thanks to our dear sponsors, the Night Bird Society.' He waited for the applause to finish and then continued. 'But I especially want to thank all of you for being here. Without you, this show could not go on.' This was greeted with still more applause. 'Yet again, my thanks are due to the participants this year for the huge effort they have made to make Avenfore's big day even bigger. Prepare to enter an imaginary world, the world of fantasy, where the fabulous is the norm. Prepare to cry! Prepare to laugh! Because the magic, ladies and gentlemen, the magic begins NOW!'

The clapping was louder than ever, but as the spotlight faded and Father Proherney left the stage, darkness filled the hall. A hush spread over the audience and the plays began.

By the time it was their turn, William was sick with nerves. As he left the hall to get ready, he checked to see if his father had arrived, standing on tiptoe to try to see over the heads of the audience in front of him. All the seats were now filled, but he couldn't be sure if Arnold was there. As he scanned the audience, a tall figure standing in the shadows at the back of the hall caught his attention. *It can't be*, William thought. Byron Mullween hadn't been at the Falcon Fair in years, or so Ernest Wiglann had told Amaranta. But there he was, William was sure of it. It had to be him: the cloak was unmistakeable

– no one else in Avenfore wore such a thing. He turned towards Amaranta, but as he did so, Byron seemed to vanish from sight. Puzzled, William looked about him once again and caught the eye of Veronica Aguevals who was sitting a row or two behind his aunt and uncle. She was staring curiously in his direction through her horn-rimmed glasses and William was reminded of the beady eyes of a rather vicious bird. Turning away quickly, he scurried after the others, glad that he had the play to concentrate on.

II

Chris's nerves worsened as the start of the play drew nearer. He paced up and down outside the dressing room where Bridget and Elsie were getting ready. 'Hurry up, Bridget,' he hissed. 'There's only two minutes left. Get a move on!'

'Hey,' William said, 'calm down, we've five minutes left yet.'

At that moment, Elsie and Bridget appeared from the dressing room in full costume and make-up. William and Chris stared in awe. They had seen them at the dress rehearsal the previous evening, but here, under the stage lamps, the girls were transformed. Elsie, as the nymph, Obrixele, looked as if she'd jumped straight out of a fairy tale, while Bridget's Yss was pale as a white rose with a blush of carmine-rosy cheeks and round blue fairy eyes, set off by a tiara of sparkling beads in her auburn hair.

'You look amazing,' Chris breathed. 'Both of you,' he added quickly looking away from Elsie.

'Thank you,' Bridget said with a knowing smile, 'It's all Amaranta's doing. We couldn't have done it without her.'

As if on cue, Amaranta followed them out of the dressing room. 'There you are, William,' she said. 'I just need to touch up your make-up.' She went over to William with her make-up bag and applied a few finishing touches to him. Then she stood back, looked him over, and nodded approvingly.

'You look stunning too,' she said, 'even if I do say so myself.'

'Actually, I look green,' he replied with a large grin. Amaranta snorted with laughter and even Elsie and Bridget had to stifle loud giggles.

'We're up,' Chris whispered as Father Proherney walked into the spotlight in the centre of the stage once again.

Amaranta squealed with excitement. 'Break two legs,' she said as she hugged them all in turn.

William turned to Chris who was looking pale and terrified again. 'You see?' he said. 'Everything's under control. Just concentrate on your breathing as you read the lines.'

They grasped each other's hands as Father Proherney announced them to loud applause. 'And next, Elsie Harckwell, William Howbbler, Bridget Durffan and Christopher Durffan in a beautiful tale of love. Ladies and gentlemen, I give you *An Odyssey in the Greenwood.*'

III

The play went as smoothly as in rehearsal. Elsie and Bridget glided and shimmered across the stage, holding their audience engrossed. In the moving final scene, Obrixele faded away as Aorr and Yss joined hands and gazed lovingly into each other's eyes. Then they kissed and ran off into the forest. The lights went out and a hush fell on the audience.

Seconds later there was an explosion of clapping like none heard before that evening. Bridget, Elsie and William came out for a curtain call and were greeted with a roar of approval. William had to drag Chris out. Elsie and Bridget grabbed Aramanta and pulled her out too. Then, holding hands, they took their bows.

A great whoop and shouts of 'Bravo' caught William's attention. Through the bright stage lights and the darkness of the auditorium, he stared down into the audience in the direction of the noise and saw his father, Arnold, standing in the row of seats next to his aunt and uncle, clapping and cheering. Beside him was Abelard Greewoof, also standing and applauding. Then others stood up: the Durffans, the Dreephys, even Mr Wiglann stood solemnly clapping, and suddenly the whole audience was on its feet, applauding. William gasped. It was a standing ovation!

He glanced over at his friends beside him on stage. Chris was staring down at the audience in shock and the girls were beaming with delight.

'Psssssst!'

William looked over into the wings to see Pat Aguevals gesturing at him in a not-so-friendly way. The Aguevals triplets were next on and they were getting impatient as they waited in the corridor for the applause to end.

'Get off, it's our turn,' Pat hissed as Tom made rude gestures at them; they were both clearly jealous of the success the others were enjoying.

The five friends hurried off stage as Father Proherney thanked the audience for their rapturous applause before going on to introduce the Aguevals.

'Prepare yourselves now to watch the most amazing magician the world has ever seen. The incomparable, the brilliant, the one and only ... *Pitt the Magician*!

The play was a parody of a magician – played by Tom Aguevals – whose clumsy magic meant that he never got any trick right. Pat and Jack asked him to grant them a wish, until they realised that whatever they asked for the result would be disastrous. It was all rather silly, but William had to admit that it was very funny, although from the look on Tom Aguevals' face, he reckoned some of the jokes against poor Pitt had not been in the script, and his brothers were enjoying the opportunity to make fun of him a bit too much.

As the curtain fell, Veronica Aguevals was the first to applaud and the rest of the audience soon joined in. The triplets' performance received a good ovation but nothing like that of their predecessors.

Once all the plays had been performed, Father Proherney appeared again to repeat his thanks and to announce that there would now be a pause of thirty minutes to allow the judges to deliberate and choose the winners.

After removing his costume and make-up, William hurried to the hall to greet his father. Elsie was already in the auditorium being congratulated by her parents. Arnold beamed at his son as soon as he saw him.

'That was fantastic, William' he said. 'I'm just sorry your mother and Kristyn weren't here to see it. They would have loved it too.'

'How are they doing, Dad?' William asked. 'I really do miss them both.'

'They miss you too, very much. Mum sends you this, by the way,' Arnold said, pulling William into a large hug.

William could feel a lump in his throat as he hugged his father back. Avenfore was like home to him, but this was the downside of being separated from his mum and sister. They weren't there when all the good things happened. But it wouldn't be for too long, he hoped. 'We'll be together at Christmas, won't we, Dad?' he murmured in Arnold's ear.

Over his father's shoulder, he saw Amaranta watching him and he smiled at her. She smiled back, but it was a sad smile. The same sad smile he had seen on that first day in Ravenwood Castle. She must be missing her parents too, he thought.

But William hadn't any time to think about this. The judges had reached their decision and the audience clapped as Mr Mestfinn, made his way onto the stage to announce the winners. A silence fell on the hall as he opened the envelope which contained the details of the third-placed plays.

'The third prize goes to the play … *One Summer Day* performed by Gladis and Arline Arinduff and Marie Ballygarin!' There was much clapping as the girls went up onto the stage, where they each received an envelope and a small trophy. The three girls waved to the audience and went back happily with their prizes.

'For its originality and imagination,' Mr Mestfinn continued, 'the judges have decided that the second prize should go to … *Pitt the Magician* performed by the three Aguevals brothers, Tom, Pat and Jack!'

Veronica Aguevals was up on her feet and applauding her nephews as they received their prize. William could see Pat and Tom were disappointed not to have won and as they came off the stage their eyes strayed over towards him and his four friends betraying a mixture of arrogance and envy. They clearly couldn't bear the idea that the others might be the winners. Jack, on the other hand, looked pleased and threw William a friendly grin as he sat back down in his seat beside his brothers, clutching his second-prize trophy.

Now all attention was back on Robert Mestfinn.

'Ladies and gentlemen,' he began, 'it is a great honour for me to announce the winners of the first prize in the Falcon Fair short play competition. I've helped organise this competition for many years now, but never, in all these years, have I seen such a high standard of performance and production as we have seen in all the wonderful plays tonight. I would like to thank all the young participants for all the hard work they have put into these plays for us over the past weeks. You should all be very proud of yourselves.'

The five friends gripped each other's hands, hoping against hope that they had won. William caught Tom Aguevals glaring at them jealously, obviously hoping, William guessed, that someone else would win.

'But I will not keep you – or myself – in suspense any longer,' Mr Mestfinn continued as he quickly opened the first-place winners' envelope. Then, with a broad grin, he announced, 'This year's first prize winner in the Falcon Fair short play competition is … *An Odyssey in the Greenwood.*'

The audience erupted into applause once more as Bridget, Elsie, William, and Chris walked up onto the stage to receive their trophies, Chris making sure he positioned himself behind the girls, as he tried to make himself as unnoticeable as possible. Amaranta too wanted to stay in her seat, but to the amusement of the audience, Aunt Edna pushed her up the steps and onto the stage to join the others. Then, as they took another bow, the applause rang out louder than ever, the audience rose to their feet as all the lights came on and William saw that his father was clapping most heartily of all.

River Lane

I

THE FALCON FAIR PLAY COMPETITION WAS followed by a supper for all the contestants and their families. William had never seen so much food in his life – savoury pies, sandwiches, cakes and biscuits, and his favourite: fruit crumble with huge dollops of cream and thick, yellow custard to be washed down by a large jug of tangy lemonade.

'I could eat a horse,' Chris murmured as he surveyed the feast spread out before them.

'Me too,' William said. 'I'm so glad they didn't ask us to eat before the show. I was so nervous I felt sick. I wouldn't have managed a mouthful.'

'Well, you'd better tuck in now, boys' Arnold Howbbler advised.

William and Chris needed no further encouragement and pushed their way towards the tables to grab their own plates.

After supper, everyone piled out of the hall into the nearby park where the Drunfarnam brass band were playing their final set of the evening. It was a balmy evening and stars twinkled in the dusk sky as the band played a medley of popular tunes and merry waltzes. People began to dance in time with the music, including Aunt Edna and Uncle Walter, who were, as Arnold put it, 'very light on their feet'. They were soon joined by Elsie and Bridget who twirled each other around the grass laughing happily, watched by a smiling William and Chris. If his mum and Kristyn had been there, William felt sure it would have been one of the happiest moments of his life.

From the corner of his eye, he saw Mr Wiglann standing on the opposite side of the bandstand staring into the dancing crowd.

Amaranta was not with him. Now that William thought about it, he hadn't seen Amaranta in a while. He looked about him but couldn't see her anywhere.

Then he spotted her. On the street outside the park, heading in the direction of the town square. Something about her worried him: she had that same sad air about her he had seen in the hall after the play, and, on impulse, William decided to follow her. She certainly looked as though she could do with cheering up.

As he reached the park gates, a tall, thin figure suddenly blocked his way. Veronica Aguevals was as impeccably dressed as ever: not a blonde hair out of place, her plain grey summer dress with lace collar and cuffs as neat and crisp as if it had just been ironed. William couldn't help thinking she would have been an attractive woman if it wasn't for the cold calculating look in her eyes and the thin upturn of her mouth at one side which gave her face a permanent sneer. She was smiling at him, but there was no warmth in her and William felt a chill run down his spine as she caught his eye.

'I note congratulations are in order, young Howbbler,' she piped in her high, fluting voice. 'An excellent performance this evening, even if I must say so myself. Although' – at this, Miss Aguevals leaned forward conspiratorially, a move William found even more intimidating than he would have thought possible from a librarian – 'please don't tell my three dear nephews I said that. They're such sensitive boys, you see.'

William couldn't imagine anyone less sensitive than the Aguevals triplets – well, Tom and Pat, anyhow; Jack, he wasn't so sure. Sensitive people didn't chuck stones at innocent birds for sport, for a start. But he had no intention of discussing the merits or otherwise of the Aguevals boys with their scary aunt. 'Don't worry, Miss Aguevals,' he said, 'I won't say anything to your nephews.' In fact, he thought to himself, if I never have to speak to any of them again, it'll still be too soon. To Veronica, he continued, 'Now, if you'll excuse me, please, I have to meet someone.'

'Of course, I wouldn't dream of detaining you,' Veronica was smiling at him, but she remained in his way.

William was puzzled. Did she expect him to push her out of his path or what? 'I'm sorry, Miss Aguevals, I really am in rather a hurry,' he said, edging his way towards the gate as best he could. To his relief, Veronica stepped out of his way just as he reached it. He heard her call after him as he fled out the gate.

'Congratulations again. I shall definitely be keeping my eye on you in the future.'

Even at a distance, as he hurried up the street in the direction of the village square, there was something in the tone of her voice which made William shiver once more.

II

By the time William reached the village square, there was no sign of Amaranta. He stood by the high cross and surveyed the square from all angles, but he could not see her amongst the passers-by slowly making their way along the village streets. Surely Amaranta had not gone all the way back to Ravenwood Castle by herself? He couldn't imagine Mr Wiglann being happy about that at all.

He continued walking towards River Lane. In the distance he could make out a solitary figure sitting hunched over at the end of the jetty, legs dangling over the edge of the pier, staring at the reflection of street lamps on the dark water below. It was Amaranta and, even though she made no noise, he could tell from the shake of her body that she was crying.

'Amaranta,' he cried. 'What's the matter? Are you all right?'

She turned around, clearly surprised, and he saw her quickly rub her eyes with her hand to wipe away her tears.

'There's nothing the matter,' she called back to him. 'Everything's okay. Please go back to the party, I'm fine here.'

'Don't be silly.' William made his way along the jetty towards Amaranta. 'I'm no genius,' he said as he sat down beside her, 'but I do know that people who cry at the end of jetties are clearly not fine.'

Amaranta smiled softly. 'You're the one being silly,' she said, but he could see fresh tears well up in her beautiful green eyes.

'Seriously, Manta, what's the matter?' William asked softly. 'If there's something bothering you? If there's something I can do to help?'

Amaranta stared him directly in the eyes for a few moments, until finally, she spoke. 'You and I are quite different, William, yet there's something about you that makes me feel I can trust you.'

William stared back at her, unsure of what to say next.

Amaranta sighed. 'I need a friend, William. Someone I can trust.'

William was perplexed to hear these words. Amaranta always seemed to be so sure of herself, so full of confidence. But looking at her now, he saw how much effort this was costing her. Taking her hand in his he said. 'You can trust me, I promise you.'

'There's something that's been troubling me for some time,' Amaranta continued, 'something I'd like to share with you.'

William gave her an encouraging smile, and she went on. 'Three months ago, on my fourteenth birthday, my mother told me that I had been adopted as a baby; that she and my father were not my real parents. As a baby I was left outside the door of Ravenwood Castle. Uncle Ernest had found me and looked after me before sending me to live with his sister, Aileen, in Scotland.'

William stared at her. 'Seriously?' That was all he could think of to say.

'Yes,' she said. 'Seriously. Of course, all these years, I had no idea that I was adopted. Until three months ago I was a happy person, living with my family, just like everybody else. I just thought my parents were my parents and my older sister was my sister. Mum and Dad never gave me any indication until then that I wasn't their daughter. Still, you can imagine the shock.'

'Uh, yeah.' William couldn't even imagine how he would feel if his mother dropped a bombshell like that on him. It didn't even bear thinking about. 'So what happened?'

'I didn't know what to think at first. I tried so hard not to let the news affect me. I mean, they were my family, my only family, and I loved them just as I always have. I didn't – couldn't – stop loving them, even if I'd wanted to. And I was scared. Terrified. I thought maybe this meant they wouldn't love me.' Amaranta gulped and a large, soft, fat tear rolled down one cheek. 'Or worse. That they didn't love me and they didn't want me anymore.' A large sob escaped her and, unsure of what else he should do, William squeezed her hand tightly, hoping it would comfort and reassure her.

'I'm sure they would never think that, Manta,' he whispered.

The girl breathed in deeply. 'You're right, William, of course, you are. My parents didn't stop loving me. In fact, my mother told me that she loved me even more, if that was possible. And that they were as scared of losing me as I was of losing them. But I was growing up and they felt it was important that I should know before …'

'Before what?'

'That's just it,' Amaranta said, sounding as puzzled as he felt. 'Mum never said. She just said, she felt I needed to know. Nothing more than that. No explanation.'

William was intrigued. 'But did you ask?'

'Of course, I did, silly. But Mum wouldn't say. She told me to forget about it. I knew the truth, but it made no difference. I was still their daughter and that's what mattered. And I tried so hard to do as she asked. But as the days went by, I found myself wondering more and more about who my real parents might be, and why they had abandoned me. Then Uncle Ernest suggested that it would be a good idea if I were to come live at Ravenwood and study at St Clem's and I accepted. I thought it might do me good. Be a distraction from all the millions of questions hammering away inside my head. And maybe by coming to Ravenwood, I might find out something about my birth parents. You know, find out who they are and where they might be, and why they left me at the castle.' Amaranta's green eyes glistened with tears and longing.

'And your parents agreed to you coming to Ravenwood?'

'Yes, they agreed with Uncle Ernest that a change of air might be a good idea, so they consented to my coming to Avenfore to study. My sister and I were educated at the best schools. We both had piano classes, swimming classes – it all seemed so normal. Now, however, I don't understand how. How could my family have paid for our expensive education on a civil servant salary? Somebody must be paying for my sister's and my education? But who? It's all such a mystery.'

Amaranta stood up slowly and peered out over the river Inni and Ravenwood Forest toward where the dark shape of Ravenwood Castle could be seen on a hill in the distance.

'William,' she said suddenly, 'please help me find out who my real parents are.'

William got up and stood beside her. 'Of course, I will, Manta. I'll do whatever I can to help.'

She was looking at him now.

'But I want everything I've told you to remain secret. Please don't mention it to anyone else. Promise me you won't?'

'You can trust me, Amaranta,' William said solemnly. 'You're not alone. I'm with you and I promise to help you find your real parents.'

Without warning, Amaranta leaned in and kissed him softly on the cheek and William's heart gave a strange joyous leap.

III

The village felt quiet and deserted as William and Amaranta made their way back along River Lane towards the main square, although the sound of a slow waltz could still be heard floating on the night air in the distance from the direction of the village park.

Ernest Wiglann was waiting for them in the square. 'Was looking' for you,' he growled as they crossed the road to join him at the base of the high cross, which towered above them, the soft glint of its granite quartz in the glow of yellow street lights mirroring the pinprick gleams of starlight across the black sky above.

'I'm sorry, Uncle Ernest,' Amaranta said, giving the old man a peck on the cheek. The old man grunted, but it was a softer, more forgiving grunt than was normal for the caretaker. All the same, he glowered at William.

'You shouldn't be wandering about on your own like that. You're lucky if I don't tell—'

But they never found out what it was that Mr Wiglann wasn't going to tell because, that moment, Arnold Howbbler came into the square from the direction of the hall.

'Ah, there you are, William,' Arnold cried as he strode towards them. 'It's high time you were home, I think. You too, Miss Bonclane.'

'Just leaving' now, Mr Howbbler,' Mr Wiglann replied.

CHAPTER 16

Annual General Meeting

I

F ROM THE MOMENT HE AWOKE, WILLIAM felt a surge of energy flow through him. Today was one of the most exciting days of his life: later this evening he would be sworn in as a Knight Postulant and join his father and Mr Greewoof as a member of the noble Order of the Alliance.

He leaped out of bed, washed quickly and raced downstairs to the dining room where Aunt Edna had insisted on serving breakfast in honour of his father.

Arnold Howbbler and Elsie were already seated at the breakfast table.

'There you are, sleepyhead,' Elsie exclaimed as William plopped himself down on an empty chair beside Arnold. His father smiled at him, but William thought he looked weary and disgruntled.

'Did you sleep well?' Arnold asked

'Yes, thanks. How about you?'

'Not as well as I would have liked, I'm afraid.'

Aunt Edna now entered the room carrying a tray piled so high with toast, crispy rashers of bacon, black and white pudding, sausages and eggs that William wondered how they would manage to eat it all between them. But he felt his stomach rumble at the sight and decided he was looking forward to giving it a good try.

As William tucked into his breakfast, Aunt Edna was still telling her younger brother off. 'Staying up until all hours reading. And after all that travelling from Marburg, Arnie, you were bound to be overtired. Not to mention sleeping in a strange bed.'

'Rest assured, Ed, it wasn't the bed or the room. They are both perfect. It was a long journey from Marburg and I had had a lot of excitement when I arrived in Avenfore. I couldn't fall asleep,' Arnold laughed. 'Thanks to these two young people and their friends. Falcon Fair play champions no less! What an achievement!'

'It was wonderful, Uncle Arnie,' Elsie said happily. 'Chris is such a brilliant playwright, isn't he? He has such a way with words. And the soul of a poet.' William nearly choked on his bacon as Elsie let out a long, dramatic sigh.

'Chris is a very talented young man,' William's father replied with a quick grin at his older sister, who rolled her eyes and shook her head behind Elsie's back.

'A wonderful achievement, indeed, Elsie dear, for all of you,' Aunt Edna continued, 'But, Arnold, it's such a shame you can't stay here tonight also, instead of up at Ravenwood Castle, as you really need to catch up on your sleep and I'm sure another strange bed will unsettle you even more.'

Arnold Howbbler shook his head. 'Don't worry, Ed, I'll be fine. Besides, I'll have William with me to keep me company.'

'William?' Aunt Edna and Elsie cried in unison.

'But why is William going to Ravenwood Castle?' Elsie demanded. 'He's not part of the birdwatching society.'

'Not yet,' Arnold said, 'but after tonight he will be.' William felt a rush of excitement at the thought of belonging to the same Order as his father, who he admired so much.

'Seriously?' Elsie was clearly unimpressed. 'But what does William know, *or care*, about birds?'

William felt himself becoming indignant, but at the same time, he knew that was unfair on his cousin, who knew nothing about the true nature of the birdwatching society. Even still, he wasn't going to sit idly by. His father beat him to it.

'What he doesn't know, Elsie, he'll learn. And he's eager to learn, which is all that matters. Besides, it'll be good having another Howbbler to talk to about birds and birdwatching.'

'Urgh,' Elsie said shoving a large piece of bacon into her mouth, 'it all sounds sooo dreadfully dull.'

William had to hide a large grin as Arnold winked at him. *If only you knew, Elsie*, he thought, *if only you knew.*

II

Arnold and William arrived at Ravenwood Castle at four o'clock on the dot. The whole castle had been turned over to the Order of the Alliance for their annual general meeting, although Arnold explained to William that the owner, Byron Mullween, usually made himself scarce while the meeting and dinner were taking place.

'So Byron Mullween's not a member of the Society?' William asked. He thought it odd given the castle's connection with the Order.

'No,' Arnold said, 'well, he is, but he no longer takes part.' A look of sadness passed over his face. 'It's such a shame, Will. The Mullweens are one of the oldest families in the village and have a long association with the Order. There had always been a Mullween in the Order. Until now.'

'But why would Byron not want to be in the Order, Dad?' William asked. 'It's such a wonderful thing. I can't imagine why anyone would want to turn their back on it.'

Arnold sighed. 'I don't know why, Will. To be honest, I don't think that any one knows other than Byron himself. One day he simply said he no longer wished to perform his duties as a member of the Order. He gave no explanation, but the brothers chose to respect his wishes, in the hope that eventually he would return to us and take up his rightful place at our table. But that was many years ago.'

'And he hasn't returned?'

'No. Not yet. We have tried to persuade him back, but to no avail so far and the choice to re-join us is his alone. Now, let's get inside and get you settled in for the big evening ahead, shall we?'

Arnold, put his hand on his son's shoulder. 'Your turn will come, William, to help the Order,' he said, 'and I have no doubt that when it does, you will serve well and every member will be as proud of you then as I am now.'

William heard a well-known and familiar voice calling to him. 'There you are, Will. Welcome to Ravenwood Castle. More importantly, welcome to the Order.'

William spun around in disbelief as the owner of the voice gave him a friendly slap on the back and a quick hug.

'Chris,' he stammered, 'what on earth are you doing here?'

'Of course, you'll understand how hard it's been for me not to say anything these last few weeks,' Chris said, as he and William followed Mr Dreephy up the main stairway of the castle to the first-floor bedrooms.

William did know how hard it had been. He had found it very difficult not to share his excitement about the Order with Chris or Elsie and Bridget. Or Amaranta. Which reminded him, he hadn't seen any sign of Amaranta as yet. Perhaps Byron Mullween had brought her with him when he went off for the day? Or perhaps she had made plans with Elsie and Bridget to go to the Falcon Fair's ceili and set dancing exhibition.

'I really had no idea you were the other postulant,' he said to Chris.

'I'm not,' Chris said. 'I joined last year.'

'But Mr Greewoof said there would be two new postulants, this year, so I assumed …?'

'Well, it's not me. But the full Knights make the decisions, so I won't necessarily know everything myself until the meeting tonight.'

William was puzzled. He really had thought Chris must be the other postulant. But if it wasn't Chris, then who could it be? But before he could try to figure it out, they were at the top of the grand staircase and Mr Dreephy was leading them along a long corridor with a series of arched doorways on either side. William noticed that each doorway was designated with a modest brass nameplate bearing the name and silhouette of a bird – fitting, William thought, for an Order pretending to be a birdwatching society. He read the names as he passed: mallard, magpie, wren, nightingale, siskin and chiffchaff.

Mr Dreephy came to a halt outside a door marked KINGFISHER. 'Your room,' he said, indicating towards William. William stepped in and looked about him. The room was large, with high vaulted ceilings. Its tall windows looked out over the lush green grounds of the castle towards the lake of Lesciern. Although the furnishings were dark and heavy, including a large four-poster bed to his right, the amount of light spilling into the room gave it a pleasant and airy feel and William felt his spirits rise. Strange as it might seem, he felt at home in this room – in the castle overall – as if he'd lived there all his life. Like a traveller who had finally come home.

'Dinner will be served in the Society dining room at eight o'clock sharp,' Mr Dreephy intoned. 'Dress is formal. It is not considered good form to be late.'

'Don't worry, Mr Dreephy, I'll make sure he shows up on time,' said Chris.

CHAPTER 17

The Isle of Lesciern

I

CHRIS COLLECTED WILLIAM FROM HIS ROOM at quarter past seven that evening. William had been dressed and ready for almost an hour, so anxious was he not to be late. He'd spent the intervening hours in his room, going over the Latin oath again and again so that he was word perfect.

'Nice suit,' Chris said when William opened the door to him.

'You don't look too bad yourself,' William laughed. And, indeed, he had to admit that Chris looked very grown up in his sleek black tuxedo with a dark-wine coloured bow tie. William's own dinner jacket was double-breasted and he wore a black bow tie, like his father's. He hadn't seen anything of Arnold since they had arrived at the castle and Chris had explained that the full Knights had extra meetings that the Squires and other brothers were not part of. William hadn't seen Amaranta either and presumed she must indeed have left the castle for the day because of the Society meetings.

Chris led the way to the Society dining room. William followed him down the grand staircase into the entrance hall of the castle, where they stood opposite the two huge paintings – the landscape showing the castle and the isle of Lesciern in the background and the portrait of the grumpy-looking Right Honourable Fergus Mullween – which hung on the arch-shaped hollow underneath the staircase landing. Chris moved to the wall and tapped at a candelabra to the side of the landscape painting and a small lancet-shaped door in the recess between the two paintings swung open. The older boy laughed at the look of surprise on William's face.

'Well, it is a *secret* society,' he said as he stepped through the door, beckoning at William to follow him.

The doorway opened onto a narrow passageway which curved and sloped downwards towards the back of the castle. William ran his hand along the stone walls of the narrow corridor. He was actually in a secret passageway!

After a few hundred yards, the passageway opened out into an antechamber at the far end of which stood an old suit of armour, in perfect condition, on a stone pedestal. To the right of the suit of armour was another huge painting similar in style to the mural William had seen in the crypt of the old church at Hollypoint. It showed an armoured warrior next to a dragon he had slain. Beside the picture, set in the wall, there was a bronze plaque which read: FEAR ONLY WHAT IS INEVITABLE.

William watched as Chris crossed to the suit of armour and, placing both hands on one of its feet pulled it forward. He then went over to the bronze plaque beside the picture on the right and pushed it firmly. There was a loud click and the painting swung away from the wall to reveal another secret door.

William gasped in astonishment as the door opened and his father stepped out into the antechamber. With a huge smile on his face, Arnold Howbbler put his arm around his son's shoulder and ushered him into the room beyond the secret door.

As they crossed the threshold together, Arnold whispered, 'Welcome to the Order of the Alliance, William. Welcome to the oldest secret Order in the world!'

II

The dining room of the Order of the Alliance was of banquet-hall proportions with a huge wooden vaulted ceiling and walls decorated with dark wood panelling and rich tapestries. The back wall of the room was dominated by a mural which showed an armour-clad warrior on horseback, his sword raised, and a falcon flying above his head.

Enormous crystal chandeliers spilled their light down onto an elegant dining table which ran the length of the room, set with sparkling glassware, porcelain and silver cutlery in amongst the extravagant candelabras and elaborate vases of flowers. Doing a quick count in his head, William noticed place settings for twenty-four diners, just as Mr Greewoof had explained: twelve Knights and twelve Squires. He supposed that they always set a place for Byron hoping one day he would change his mind.

Almost dazed by what he saw, William now realised that the room was full of people. Some were familiar faces: Mr Greewoof, Chris's father, Mr Durffan, and Mr Mestfinn, the St Elms' music teacher. But there were many other faces he didn't recognise and Arnold now brought him around the room, introducing him to some of the other members.

First up was Mr Millmelan, the headmaster of St Elm's who William had not yet met despite his place at the school. 'Pleased to meet you, William, and welcome to the Alliance,' Mr Millmelan said brightly as he shook William's hand.

'Delighted to meet you, Mr Millmelan. I've heard so much about you.'

'Nothing bad, I hope' the headmaster chortled.

Next up was Valcott O'Neill. 'Valcott runs the Alliance's bookshop in Drunfarnam,' Arnold explained. 'If you ever need anything, he's the chap to get in touch with.'

Valcott smiled and clarified things by adding, 'What Arnold hasn't said is that the shop is also the main contact point for members of the Alliance. And you're welcome whenever you want to come, whether you need my help or not.'

Then Arnold introduced him to Alastair Malblenar, who had just arrived from Scotland, Harry Smith, who had travelled from London, Frederick Boarnys, the Avenfore church sacristan, and Mr

Brady Grayling, who worked in Drunfarnam library. By the time William had met them all, his head was in a spin and he had no idea how he would remember everyone.

'Don't worry,' Arnold said. 'You don't need to learn them all. Just a few ones in case you need to contact them. And we always use codenames in any event.'

'Codenames?' William asked.

'That's right.' It was Mr Greewoof who answered, 'your father's Corncrake and I'm Magpie.'

William thought about the bird on the door of his bedroom. 'And I'm Kingfisher?'

'Well deduced, young man,' chuckled Mr Greewoof.

William was just thinking of how appropriate bird codenames were when his father turned to Mr Greewoof. 'Abelard, I must ask, where's our second new recruit got to?'

'Should be here any minute now, Arnold. I bet William wants to know who it is.'

'At this stage, I'm fairly dying of curiosity, Mr Greewoof.'

'Not long to wait, William,' Mr Greewoof said glancing at his wristwatch. 'In fact, I reckon our second Knight Postulant should be arriving just about … now.'

As Mr Greewoof spoke, the door of the dining room opened, and all eyes turned to see who had arrived.

Ernest Wiglann stood in the doorway. On his arm, resplendent in a midnight-blue evening gown and a pearl necklace around her slender neck, smiling, but clearly nervous, was Amaranta Bonclane.

III

Amaranta's acceptance into the Society was a great source of excitement even for those Knights already in on the secret.

'I'm the first woman to be admitted into the Society since it started,' she whispered to William and Chris proudly during dinner.

'Uncle Ernest proposed me last year to fill one of the empty seats, which was when we discovered that there was nothing in the rules of the Alliance to say that women could not be members. Apparently, it had just always been taken for granted that the Order was only for men. But from now on there will be women as well.'

William smiled at the thought. He couldn't help thinking of his cousin, Elsie, whose intelligence and capabilities, despite being bossy and annoying at times, could prove of great use to the Society and it seemed to him a crazy idea for anyone to object to Amaranta or Elsie joining the Order simply because they were girls.

Abelard Greewoof rose to his feet to propose a toast.

'To our two young candidates, who this year will join our noble Order,' he cried. 'To William Howbbler and Amaranta Bonclane.'

'To William Howbbler and Amaranta Bonclane,' they chorused raising their glasses.

Amaranta and William stood to join the others as Mr Greewoof raised his glass again and declared. 'For the good of the Alliance and its brethren!'

After the meal Abelard suggested they all go outside and enjoy the beautiful evening before setting off to the island of Lesciern for the ceremony.

Amaranta gave a whoop of delight as they wandered out into the castle grounds. The summer sun was beginning to set and paper lanterns shone bright in the growing gloom, illuminating their way, with white pennants bearing the falcon insignia fluttering among the lights. They strolled about the gardens chatting until Mr Dreephy sounded a deep sonorous bell from somewhere inside the castle and the brethren slowly gathered together in the entrance hall of the castle.

The atmosphere in the entrance hall was now sombre and attentive as Elwood and Mary Dreephy quietly handed each of them a long white hooded cloak from two trunks which now stood beneath the paintings underneath the stairway. Then, one by one, the brethren began to make their way slowly out into the garden again, following the lantern-lit pathway to the castle mooring by the lakeside.

There, to William's surprise, a row of six boats was waiting for them. Arnold Howbbler stepped into one of the boats and beckoned to William and Amaranta to join him. Beside them, Chris joined his father, Edmund Durffan, Robert Mestfinn and Brady Grayling in another boat and all along the mooring, other brethren waited their turn to board their vessels.

The last to board were Abelard Greewoof, Harry Smith and Alastair Mablenar. Their fourth was missing, William thought, remembering the empty place setting at the dining table earlier – Bryon Mullween's place setting – and it made him sad that Mr Mullween had chosen not to be a part of all of this.

When everyone was in their boats, Ernest Wiglann slipped the ropes from their moorings and pushed the boats off out over the lake before joining William and Amaranta in Arnold's boat.

The six boats cut through the calm waters of the lake, their way lit only by the light of the full moon. Amaranta sat on the prow of the rowing boat. In her white cloak, and with her pale face and green eyes, William thought, she looked more hauntingly beautiful than ever.

'Don't you think this is exciting?' Amaranta whispered to him. 'We're retracing a journey the original knights made more than six hundred years ago.' William nodded, unwilling to speak and break the magical spell of the evening.

Theirs was the last boat to reach the island. Mr Wiglann tied up the boat and they walked along the lake edge and up a short dirt path to join the others.

All the brethren were gathered in a clearing in the centre of the island at the middle of which stood a mighty granite standing stone. It was over eight feet tall and about four or five feet in diameter and towered above even the tallest of the Brothers. Like the Avenfore high cross, it was covered with intricate carvings of runes, beasts, geometric shapes and spirals. In front of it was a granite fire pit, the burning fire sending flames and sparks shooting up towards the night sky.

As he and Amaranta watched in silent awe, the twelve Brothers stepped forward, each with a torch in each hand. One by one, they lit the twenty-four torches – one for each Brother of the Alliance – from the fire. The twelve Brothers, who William now surmised were the Squires of the Order, moved around the standing stone, each one positioning one of their torches in twelve equidistant spots to form a circle around the standing stone. They themselves then formed a second circle behind this first circle, each man holding a flaming torch in his hand. Then, as one, the company began to chant the Latin oath inscribed on the base of the stone – the very oath that William had spent so long learning over the past weeks.

'The flame that our ancestors ignited one day is the same one that we will ignite today. May this fire serve to remember and keep alive that which united them in the hope that our children and the children of our children will continue to serve this noble cause. So that good may never bow to evil, we ask God to give us strength to fight it.'

As the last words of the chant rang out across the island of Lesciern, Harry Smith, clearly the eldest of the Knights, opened a large trunk which was set near to the entrance to the clearing. Reaching in, he took out a sword, and William gasped. It was a long, two-handed sword with the shamrock-leaf cross symbol on its pommel, which William now knew from the *Chronicle of the Noble Order of the Alliance*, to be a cross bottony. At the top of the blade, directly underneath the simple cross guard, was engraved a falcon. William had no doubt that what he was looking at was one of the twelve swords of the original Knights of the Order of the Alliance.

As Harry drew out the sword, Abelard Greewoof approached and knelt on one knee before him. 'On bended knee as a sign of acceptance and respect,' whispered Arnold to William and Amaranta, who simply nodded in awe and watched as Mr Greewoof, sword in hand, stood up and took up his position beside one of the torches around the standing stone, in front of a man William had been introduced to as John Cloondale from Drishlean, who was clearly Mr Greewoof's Squire.

One by one the other Knights also received their swords and took their place around the stone until only William and Amaranta remained. Three men stood alone behind their Knight's torches and it struck William that they were the Squires without Knights – Brady Grayling, Frederick Boarnys and Ernest Wiglann.

Then Harry Smith began to speak. 'Before we begin, let us have a moment of silence for those who have left us these years past. Aaron Seblean, who gave his life in service to the Alliance' – at this Brady Grayling bowed his head – 'and Benjamin Greether' – now it was Frederick Boarnys' turn to bow – 'another Brother lost to us this year who, despite his great age, never wavered in his service even to the very end.'

'*Aeterna vita iustis!* – eternal life to the just,' shouted the assembly in one voice, the Knights raising their swords high as they did so. The sight of the brethren in their white cloaks, hoods up, their faces lit only by the flickering flames of the torches sent a shiver of excitement down William's spine. Looking over at Amaranta, he could see she was feeling the same way too.

With that, Harry signalled to the two postulants that they should accompany him to the stone. 'Worthy disciples,' he continued, 'on an occasion similar to this six hundred and thirty years ago was the noble Order of the Alliance founded, an alliance of which today you will become part. As we do every year, we are gathered here on the island of Lesciern to celebrate the founding of our order and to name new fellow members. It was around this very stone that our forefathers took an oath to serve just and noble causes and for over six hundred years both the stone and the order remain in place. During those years, the Alliance faced many and diverse dangers. History teaches us that evil is temporary and that good finally prevails. I wish you to know that if our Order has survived through to this day it is in no small part because it has continuously adhered to the wise precepts of the Alliance: discretion, prudence and patience.'

As he finished, Harry signalled to Abelard Greewoof and Arnold Howbbler, each of whom went to the trunk and pulled out a sword. Together they approached the stone where William and Amaranta were standing.

'Please kneel now to acknowledge your acceptance of this sword and your obligation and duty to the Order,' Harry said, and William and Amaranta dutifully did as they were asked.

Abelard then brought forward the sword that had belonged to the late Aaron Seblean and handed it over to Harry, who took it by the ridge of the blade. Brady Grayling stepped forward with his torch as William went down on one knee and bowed his head slightly forward and again recited the oath of the Templar fire.

As soon as he had finished, Harry touched him with the pommel and declared, 'In the name of all that is good do I name you Knight Postulant of the Alliance.'

William then rose to receive his sword. Holding the blade in both hands, Harry held out the sword to William, who took it firmly by the grip, and then, raising it high, declared, *'Fides et ratio!'*

The other Knights also lifted their swords and together exclaimed once again, *'Fides et ratio!'*

His heart pounding with excitement in his chest, William watched as Amaranta then received the sword which had once belonged to Benjamin Greether in similar fashion – knee bent, head bent, and a solemn, passionate look in her bright green eyes – beneath a torch held aloft by Frederick Boarnys.

Harry Smith pushed back his hood and thrust his sword into the ground, his hands resting on the pommel. 'Dear Brothers …'

He paused as Abelard Greewoof inclined his head slightly towards Amaranta. 'Dear Brothers and, eh … Sister, as you all know, this year we were very close to recovering the *Book of the Knights Templar Errant*. Alas, it was not to be, and poor Aaron Seblean was the only one to know its whereabouts – a secret he unfortunately took with him to the tomb. We do not know if it is in the possession of the evil Ignatius Nosmorum or at the bottom of Lochbury Lake. Wherever it is, our mission is to seek it out, and that must, perforce, be our task this year, too.'

A sharp buzz of energy seemed to flow around the group of Knights and Squires gathered around the great standing stone at the mention of the lost *Book of the Knights Templar Errant*. Harry motioned them to silence by raising his sword.

Unbidden, the Knights and Squires formed circle around the menhir and taking their swords in both hands raised them high, proclaiming in one voice, 'While that which united us unites us, nothing will ever be impossible.'

William too repeated the cry that he had memorised a few days earlier, as he gripped his sword with all his might and made a silent vow that he would not rest until the *Book of the Knights Templar Errant* was found.

CHAPTER 18

Drunfarnam

I

Following Mass on Sunday morning, William and Arnold Howbbler returned home to Aunt Edna's for lunch. While Uncle Walter ate his dinner, read the newspaper and ignored them all, all at the same time, William was amused and amazed in equal measure at the way in which his father was able to field questions about the Night Bird Society.

Had they enjoyed the meeting? Was it very boring? – That was Elsie's question. Who else was there? – That was Aunt Edna's. Arnold answered all their questions politely and as truthfully as he could without giving anything away.

Arnold did blanche when Elsie suggested watching birds might be a good hobby for Aunt Edna, but fortunately, her mother dismissed that idea immediately. If she wanted to watch birds, she could just look out the kitchen window. She didn't need to go traipsing into forests to spot them, thank you very much. Besides, Edna mused, from what she could see birdwatching was an all-male preserve.

'Actually, that's not true,' William said. 'The Society does admit women. Amaranta's a member.' He only realised his error when he saw Arnold throw him an exasperated look.

Elsie was scowling also. 'Really,' she said. 'So that's why Manta couldn't come to the set dancing exhibition with Bridget yesterday evening? She was at the birdwatching meeting.' William gulped. All he needed now was Elsie to start asking even more awkward questions and he would be in trouble.

But Elsie rolled her eyes and sighed. 'To be honest, I don't really blame her. If I had a hobby that tediously dull, I'd probably lie about it too.' William breathed an inward sigh of relief, and from the look on Arnold's face, that was the case with him too. 'Although,' Elsie continued, 'I don't ever remember anyone asking *me* to join.'

'That's because you keep telling us it's really boring,' muttered William through a mouthful of shepherd's pie. Elsie glared at him and was about to make what William was sure would be a smart retort, when Aunt Edna piped up.

'I was just thinking that we should go to the pictures after we drop Arnold to the railway station to get his train back to Dublin this evening.'

Elsie squealed with delight. 'Oh, yes,' she said, 'please, Mum, let's do.'

'Sounds like a great idea, Ed,' Arnold said, winking at William. 'What will you go and see?'

'Give us the paper, Dad, please,' Elsie cried, jumping up from her chair and snatching the newspaper from her surprised father.

'Do you fancy coming with us, Uncle Walter?' William asked.

'Uh,' Walter looked confused.

'To the cinema, dear; to see a moving picture,' Aunt Edna explained.

Walter's normally placid face wore a look of horror. 'Uh, no thank you, Edna, dear,' he said, 'but you and Els go and enjoy yourselves.'

'Look, Mum, *Darby O'Gill and the Little People* is showing at the Odeon in Drunfarnam at six thirty. Can we go?'

'What's that about?' William asked unconvinced.

'About little people, dear,' Aunt Edna replied, although William got the feeling she didn't really know what it was about herself.

'Leprechauns, I think, Ed.' Arnold couldn't help a smirk.

'Oh dear,' Edna said. 'Perhaps we should see something else?'

Elsie glowered at William, although he had no idea why. 'Don't be silly, Mum,' she insisted. 'It's a love story and you'll love it.'

'That's true,' she said. 'I do love a good love story, Arnie.'

William could see his father was now trying very hard not to laugh. 'Well, then, it all sounds just about right,' he said at last.

'That's all settled so,' said Elsie, beaming triumphantly. '*Darby O'Gill and the Little People* it is!'

II

The film was every bit as saccharine as William had feared. However, he had to admit it wasn't the worst he'd ever seen. Besides, sitting in the dark cinema staring up at the screen had given him time to think over the events of the past few days.

Saying goodbye to Arnold had been tough. He'd hugged his father tightly, made him promise to give Prudence and Kristyn more hugs and kisses from him and then stood on the platform waving until Arnold's train disappeared around a curve in the direction of Dublin. He'd been grateful for Elsie's comforting hug as they left the station. For all her bossiness, Elsie really was one of the kindest-hearted people William knew.

On the journey back to Avenfore, William sat in the back of the van and stared out at the darkening countryside through an open slit of canvas. The road outside Drunfarnam town followed the course of the river Inni on one side and was bordered on the other by a large embankment punctuated by hedgerows of thick hawthorn trees and the occasional sycamore or silver birch tree. The air inside the canvas awning covering the back of Aunt Edna's van was hot and muggy and William could feel his eyes grow heavy.

He yawned to keep awake and opened the awning a bit wider to let in more air. The bright headlights of a car behind the van caught his attention. He watched it approach, its headlights casting an eerie illumination over the hedgerows and trees lining the road, making them look sinister and menacing. Then suddenly, the car was directly behind Aunt Edna's van, travelling at such speed that

William felt as though it might actually hit them. He shrank back into the van and put his arm over his eyes to shield them from the blinding light as the car roared towards them with an angry shout of its horn.

As it careered around and past them, William shifted so that he could peer out through the windscreen of the van. As he did so, the car swerved so close in front of the van that, despite the fact that Aunt Edna was driving slowly, she had to break suddenly to avoid colliding with it. Aunt Edna and Elsie gasped in shock.

'What on earth does that idiot think he's playing at?' Elsie thundered as the car disappeared up the road in front of them.

'Are you all right, William?' Aunt Edna called.

'I'm fine, Aunt Edna,' William said, trying to reassure her.

'Oh dear,' his aunt said, 'I really don't know why people have to drive like that. It's really not very pleasant at all. Quite takes the good out of driving, don't you think?'

Aunt Edna trembled as she spoke and Elsie put a hand on her mother's arm. 'Don't worry, Mum,' she said gently. 'We're all right, that's the main thing. Just relax and you'll be as right as rain in a minute.'

'Elsie's right, Aunt Edna,' William said. 'Don't worry about us. Take it easy and you'll feel better soon.'

'Thank you, dears,' Aunt Edna said with a break in her voice which told William she was near to tears.

'Oh Mum,' Elsie murmured and leaning in towards Aunt Edna, she wrapped her mother in a large hug.

As she did so, William noticed the car turn off the main road to the left ahead of them and felt fear wash over him. The shape of the car from the side with its sharp tailfins was unmistakeable. He had no doubt that the driver who had almost caused poor Aunt Edna to crash was none other than Ignatius Nosmorum!

His heart pounding, William watched as the car pulled to a halt and a strange black shape emerged from the darkness lit up by the white beams of the car's headlights. It was part of a large round structure. A wheel? Like a large mill wheel or a Ferris wheel, perhaps? Around it, he could also make out the outlines of a jumble of other buildings, some squat and low, others larger and taller. As he watched, the headlights went off and the buildings in the distance were plunged once again into complete darkness. Then for a brief moment, William saw the familiar silhouette of the Wicked Crow illuminated in the light of an open doorway, before that too shut, and the evil man was swallowed up into the blackness.

CHAPTER 19

Hannah Fairground

I

W ILLIAM HARDLY SLEPT THAT NIGHT. HE tossed and turned, his dreams haunted by visions of the Wicked Crow standing in a flame-lit doorway or striding towards him only to be engulfed by thick forest mist. He couldn't wait to tell Mr Greewoof or Chris and Amaranta about the sighting, but, in the early hours of the morning, he decided to keep it to himself until he had a chance to find out as much as he could about the strange buildings and the wheel-like structure he had seen in the headlights the night before.

Usually, he would ask Aunt Edna, but she looked a little upset and subdued at breakfast after the near-accident and so he thought he'd better not. Elsie was also rather cross, but William could understand that. She was angry that someone had upset her mother with such dangerous driving.

The weather didn't help. The summer sun was hidden behind grey clouds and rain pattered against the kitchen windows.

'You look tired, William, dear,' his aunt remarked as he sat down at the kitchen table. So do you, Aunt Edna, William thought, but he didn't say it out loud.

'I'm fine, thanks,' he said, 'just tired. It's been quite a weekend and I didn't sleep too well last night.'

'No, me neither,' murmured Aunt Edna, looking distressed all over again and Elsie threw William a look of exasperation.

'It's such horrible weather outside,' his cousin declared loudly. 'And I'm feeling tired as well. I think it would be an idea if we stayed indoors with you today, Mum. What do you think, Will?'

'Um, yes, that sounds like a great idea,' William said, squirming under his cousin's firm glare.

In the end, William was glad Elsie had suggested they stay put. Mid-morning, claps of thunder pealed through the skies and the heavy rain turned to a downpour for most of the afternoon. Any reluctance William had felt about staying in vanished when he saw how much their company cheered up his aunt. But he quickly realised there was no way he could ask her about the odd buildings — it would remind her of the near-accident. When he got a chance, he'd have to try Uncle Walter instead.

II

Tuesday morning dawned bright and fresh. Aunt Edna was bustling about in the kitchen, looking far more like her old self, when William arrived down for breakfast.

'So, my dears, what are you planning to do today, then?' she inquired.

Elsie turned to William. 'What's the plan, then, Will? Any thoughts?'

William hadn't really thought about it, but suddenly he heard himself say, 'I'd like to go to Malconary's,' he said. 'Dad gave me some money to buy sweets.'

'That's a good idea,' said Elsie. 'I'll go with you. But I'll call into Bridget's first to see if she or Chris want to come with us.'

'Sounds good,' William said.

'What about Amaranta?' Aunt Edna asked.

'It's just it's a long trek to Ravenwood Castle and back again, Mum,' Elsie explained.

'I'll telephone Mrs Dreephy,' Aunt Edna replied cheerfully, 'and I'm sure Mr Wiglann will give her a lift into town if we ask.'

'That would be great, Mum, thanks.'

As Elsie and William pulled on their shoes, William said he'd like to call into Uncle Walter on the way. He'd promised to show him some new clock or other, he offered by way of explanation. Elsie rolled her eyes. Her father's obsession with clocks was clearly as incomprehensible to her as her uncle's and William's obsession with birds.

'Tell you what,' she said, 'you drop in on Dad on the way and I'll go on to Bridget's and collect her and Chris. We can meet up in Malconary's afterwards. Hopefully, by that stage, Amaranta will have arrived also.'

'That sounds great,' William said. And he meant it. It would make it much easier to talk to Uncle Walter alone.

Ten minutes later, he was sitting, open-mouthed, in the spacious, windowless, oak-panelled backroom of Uncle Walter's antique shop staring at the six-foot high shelves filled with hundreds of perfectly ordered clocks of all shapes, sizes, styles and periods. Wearing a satisfied smile, Uncle Walter was pointing out some of the models and explaining their characteristics.

'Now what about this, William! This hourglass is one of the oldest pieces in my collection, and it belonged to King Louis XVII of France, no less.'

'Amazing,' was all William could mutter. 'Really amazing.'

'Well, there we are, then,' Uncle Walter said, surveying his precious timepieces lovingly. 'Beauties, each and every one of them, don't you think?'

They truly were astonishing. So much so, William had almost forgotten why he had come to see Uncle Walter in the first place.

'Er, uh, Uncle Walter,' he said finally. 'The road into Drunfarnam, there's a building there – looks like a large wheel with other buildings around it. Do you know what that is?'

Uncle Walter frowned for a moment as he thought. 'The road into Drunfarnam?' he asked, 'on the Avenfore side, d'you mean?'

'Not far outside the town, if you were coming from Avenfore,' William explained.

Uncle Walter's brow furrowed again. 'Ummm,' he said, 'I think it must be the Hannah fairground you're talking about.'

'Fairground?' William asked, surprised. He wasn't aware of a fairground near Drunfarnam. It was odd none of the others had mentioned it.

'Well, it used to be a fairground,' Uncle Walter continued. 'It's been closed down for the past ten years or so, I should imagine. Didn't know it was still there, to be honest.'

'Do you know who owns it?'

Uncle Walter shook his head and grinned. 'No idea. Fairgrounds and their owners are not my area of expertise, I'm afraid.'

'Do you remember why it closed down, perhaps?' William asked.

'I'm afraid I don't, Will,' he replied. 'Although, now you mention it, there is something in my mind about an accident of sorts …'

'What kind of accident?'

But Uncle Walter shook his head again. 'I really don't know,' he said. 'You could ask your aunt, of course; she tends to remember these things much better than I do. Or you could try the library.'

'The library?'

'They should have archive copies of old newspapers which you can look up. They might even have other literature on it. I'm sure if you ask the librarian will be able to help you.'

'Thanks, Uncle Walter, I appreciate the help.' He glanced down at his watch. It was showing one minute to ten o'clock. He hadn't realised it was so late already. He'd arranged to meet Elsie and the others at half past ten, so he'd better hurry if he wanted to go to the library first. 'I should go, Uncle Walter,' he said.

'Er, yes, that would indeed be best,' his uncle said looking around him in alarm.

'Is something wrong?' William asked.

'Oh no, not wrong,' Uncle Walter replied. 'Just noisy.'

'Noi—?' But Uncle Walter was already shoving him out the door as hundreds of clocks began to chime the hour in a deafening cacophony of whirrs, creaks, bells, gongs and frantic choruses of 'cuckoo'.

III

Avenfore library was quiet and still and William was somewhat alarmed to find himself the only person there at that time of the morning. He had hoped to be able to find the newspaper archives without Miss Aguevals' help, but she looked up at him from behind her desk almost as soon as he entered the building.

'How can I help you this sunny Tuesday morning, William Howbbler?' she asked, her voice ringing shrill through the silent room.

Reluctantly, William made his way over to the desk. There was no way around it: he would have to tell her what he was there for.

'I'm looking for the newspaper archives, Miss Aguevals,' he stammered. He had no idea why this woman made him feel so nervous, but she always seemed to manage to do so. She was staring at him now, her eyes beady and curious.

'Really, young man? That's very interesting. Tell me, what do you need them for?'

Alarm bells rang so loudly in William's head, they almost made his head hurt. Why did he dislike this woman so? Whatever the reason, he had no intention of telling Veronica Aguevals why he was interested in the old newspapers.

'I-I-I ...'

'Y-Y-You what, dear?' Miss Aguevals had a smile plastered to her face, but William detected something nasty and mocking in her tone. Veronica Aguevals was a seriously unpleasant woman. He had no idea how he knew this; he just did.

'Come along now, boy, I haven't got all day!' The librarian's tone was sharp as a whip. William had no idea what was eating her – after all, there was no one else in the library, and surely it was her job to help people who came to the library with queries.

'I-I-I'm writing to my mother' – he blurted out the first thing that came into his head – 'I wanted to do some research on the Falcon Fair; to tell her all about it. She's really interested in it, you see.'

'Is she really? And what is your mother's name?'

William stared at her for a moment, astounded. Why on earth did she want to know that? But he didn't want to be rude either and she could as easily find out from Uncle Walter or Aunt Edna or any of their neighbours.

'Prudence,' he replied. 'My mother's name is Prudence.'

'And are you an only child?' Miss Aguevals inclined her head to eye him even more beadily than before.

'N-N-No, I have a sister; her name's Kristyn.'

'Kristyn. What a pretty name,' Miss Aguevals cooed in a way William imagined a vulture might coo at its prey before it swooped in on them.

'And where are your mother and sister? Are they also in Avenfore? I don't think I've seen them around.'

'No, Miss Aguevals, they're not in Avenfore. They're with my Dad. He's a university lecturer. In Marburg.'

'Ah, Germany,' Veronica cooed again. 'How lovely for them. But lonely for you, I imagine?'

'Yes. I miss them a lot.'

'Yes, young William Howbbler, I'm sure you do.' Her eyes were boring into him as if she was trying to look through him. Then she flashed him a brilliant smile that seemed to come out of nowhere.

'Well, that's enough chit-chat for one day, William Howbbler; you shouldn't be keeping me from my work, you know. The newspaper archives are over there.' She indicated with a long, slender pointed finger towards the back of the library. 'Along the back wall behind the history section, L to H; you can't miss them. And be careful with them. They're fragile items. If you damage them, you will be sorry.'

The thought crossed William's mind that he was already sorry – sorry he'd had to have that conversation with the librarian in the first place – but he thanked her and, with a sigh of relief, trotted over to the archive section as quickly as he could.

The newspaper archives were held in sets of large, leather-bound volumes on a number of shelves lining the back wall. Each volume held six months' worth of editions of the local monthly newspaper, the *Avenfore Chronicle*. William stared at them in dismay. There were so many of them and he had no idea where to start.

He took a deep breath and tried to remember his conversation with Uncle Walter. Ten years or so, his uncle had said. So let's try 1949, William thought. As good as place as any to start. He pulled the first large volume out of its place on the shelf and heaved it onto a nearby desk where he could open it out at full width to read its contents.

The newspaper itself was quite fascinating. Local news and adverts mixed in with national and international events. But nothing about the Hannah fairground in Drunfarnam.

William glanced at his watch – twenty-five minutes past ten. He was almost at the end of the second 1949 volume. He'd need to finish up soon and go to Malconary's to meet Chris and the girls. Then, just as he was finishing one of the November issues of the newspaper, a picture of a Ferris wheel caught his attention. His heart gave a leap as he read the advertisement beneath the picture:

Be amazed at Hannah Fairground. Fire-eaters, jugglers, carousels and Dodgems, Hoop-la stalls and a helter-skelter. See the amazing Snake Lady. Let Madame Ophelia, our mystical Fortune Teller, see into your Future. Candyfloss and toffee apples. Entertainment galore for young and old. buy your tickets now.

Excitement building, William thumbed through the rest of the paper so firmly that, despite its age, the inky residue rubbed off on his fingers and smudged the pages.

'What did I tell you about damaging the newspapers, William Howbbler?' The librarian's voice rang out above him like a clap of thunder, making William jump in fright.

'I-I-I ...'

'Really, young man, you will have to do better than that.' Veronica Aguevals was bearing down on him, that beady curious look in her eyes again.

William snapped the volume shut suddenly and jumped up.

'You're right, Miss Aguevals,' he said. 'I'm sorry about the newspaper, but I have to go now.'

'Wait a minute, William Howbbler, I haven't finished talking to y—'

But William had already replaced the archive volume on its shelf and was running for the front door without looking back.

IV

Elsie, Bridget and Amaranta were seated at a table waiting for William when he arrived at Malconary's.

'There you are,' Elsie exclaimed. 'What took you so long?'

'I was with your dad,' he said. 'And afterwards, I went to the library.'

'Why?' Elsie demanded. Her tone was sharp and William bristled. He was tired of people trying to interrogate him today about stuff that was, frankly, none of their business – even if the interrogator this time was Elsie. Much as he loved his cousin, William heartily wished she wasn't in the habit of asking so many awkward questions.

'I was looking something up,' he snapped. 'For the Night Bird Society, if you must know.' *Which is true*, he thought, *just not the whole truth*. He saw Amaranta perk up at the mention of the Order's public name.

'Nothing of interest to you, Els,' he continued.

He realised almost immediately that he'd said the wrong thing. Elsie glared at him.

'Suit yourself,' she said. 'I was only trying to be friendly.'

'I'm sorry, Els,' he said, throwing her a repentant grin. 'But I've just had a grilling from Miss Aguevals and, believe me, it wasn't very pleasant.'

Elsie shuddered dramatically. 'Ugh,' she said. 'All right, then. I'd feel scrappy myself if that old bird had been hounding me. So, did you find what you were looking for anyway?'

'Actually, no. I got some information, but not all of it.'

'What is it you're looking for?'

'Eh' —It was as difficult to lie to Elsie as it was to lie to Veronica Aguevals, although for totally different reasons — 'just boring bird stuff, really. It's not that important.' Again, he caught Amaranta's eye as she shifted forward slightly to stare at him curiously.

'Try Drunfarnam,' Elsie said.

'Drunfarnam?'

'Drunfarnam library, silly. It's a much bigger library, so they're bound to have lots more than here in Avenfore.'

Of course, William thought. And he could ask his Squire, Brady Grayling, for help, if needs be.

He beamed at his cousin. 'That's a brilliant idea, Els. I'll definitely check it out. Thanks.'

To his relief, Elsie smiled back at him — all was forgiven. But it didn't last long.

'All that boring bird stuff is right,' said Bridget suddenly. 'And now Manta's joined, I hear. Well, I hope you two aren't going to be as dull about it as Chris is. He's always off with Dad on those silly birdwatching trips. Too much fuss over nothing. Don't you agree, Els?'

If Bridget was expecting Elsie to agree, she was sorely disappointed. William looked at his cousin's face — it was thunderous.

'Chris is a birdwatcher too, is he?' Elsie hissed.

'I—'

'You never thought to tell me?'

'You never asked.' Bridget stared at her best friend nonplussed. 'Besides, I—'

Elsie wasn't listening. She glowered at William and Amaranta.

'So, is everyone else in this village a member of the Night Bird Society too – or is it just me and Bridget who aren't?'

'Why don't we all go to Drunfarnam?' It was Amaranta who spoke.

Elsie stared at her coolly. 'Why should we all go?' she said. 'After all, Bridget and I don't have any birdwatching stuff to look up.'

Amaranta went bright red, but Bridget squeaked with excitement.

'Ooh, yes, Els, let's all go! We could go see that fortune teller. You know, the one Gladis and Arline told us about – the one their cousin's sister's aunt went to. Oh, please say yes, Els; it would be such great fun! Besides, I'd be far too scared to go on my own! Say you'll come with me? Please??'

Elsie didn't respond. She continued to glare at William and Amaranta as Chris appeared at the door of the sweet shop and waved over at them.

'Sorry I'm late,' he called. 'Got delayed doing stuff for Dad!'

Elsie stared at Chris as he joined them at the table. For one awful moment, William thought she might burst into tears, but then, to everyone's surprise, she stood up.

'I think the fortune teller's a great idea, Bridget,' Elsie said. 'We've probably both lots of questions for her. We should invite the twins along also – I'm sure they'd love to come. And you're welcome too, Amaranta' – Elsie's smile was sweet but slightly venomous – 'unless, of course, you're not too busy looking up "bird stuff" with the boys here.'

Chris stared in astonishment as Elsie swept past him and made for the door, his sister scuttling anxiously after her.

He turned to William, a look of complete bewilderment on his face. 'What on earth's got into Els?' he asked.

William looked at Amaranta who groaned, put her head on the sweet shop table and buried her face in her hands.

'Long story,' William replied with a sigh. 'A long story about boring bird stuff.'

CHAPTER 20

A Near Miss

I

E LSIE WAS STILL UPSET WHEN THEY all set off for Drunfarnam that afternoon. For once, she let Aunt Edna sort out the travel arrangements and didn't object when Chris suggested that he, Amaranta and William make the trip by boat as there wasn't enough room for them all to go with Aunt Edna.

William's stomach clenched with guilt as he watched the van trundle to the end of Fern Lane and indicate right in the direction of the village square and the Drunfarnam road. From the looks on Amaranta's and Chris's faces, they felt much the same way as he did.

They made their way to the Avenfore jetty where Mr Richie Oblane, the village boatman, was waiting. They hired a row boat for two shillings and sixpence and confirmed they understood Mr Oblane's strict instructions to return it by seven thirty p.m. sharp.

The afternoon was fresh and bright, the air cleared by the previous day's thunderstorm. Chris rowed, while Amaranta sat at the back of the boat, and stared into the clear water of the Inni River beneath them. William sat in the middle, enjoying the warm sun on his face and listening to the gentle rhythmic splash of the oars as they hit the water. William glanced down at the brown and green river algae streaming beneath them as the boat forged its way upstream, following the meandering curve of the Inni.

William's reverie was broken as the row boat turned a corner a little way out from Drunfarnam.

'Look! That's the place!' he shouted.

'Where?'

'What?'

Chris and Amaranta asked together.

William was sitting up now. 'Over there on the riverbank. Look!'

The others looked over to where he was pointing in the distance to the south-western bank of the river where a group of low, shabby-looking buildings lurked on a plateau above the river and below the main road on the other side. At their centre was a lopsided and rusted Ferris wheel which looked as though it would topple over any minute if swept by a stiff summer breeze.

'What is that place?' Amaranta asked.

'It's the Hannah fairground.' This time it was William and Chris together.

Amaranta shivered. 'It's derelict.'

'Sure is,' Chris said, 'for as long as I can remember. It's been shut down so long I'd forgotten it was there.'

'It's been closed ten years,' William said, 'or thereabouts. At least that's what my Uncle Walter says.'

'Why did it close down?'

The boat was now parallel with the buildings and Amaranta stared at them, shielding her eyes from the sun as she did so.

'Some sort of an accident,' William replied. 'But I don't know any more than that. That's what I was trying to find out in Avenfore Library this morning. I reckon we might have better luck in Drunfarnam, though. There's bound to have been a report in the *Drunfarnam Tribune* about it at some stage.'

Chris had pulled up the oars, allowing the boat to drift slowly upstream by itself for a while. 'But why the interest, Will?'

William hesitated. In all the upset about the argument with Elsie, he hadn't thought to tell Chris and Amaranta about the sighting of Ignatius Nosmorum. He told them now and watched their stunned faces as he did so.

'So you think this place has something to do with the Wicked Crow?' Chris asked.

'I think so, yes.'

Amaranta's eyes were shining with excitement. 'We should go and take a look,' she squeaked. 'Look, there's a path from the riverbank that leads right up to it.'

'No!' Both boys spoke together.

'Why not?'

'It's too risky,' Chris said, 'I think we should find out more before we go in there, Manta. Just in case. With any luck we'll find what we're looking for in Drunfarnam library.'

William nodded – for once, happy for the older boy to prevail as the voice of reason.

'And Mr Grayling, the librarian is one of us, so he can help us,' Chris said. 'We'll have to tell the Order about this immediately, anyway.'

'I don't think we should.' William could see a strange reckless look in Amaranta's eyes.

'Mant—'

'It's like you say yourself,' Aramanta continued, 'let's just keep everything to ourselves until we get more information.' She looked at the two boys. 'Agreed?'

Chris shrugged and William sighed. 'Agreed,' they chorused.

II

Drunfarnam library was a solid building with a grey granite façade that time had blackened.

There was no sign of Brady Grayling, the Brother of the Order of the Alliance, who had stood as William's Squire during the investiture ceremony on the Isle of Lesciern. William was relieved about that. If Brady wasn't there, he couldn't ask any awkward question about what they were doing and William had had enough of telling people fibs for one day, at least.

Instead, he and Amaranta started to walk through the endless ceiling-high rows of bookcases, leaving Chris to inquire about the newspaper archives.

Moments later, Chris led the way over to the section of the library, where, as in Avenfore, the large, leather-bound volumes of the *Drunfarnam Tribune* were housed. They each took a volume – the two volumes for 1949 and the first volume for 1950 – and started to read.

After about half an hour, Amaranta closed over her 1950 volume and yawned. 'Nothing,' she said. 'Absolutely nothing. Have either of you had any luck?'

William shook his head, disappointed that he hadn't yet found anything. Chris shook his head too, then gave a small cry and pointed to the late 1949 newspaper he had been reading.

'Look,' he said. 'It's not much, but it's something.'

Crowding around him, Amaranta and William stared eagerly at the article Chris had been reading. It was short, but hugely intriguing.

Hannah Fairground to remain closed following fatal accident.

The Hannah fairground will remain closed for the foreseeable future following the accidental death of a visitor to the fairground last month. 'We greatly regret this terrible occurrence,' the owners of the fairground told the *Drunfarnam Tribune* today. 'Visitor safety is paramount and we are doing all we can to ensure this never happens again.' The inquest into the death of the man, named as journalist, Jerome C. Caplan, will be held in Drunfarnam Coroner's Court early in the New Year.

'Is that all?' sighed Amaranta. 'There must be more, surely?'

'Perhaps it's in the later volume,' William suggested.

'I've just read through all the papers for early 1950, there's no mention of the accident or the inquest.'

'All very odd,' Chris said. 'You would imagine there would be something there about the inquest at least.'

'The whole thing is odd,' said William. 'But perhaps the fairground owners, whoever they are, managed to keep it out of the papers. After all, it wasn't good for business.'

'But closing the fairground down for good isn't good for business, either,' said Chris thoughtfully. 'So something's not right, no matter which way you look at it. Amaranta, what on earth are you doing?'

William glanced over at Amaranta – she had her nose in the air and was sniffing loudly.

'I can smell a strange perfume. It's really strong, but not unpleasant. I've never smelled anything like it before.'

William breathed in and, without knowing why, he gave a shudder. He sniffed again, moving in the direction of the scent, towards the nearest aisle of books and trying to remember where and when he'd smelled that strange perfume before. Then it came to him and he gasped. Someone in the next aisle was wearing the same, unmistakeable patchouli perfume as the Wicked Crow.

'What's the matter, William?' Amaranta had come up behind him. 'You look as if you've seen a ghost.'

William gestured to her to keep quiet. He cautiously took a few books out of the shelf in front of him to see who was on the other side. But, as he did so, he accidentally dislodged some further along the shelf and they fell to the floor with a crash. William hastily picked up the fallen books and went to put them back on the shelf. But the person on the other side had also removed a book to see what was going on and two, black hawk-like eyes gazed at William through the gap. William quickly pushed the last books back into place – but he had no doubt who he had just seen – those cruel eyes belonged to Ignatius Nosmorum. He couldn't be sure if he'd been recognised, but he wasn't going to wait to find out.

He grabbed Amaranta's wrist and beckoned urgently to Chris.

Amaranta was glaring at him. 'I'm not going a step further, William, until you tell me what's going on!' she cried.

'Shhhhhh!' William said. 'The Wicked Crow is here! In the library! I just saw him! And that smell, It's patchouli – that's the perfume he uses. We should get out of here. Fast!'

Amaranta gasped. Chris, who had arrived in time to hear what William had said, looked worried.

'You're right, Will,' he whispered. 'We should make a break for it. Do you know where he is now?'

William shook his head, but as he did, the sound of raised voices cracked suddenly through the silence of the building. Everyone in the library, including the three friends, turned to look around in the direction of the front desk where Brady Grayling appeared to be arguing with a tall, black-clad figure with dark, lank hair and an evil-looking cane topped with a crow's head in his right hand. Ignatius Nosmorum was pointing angrily towards the locked manuscript room, but Mr Grayling kept shaking his head and was standing his ground.

'C'mon,' William said, 'let's go while he's still arguing with Woodpecker.'

Slipping between the book aisles as quickly and silently as they could, the three made their way to the front door of the library. They hurried past the corpulent man in a badly fitted suit standing just inside the front door, who clearly had Wicked Crow goon written all over him, and burst out into the sunlit street. Only then did they breathe a collective sigh of relief.

Casa del Misterio

Let Madame Ophelia see into your future

Ask my Crystal Ball any questions

Crystal Ball Reading

Palmistry
(palm reading)

8, Red Dragons' Lane
Drunfarnam

CHAPTER 21

Casa del Misterio

I

THEY HAD ARRANGED TO MEET ELSIE, Bridget and the Arinduff twins at the fortune teller's place. On reaching Red Dragons' Lane, William took out the piece of paper from his shorts' pocket on which he'd jotted down the address.

'It's number eight,' he said, pointing to the end of the street. 'It must be down there.'

Madame Ophelia's *Casa del Misterio* was indeed the last house on Red Dragons' Lane and the only one with a balustrade, just as the Arinduff twins' cousin's sister's aunt had said. Two large plant pots with purple hydrangeas flanked the doorway. The door itself was dark green with a giant burnished brass number 8 and a door knocker in the shape of a dragonfly.

Elsie, Bridget and the Arinduff twins arrived shortly afterwards. Marching past William and the others without saying a word, Elsie lifted the dragonfly door knocker and knocked twice. The sound seemed to reverberate along the street and Gladis Arinduff jumped nervously.

'Maybe this is not such a good idea after all,' she whispered.

Elsie patted her arm. 'Don't worry, Gladis,' she said, 'there's nothing to worry about. You'll be fine.'

Before Gladis could reply, the door of *Casa del Misterio* opened suddenly and a husky voice from within boomed, 'Welcome, dear ones! Welcome to *Casa del Misterio*, the house of Madame Ophelia, medium and mystic extraordinaire!'

The group of friends stared in amazement. Standing in the doorway was a short, middle-aged woman with a plump, moon-shaped face and a mass of curly hair in an improbable shade of red. She was wearing a purple velvet robe, a diadem on her head and a large silver pendant around her neck in the shape of a pyramid with an all-seeing eye at its centre. She was beaming at them.

'This way, my dears,' the woman boomed again, before heading down the narrow hallway of the house and gesturing for them all to follow.

No one moved and Gladis gave an anxious squeak.

'Oh, for goodness sake! We're here now, so let's get on with it!' Elsie snapped. Grabbing Gladis by the hand, she stepped across the threshold and disappeared into the house after the strange-looking woman.

William and the others followed them into the house and along a short corridor towards a conservatory that looked out onto the back garden of the house. Ivy tendrils had covered all the brick walls; tea roses and night-scented stock flourished at its feet. At the bottom of the garden grew raspberries, gooseberries, blackcurrants, blackberries and redcurrants. There was also an abundance of summer flowers and clover.

'Make yourselves comfortable, my dears,' Madame Ophelia told them, indicating at the chairs and sofas dotted around the conservatory. 'I won't be a moment.'

For a while, nobody said anything, all spellbound by the curious objects that decorated the room, including skull bookends on the shelves. Gladis Arinduff shuddered.

'Really, Els,' she insisted. 'Don't you think it was too daring coming to a place like this? I think we should leave now.'

'I'm sure it will be fine,' William said, trying to be helpful.

'Of course it will, Glad, you'll see.' Arline Arinduff piped up, also trying to calm her twin sister.

'Oooh, I'm sure it will be thrilling!' Amaranta exclaimed, which, rather than helping Gladis, seemed to make her panic even more.

'Elsie ...?' she appealed.

But before Elsie could respond, Madame Ophelia came back into the room. She placed an incense burner on a low table in the middle of the conservatory and produced a box of matches from one of the pockets in her purple robe, with which she lit some incense sticks.

Bridget wrinkled her nose. 'What's that smell?' she asked Elsie uneasily.

Elsie reassured her. 'It's nothing to worry about; it's just oriental incense. Some people use it to perfume their houses.'

Bridget looked at her best friend doubtfully, as if to say how anyone could actually *want* that smell in their house, but Madame Ophelia beckoned to them all to sit down, before she herself sat down on a large high-backed, throne-shaped wicker chair facing them all.

'I suppose you have come,' she began, 'because you are troubled.' She glanced around the conservatory, before adjusting the diadem in her hair, which made Arline Arinduff giggle nervously. 'That is natural enough,' Madame Ophelia continued in her deep, husky voice, 'for we are all troubled by something. The moment I set my eyes on you all, I had a very special feeling. It's as if you keep or protect some great secret. But you have nothing to fear. I am to be trusted and your secrets will never be heard outside these walls.'

Amaranta glanced at Chris and William in surprise and even William found himself wondering if he had underestimated the fortune teller.

'So,' Madame Ophelia cried suddenly. 'Who is to start?'

The seven friends looked at each other, each one clearly willing everyone else to go first.

The fortune teller stood up and lit a candelabra with seven candles that stood in a corner. 'You seem uneasy, dear ones,' she said, 'but there is no reason to be so. You are safe here.' She pressed her hand firmly against one of the walls. There was a sharp click and a narrow door opened, showing a set of steps leading down into a room on the house side of the conservatory.

Madame Ophelia picked up the candelabra. 'This is my consulting room,' she said. 'Come in when you feel ready. Alone or in pairs, as you wish.' Then she paused theatrically in the doorway for a few seconds before vanishing into the darkened room beyond.

There was a short silence in the conservatory, then Amaranta jumped to her feet.

'I guess it's me to go first, then,' she said. She grinned and disappeared into the consulting room, shutting the door behind her.

II

The others waited in nervous silence. Bridget and Arline Arinduff whispered together, giggling every now and again. Poor Gladis Arinduff looked so unsettled William thought there was a danger she would bolt for the front door at any moment. Elsie noticed it too, sat beside her and held her hand. Watching his cousin, William felt guilty about their argument all over again. It wasn't fair, he thought. We shouldn't have to exclude Elsie or keep secrets from her. But he also knew it wasn't his place to make that decision.

Chris too was watching Elsie, rather glumly. He became even glummer when she looked away and wouldn't catch his eye. Poor Chris, William thought. He missed the whole argument, so he's probably no idea what he's even done to offend her at this stage.

At that moment Amaranta returned looking thoughtful. William easily guessed what she had asked and went up to her and murmured gently, 'Surely you knew the crystal ball couldn't answer that question?'

Amaranta didn't reply, but she did smile. Then, without a word, she went outside into the garden and William watched her bask in the summer sun with her face upturned as she drank in the sweet scent of the roses and the night-scented stock.

The Arinduff twins went in together – that was Elsie's suggestion – and they were all relieved to see them both smiling when they came back out. Bridget was next, she returned looking flushed, but not unhappy. Then it was Elsie's turn. She too came out looking happier than when she went in and Chris bounded down the steps to the consulting room, when Elsie finally caught his eye and gave him a shy smile. He too returned looking pleased and a bit embarrassed.

William was the last to go in. Reassured that almost everyone else had come out looking reasonably happy, he still couldn't help the nervous butterflies flittering about in his stomach as he made his way down the stone steps into Madame Ophelia's consulting room. It was a scary thing wondering what your future might hold for you, especially when there was so much at stake.

The room wasn't very big but large enough to contain a coffee table, two chairs and an armchair, where Madame Ophelia sat. The table was covered in a navy-blue cloth adorned with golden moons and stars. The wallpaper was similar, although a slightly lighter shade of blue. A large crystal ball resting on a silver base sat in the middle of the table.

Madame Ophelia indicated to William to sit in the chair by the table opposite her. She closed her eyes for a few moments, breathing deeply with her hands resting on the table. Then, she took William's hands and looked into the crystal ball. Her eyes darted about here and there, giving William the impression that she was struggling to understand what she was seeing.

'You seek something,' she said at last. 'I don't know what, but it is something that will make many people very happy. However, you must be careful, child. I also see a very unpleasant event ... something disastrous, something unexpected. Someone is searching for you ... they want something from you ... there is much darkness, and—'

Suddenly Madame Ophelia let go of his hands, and shrieked, 'Noooo!'

William jumped up in alarm. 'What is it, Madame Ophelia? Are you all right?'

The medium didn't reply. She took a few deep breaths and then stared at William for a moment.

Finally, she spoke. 'Why, yes, I'm perfectly fine now. Thank you, young man. I must apologise. Sometimes the spirit moves me in … eh … unsettling ways, you know.'

William wasn't entirely sure that the whole thing hadn't been just one spectacular performance for his benefit, but he had no intention of saying that to Madame Ophelia. Besides, he was also not sure that she didn't believe the entire thing herself, so it would be churlish of him to make fun of her. Indeed, he wasn't sure at all that she wasn't quite batty as she now appeared to have forgotten he was there and was muttering away to herself.

'The crow chases the falcon. That cannot be, but it is. I see it. I see it. The falcon flees, but the crow chases it. A dark, black beast with black, terrible eyes. Claws and, oh, that beak – sharp and black as night. That terrible, terrible beak – oh, save us from the darkness!'

'Are you sure you're all right, Madame Ophelia?' William asked once again.

She looked up at him, almost surprised to see him there. 'Yes, thank you again, dear boy. Perfectly fine, I can assure you.' She settled herself back in her armchair and smiled at him. 'So, tell me, is there anything else I can tell you?'

It occurred to William that she hadn't actually told him *anything* yet, but, again, he kept that thought to himself. However, there was something he was now sure Madame Ophelia could help him with. It had struck him just as he had stood up to come into the consulting room. The name – Madame Ophelia – he remembered now where he had read it: in the advert in the *Avenfore Chronicle* earlier that morning.

'You were the fortune teller at the Hannah fairground,' he said. The look of terror that spread across the medium's face was so intense it startled him.

'I-I-I-I don't think so, young man,' she finally stammered.

William held his ground. 'I know you were, Madame Ophelia,' he said. 'I saw the advertisement in the *Avenfore Chronicle*. You were the fortune teller there.'

The older woman's mood darkened and she glared at him suddenly.

'So what if I was?' her tone was defensive now.

William kept his voice calm and polite, trying to reassure her. 'It's nothing bad, Madame Ophelia. I just wondered if you could tell me anything about the fairground. Who owned it and why it closed down? I know there was an accident and somebody died, but there's nothing much about it in the local newspapers, so it's all really a mystery. But mystery's your thing, so I thought you could help.'

Madame Ophelia stared at him for a moment.

'The Hannah fairground is a bad place,' she said. 'If you care about your future, you will stay well clear of it and anyone associated with it. Do you hear me?'

William wasn't intimidated and returned her stare innocently.

'Why? Why should I stay away from it?'

The medium bit her lip, then taking hold of William's hands, she leaned across the table towards him until she was directly over the crystal ball, both she and her distorted reflection from the ball glaring at him in the dim light of the candelabra-lit room.

'Hannah fairground is a very bad place,' she said. 'A man died there, horribly. I saw him. All those incisions ... they coiled up his body... I thought I would die too of the horror. But I said nothing, no, no. Best say nothing, or else. And the same goes for you also. Powerful people, you understand? People who have money and means and the will do to evil ... do you understand?'

Despite himself, William was rattled. He knew what the woman was telling him had nothing to do with crystal balls or clairvoyance. He truly believed Madame Ophelia when she said she'd seen the body. And it all sounded truly terrifying.

He felt Ophelia shake his arm roughly. 'Promise me you'll stay away, boy. Promise me you won't go anywhere near that accursed place or that accursed—' She stopped and looked at him. 'Oh, well,' she said, with a sigh. 'I tried. I really did try. At least, promise me that you'll be careful.'

Bemused, William promised her that he would. He stood up to leave. As he reached the doorway, he glanced back. The woman was sitting upright again, her hands over the crystal ball, her eyes distant and far-away as if she was in a trance.

'What you seek,' she was saying, 'lies hidden in a very dark place. There are no windows … there is an opening … thrice covered.'

CHAPTER 22

Gallery Avernus

I

I T WAS A FEW DAYS BEFORE William had a chance to discuss the visit to Madame Ophelia with Amaranta and Chris. As the group of friends left *Casa del Misterio*, Elsie suggested that she and Gladis return to Avenfore in the rowing boat with Chris; and the others readily agreed. So, while Amaranta chatted to Bridget and Arline in the back of the van behind him, William found himself in the front passenger seat beside Aunt Edna for the journey home. He leaned back in his seat as they left Drunfarnam, the medium's words still echoing in his head: 'What you seek lies hidden in a very dark place … thrice covered…'

He was still mulling over everything she had said on Thursday morning as he walked through the village square to the Drunfarnam road. He'd arranged to meet Amaranta and Chris at the green by the riverbank opposite Avenfore church – Bridget and Elsie having been invited to spend the day with a classmate in Drishlean.

'What do you think she meant by 'an opening, not covered'?' Amaranta asked, plopping herself down on the wooden bench next to William and pulling idly at the low-hanging branch of a blossoming rowan tree above them.

'I don't know,' said William shaking his head. 'I've been trying to figure it out, but I can't.'

'To be honest, it all sounds so vague,' said Chris. 'Perhaps she just made it up? I mean, it is possible …'

William shrugged. 'You're right, I expect. But … it was just the look on her face when she said it … it looked, well … real, if you know what I mean.'

'I'm sure it is real,' Amaranta said solemnly. 'But it's like all prophecy, it's meant to be a bit vague.'

'Prophecy?' Chris gave a sceptical snort of laughter. 'I wouldn't call it that.'

'All that stuff about the crow chasing the falcon? Of course, it's prophecy,' she replied. 'But you don't have to believe if you don't want to.'

'Look, I don't know about prophecy,' William continued, 'but the meaning is pretty clear either way. Ignatius Nosmorum wants the secrets in the *Book of the Knights Templar Errant* and he won't stop chasing the Order until he gets them. And we have to stop him.'

Now it was Chris's turn to look sombre. 'You're right, Will,' he said at last. 'And I'm sorry for laughing, Manta, but it all seems so incredible.'

'Oh, don't worry,' Aramanta replied chirpily. 'What's important is figuring out what we need to do next. I think we should go investigate the Hannah fairground.'

'That's not such a good idea.' Chris looked worried. 'Don't you think we should tell one of the older members of the Order what we know and let them deal with it?'

'I suppose we could tell Mr Greewoof …' said William.

'But that's just it,' Amaranta insisted. 'What do we know? We don't really know anything yet. So I think we should find out more before we tell them.'

'He's away,' Chris said.

'Who?'

'Mr Greewoof. He's gone to a symposium on herbology in Edinburgh with Alastair Malblenar. I heard him talking to my dad yesterday and he said he wouldn't be back until next week.'

'There you go!' she said looking at Chris triumphantly. 'We can't talk to him, even if we wanted to.'

'Yes, but we could tell your uncle,' he replied.

Amaranta glowered at him. 'No, we couldn't,' she snapped.

'I promised Mr Greewoof and my dad I wouldn't go off investigating on my own,' William piped up, in defence of Chris.

'But you won't be on your own; you'll be with us,' Amaranta insisted.

'Will's right,' Chris said. 'It's too dangerous, Manta; we should leave it for the Knights to deal with.'

'Look,' she said, with the same reckless look she'd had on the boat, 'I know it's risky and you've – we've been told not to get involved in anything dangerous … but all we have to do is some scouting around. Now. In broad daylight. And if anyone sees us, we're just three youngsters looking around an old fairground we've spotted from the river. All totally innocent. Nobody could suspect us.' Her large green eyes were fixed intently on the boys. 'I promise, if you do this with me today, I will never ask you again.'

William glanced over at Chris. He didn't look happy, but William could see the struggle in his face: Amaranta's eagerness was winning over his friend's natural caution.

'Oh, come on, you two; please say yes.' Aramanta was jigging about with excitement. 'You said yourself, Will, we have to stop the Wicked Crow from getting what he wants. We have a chance to find something out that can help the Knights. Or do something useful for the Order. We're Knights Postulants, for heaven's sake; we can't back away from it like a bunch of babies. So, what do you say? Are you both in or out? Do we go and take a look around the fairground or not?'

William knew exactly what he wanted to do, but it all depended on Chris.

The older boy was staring down at an ugly patch of scuffed dried earth beneath the bench William was sitting on. Then he looked up at Amaranta with a smile. 'Yes,' he said, 'we're in. Let's do it.'

II

They moored the rowing boat Chris had hired again from Mr Oblane out of sight under the trailing branches of a large bramble bush and clambered up the narrow dirt path leading from the riverbank to the fairground site.

It stood on a dirt plateau halfway between the river and the main Drunfarnam road which snaked its way past at the top of a steep escarpment, covered in tall trees and huge clumps of prickly furze bushes, topped with a bright glow of yellow flowers, all of which did an excellent job of masking the view of the fairground below to general passers-by. Even the Ferris wheel, which from the angle where the three friends were now standing, loomed large into the sky, was almost invisible from the road. Now that William thought about it, it had been the light from the open doorway that had caught his eye on the evening the Wicked Crow had almost run poor Aunt Edna's van off the road. Otherwise he might have seen nothing. Thinking about that incident made him even more determined to find out what was going on here.

Cautiously, he, Chris and Amaranta moved towards the Ferris wheel and the group of long, low buildings clustered at its feet. The buildings were dilapidated and uncared-for, with piles of moss-covered wood stacked up against them, dirty oil barrels and torn tarpaulins lying strewn about and, here and there, rusty tangles of barbed wire fencing barring the way.

Like everything around it, the Ferris wheel itself was decrepit and derelict, and looked unsteady on its rusted iron legs. It appeared to be propped up inside by a large wooden structure, reaching high up towards the centre of the wheel, while the entire base was encircled by a fence of barbed wire, preventing anyone from getting too close.

As they stood beside it, the wheel above them clanked and groaned in loud protest as the fresh summer breeze passed across it from Dronfore Lake. William thought he could hear another strange noise, like the loud, harsh rush of angry birds, but, looking about, he couldn't see any rooks or crows in the nearby tree-tops. Even more peculiar was that the sound seemed to be coming from inside the wooden Ferris wheel structure, but there was no way of getting near it to investigate.

'I think we're wasting our time.' It was Chris who spoke. 'This place looks as though no one's set foot here in years.'

'That's what they want you to think,' said Amaranta. 'But we know that's not true, because Will saw someone here. So there must be a way into one of these buildings; we just need to find it. Where did you see the light, Will?'

William thought hard, trying to picture the scene in his mind's eye again. 'Over there,' he said at last, pointing to the end of a long, low building which led away from the Ferris wheel. 'But around the other side, I think.'

At the end of the building William pointed to a wide double door padlocked shut with a heavy rusted chain. Amaranta ran towards the door with a cry.

'Look! See, someone has been here! The padlock is new!'

William and Chris had to agree that Amaranta was right. The chain was old, but the padlock was bright, shiny and obviously new.

'Which leads us to another problem,' said William. 'How do we get inside?'

'Easy,' said Chris. He plucked a piece of wire from a nearby barbed wire tumbleweed and began to jig it about in the padlock. 'I read about it in a book.' The padlock clicked open and Chris slipped it off the chain with a grin. 'I thought it might come in handy someday.' He blushed as he realised Amaranta and William were staring at him in astonishment. 'But only for situations like this,' he explained. 'I wouldn't normally pick people's locks, of course; that would be totally wrong.'

'Totally,' echoed Amaranta, but she was smiling.

The large door creaked loudly as they opened it. It was dark inside, but with the help of the daylight pouring in from the open door, the three friends saw that they were at the top end of a long narrow, low-roofed passageway sloping downward towards a second doorway at the other end, barely visible in the gloomy distance.

'Is there a light switch?' Amaranta asked.

'I can't find one,' William replied.

'I've got a torch with me,' Chris said.

'You really are prepared.' Amaranta laughed.

The passageway was cold and William's skin prickled with goose bumps as he stepped from the warm summer air outside into its dank chill. Beside him, Amaranta sniffed loudly and wrinkled her nose in disgust.

'Ugh,' she said. 'It smells horrible in here.'

'It's damp,' said Chris.

'It's musty, all right,' William agreed. He was sure there was something else in the air. Something unpleasant, something animal-like. Something he couldn't yet identify. But he didn't want to spook the others, so he stayed silent as they made their way along the passageway towards the second doorway.

The slope became steeper and narrower as it neared the end of the passageway. As the beam from Chris's torch alighted on the second doorway, all three of them gasped in unison.

'Wow!'

'Ohh!'

'Crikey!'

The heavy door was made entirely of dark ebony wood, mounted with two old-fashioned black iron door handles, each in the shape of a rather wicked-looking bird holding a writhing circular worm in its sharp beak. Arched above the doorway in carved Gothic letters were the words GALLERY AVERNUS and below this ran a carved frieze showing a procession of bizarre animal-like creatures being attacked from above by a fierce swarm of large, flying birds with beaks as sharp as scythes.

'How horrible,' Amaranta said with a shudder. 'Those birds look terrifying. And what on earth are all the other things?'

'Mythical creatures,' said William. 'The snake one is a basilisk; the winged thing over there is a griffin – it's half-lion and half-eagle.'

'That one's a harpy,' Chris added, indicating towards a strange half-bird, half-human creature with an agonised, tortured look on its face. 'And the man-goat is a satyr.'

'It's like some sort of horrible bestiary,' William explained. 'You know, like those in medieval times. Except they are carvings, rather than a book.'

Amaranta gave another shudder. 'It's disgusting,' she said. 'They all look like they're terrified and in pain. Who wants to see something like this?'

'Well, it was a fairground,' William replied. 'This was probably the entrance to their ghost ride or the chamber of horrors.'

'It's a chamber of horrors, all right,' Amaranta replied. 'And we've not even got inside yet.'

It was a sobering thought for all three and they stood in silence for a moment.

'So,' Chris asked, 'should we turn back, then?'

'No. We've come this far. We should go in.'

'Will's right,' Amaranta agreed. 'It's too late to turn back now. So, let's see what's inside.' She grinned at Chris. 'At least, there's no lock to pick on this door.'

'By the way,' she added as William reached for one of the nasty bird door handles to pull one side of the heavy door open, 'what does 'Avernus' mean?'

'Hell,' William and Chris chorused glumly.

CHAPTER 23

The Crow Chamber

I

T HE EBONY DOOR OPENED ONTO ANOTHER passageway, almost as dark as the last. It too sloped downwards steeply, but unlike the first, it was made of stone, not concrete, its roof was arched and vaulted, and it was not empty. Lining the thick walls on either side were mirrors, their reflections curved and bent out of shape. Each one was illuminated high up by eerie pinpricks of perpetual red lights, glowing like the blood-red eyes of some night animal in the glare of torchlight and throwing distorted crimson-drenched shadows along the length of the corridor as far as the three friends could see.

At the end of the passageway was an archway leading to a series of stone steps. Here again, high above them, a further stream of large, fiercely carved birds entwined themselves with shrieking anger between the letters of another inscription: FACILIS DESCENDUS AVERNO.

'What does that mean?' Amaranta whispered.

'The descent to the underworld is easy,' Chris replied dully.

'Hell,' William corrected. 'The descent to *hell* is easy.' Even in the darkness, he could feel Chris glaring at him and Amaranta sighed.

'Thanks, Will,' she said. 'I feel *much* better now.'

Chris pushed past her and stepped through the archway. As William and Amaranta joined him on the top step, he shone his torch downwards and William's heart began to pump faster than ever – even a first glance told him that they had indeed stumbled on the Wicked Crow's secret lair.

Below them stretched out a large chamber, dark and cavernous. It was shaped like a hexagon, with six stout carved pillars forming a circle in the centre of the room, and was illuminated only by a few dusty beams of dull sunlight streaming down from what William supposed must be a hexagonal skylight so high up in the centre of the roof, it wasn't visible from where they were standing. On a raised dais in the centre of this circle was a chair. *No, not a chair*, William thought, *a throne* – carved from the same black ebony as the door behind them and bearing a coat of arms inset into the filigreed panels on its pointed, Gothic back: a shield in red, black and grey, divided in two by a lightning bolt staff topped with a crow's heads and flanked by a large grey-black crow on either side of it – its sharp-angled arms and legs covered in intricate carvings of birds: the same evil-looking birds with sharp beaks and malice in their eyes that William had come to associate with the Wicked Crow himself.

Beyond the centre circle, the opposite end of the outer walkway was shrouded in darkness so black even the light from Chris's torch struggled to penetrate it. But closer to where they were standing, William could make out the shadowy outlines of tall, heavy glass-fronted cabinets, lining the chamber walls and pushing up against the vaulted ceiling above them.

'Oh!' Amaranta jumped as a hideous face glared out at them in the torchlight from the nearest cabinet. 'What on earth was that?'

'A gargoyle or a chimera,' Chris replied. He moved closer to the cabinet as he spoke, William and Amaranta following close behind. 'They're usually found high up on old churches.' Amaranta gasped again as he shone his torch directly into the cabinet to reveal its contents: shelves of stone gargoyles and grotesques – mostly winged devils with vicious, malevolent faces crouched as if to pounce on unsuspecting souls. 'They were used as waterspouts,' Chris continued, 'and, if you're superstitious, as protection – to ward off evil spirits. The Wicked Crow must be a collector.'

'They're pretty horrible,' Amaranta insisted. 'Certainly not the stuff I'd want in my display cabinet.'

William was surveying the row of cabinet silhouettes behind them. 'They're cabinets of curiosities,' he said. 'We should check them all out. Maybe there's something interesting in them.'

'Like what?' William could hear resistance in Chris's voice. 'What exactly is it we're looking for?'

'The book.' Amaranta and William spoke in unison.

'And you really think we'll find it here?' Chris turned to them, his face eerie and troubled in the torchlight.

Amaranta shrugged. 'Why not? "What you seek is hidden in a dark place." That's what Madame Ophelia said. And, frankly, this is about as dark a place as you can get, don't you think?'

'I'll not argue with you there,' Chris agreed. 'But would Nosmorum leave it lying around like that if he knows it's valuable? It just seems odd that there's no security or anything, don't you think?'

'Maybe there is,' William replied. 'Security, I mean. We just haven't seen it yet.'

The three friends stood, once more, silent and hesitant. Then Amaranta gave a snort of annoyance.

'Come on, we're here now. Let's see what we can find. The sooner we look, the sooner we can go. Agreed?'

William nodded and it was Chris's turn to sigh.

'All right,' he said, 'but we leave at the first sign of trouble.'

'Fair enough,' William said.

'And use codenames from now on,' Chris continued. 'Just in case. All right?'

'Okay,' William said. 'Good idea, Turnstone.'

'And you, Blackbird?' Chris was looking at Amaranta.

'Fine with me, TS,' she murmured. 'It's a nuisance that we have only one torch, though. Trust the Wicked Crow not to have electricity.'

'They probably use burning torches,' William offered. 'For their, eh … meetings and stuff.' As he said it, Chris shifted uneasily beside him.

'Ugh.' Amaranta grimaced. 'I really don't want to think about what that horrible man and his gang do in this dreadful place. Let's look for the book' – she was already moving towards the next cabinet – 'and get out of here as soon as we can.'

They moved along the outer walkway, Chris shining the torch on each cabinet as they went, Amaranta and William pressing their faces close to the glass to examine the contents of each. To their disappointment, there were no books to be seen in any of the cabinets. Instead, they were full of grotesque curiosities: reproductions of the imaginary animals carved on the arched frieze above the ebony doorway and William became more and more uneasy as they moved, cabinet by cabinet, around the outer walkway. He didn't know if he was imagining it or not, but there was a faint rustling and murmuring sound coming from somewhere – he didn't know where – that unnerved him and, suddenly, he couldn't shake the idea that they were being watched.

It was only when they reached the section of walkway opposite to the entrance archway that William's fears were realised. All three friends jumped as a harsh cawing sound broke through the darkness and echoed through the chamber.

'What the hell is that?' Chris asked, anxiety clear in his voice, swinging his torch about wildly to look for the source of the horrid noise.

'It's a bird,' William replied. 'This bird, to be precise.' He grabbed Chris's arm, directing the beam of light to what he had seen momentarily – the glinting black eyes of a large grey-and-black bird tethered to a tall perch to the right of the throne-chair, just out of reach of the desolate rays of sunlight which ventured down from the roof.

Amaranta gulped, as the bird, aware they were looking at it, inclined its head warily and fixed them with an evil stare.

Chris laughed nervously. 'That's odd,' he said. '"Avernus" doesn't just mean hell, it also means "birdless".'

'Must be Ignatius Nosmorum's idea of a joke, then,' William said, 'because that is definitely a bird. A nasty-looking bird,' he added, as they moved in closer to take a look, 'Is it some sort of a raven?'

'No,' said Chris, 'not a raven, although it's as big as one.'

'Definitely not a raven,' Amaranta chipped in. 'Ravens' tails are wedge-shaped and they croak rather than caw. This one caws and its tail is fan-shaped, so it's a crow. A grey crow.'

William stared at her. 'How do you know that?'

'Uncle Ernest taught me. But, to be honest, I've never seen one quite so big. Ever. It's rather cruel-looking, don't you think?'

As if to confirm her opinion of him, the large grey crow glared, then leaned forward all of a sudden and pecked at Chris's hand.

'Ow!!' Chris yelled as he stumbled back away from it in alarm, bumping into one of the pillars surrounding the centre circle of the room.

'Shhhhh!' William put a hand on Chris's arm to quieten him. 'Listen,' he whispered. 'It's that noise again, the strange rushing one I heard outside.'

'Blimey!'

William looked to where Chris was now pointing. Above them, invisible from anywhere in the room other than the centre circle itself, was a tall, wide tower-like structure wider at the base and narrowing to a six-sided skylight through which the gloomy sunlight fell downwards onto the crow throne beneath it. Lining the inside of the tower structure was a series of large cages filled with birds. Crows, William realised. The entire steepled roof of the chamber all the way up to the skylight was filled with crows. Black crows, grey crows; crows of all shapes and sizes. And judging by the increased noise they were making, these crows were upset and getting more upset by the minute.

'This isn't good,' William said. 'I think we should get out of here. Now. Ama—Blackbird, c'mon, we're leaving.'

'William, Chris, look, there are books over here; loads of books. We should look through them,' Amaranta called out to them. Her voice echoed through the chamber making it impossible for William to figure out where it was coming from. Wherever she was, she was too far back in the shadows for him to spot her. As he searched for her, the cacophony of cawing and squawking from the roosts in the tower became louder and more urgent. William's heart began to pound and he could feel the panic rise within him.

'C'mon, Manta,' he shouted. 'We need to get out of here. Now!'

All of a sudden, the huge grey crow behind them raised itself up on its perch, flapped its wings menacingly and pulled on a metal chain suspended above its perch, before letting out a terrifying series of caws, three times in quick succession. Its odd performance was answered by a sharp click of metal and the shrill squeak of metal gates swinging open in the tower roof above them.

'Manta!' William looked about him frantically, but he couldn't see Amaranta anywhere.

'Kingfisher, Blackbird, run! Now!' Chris was yelling at him. But William stood for a moment, transfixed by what he saw. Above him, whirring about the hexagonal skylight, a roaring, cawing, screeching mass was forming itself into a black storm cloud of agitated, angry crows.

'They're forming a mob,' Chris was pulling at him to get his attention. C'mon, Kingfisher! We've gotta run!'

William stared at him. 'We can't. Manta! Where's Manta?'

'She's ahead of us, Will; she's out already. C'mon, we've got to go now.'

As Chris spoke, William realised he could hear the sound of someone running away from them along the mirrored passageway beyond the crow archway. He also realised he had been holding his breath. As he breathed out, he glanced up, and, for a split second before he ran, he saw the murder of crows form themselves into a malicious arrow of angry birds and plummet downwards heading straight in his direction.

William could still hear the rush of crows behind him as he and Chris pelted up the stone steps towards the archway and ran as fast as they could through the steep, crimson-tinged darkness of the mirrored corridor towards the ebony doorway.

'We need to shut the door,' William shouted. 'That way they can't get out.'

'You go right; I'll take left,' Chris panted in reply. 'Close your section as fast as you can.'

They had reached the door now and William felt a violent whirr of wings brush against his face, spurring him on through the doorway. He veered right as Chris had instructed and pushed his section of the heavy door with all his might. Chris was already doing the same on the other side and, to their relief, the doors closed shut with a weighty thud just before the first birds reached it. A few thumps, shrieks, angry squawks and caws, then more thumps, followed, but the door remained firmly shut with the birds on the other side. Chris and William slumped to the floor and breathed a sigh of relief.

'All right, Kingfisher,' Chris whispered into the darkness as soon as he had got his breath back. 'Thank goodness that door's as strong as it is.'

'You can say that again, TS,' William said, with a grin. 'C'mon, then, let's meet up with Am—Blackbird and get out of here fast.'

Almost as soon as he had said that, a loud shriek rang out from outside the building.

'Amaranta!' William shouted, scrabbling to his feet in alarm.

'King—oh, for heaven's sake, Will! Wait! Be careful!' Chris shouted as he ran after him. But William was already running at full speed along the passageway towards the main door.

II

Momentarily blinded by the bright sunshine after the darkness of the underground passageways, William couldn't see Amaranta at first, although he could hear her shouting at someone to let her go. He was about to call out, when a hand shot across his mouth and two strong arms grabbed him and pulled him back inside the building.

'What the—!!' William spluttered.

'Be quiet,' Chris hissed from behind him. 'If Manta's in trouble, rushing in like a bull in a china shop won't help her. We've got to figure out what's going on first.'

The calm in the older boy's voice made William think. Of course, Chris was right. Rushing in would probably only get both of them in trouble and perhaps put Amaranta in more danger.

'What do we do?' he whispered anxiously.

Another high-pitched, angry shriek from Amaranta somewhere outside made both boys jump.

'We need to help her now, Chris!' William realised he was pleading.

'Shhhh!' Chris was peering out through the open doorway but staying back far enough to make sure he couldn't be seen. 'I can see her. She's over there and the goon's got her.'

'Which goon?'

'The one we saw outside Drunfarnam library on Tuesday. Remember, the fat guy in the awful suit?' Chris's grimace was followed by a man's howl and a shout of triumph from Amaranta from the yard outside. 'Caught him right on the shin bone, that did! Good girl, Manta!'

'Chris! Manta needs help, not a running commentary. We need to go help her. Now!'

'Calm down, Will. So, here's the plan. See that old tarpaulin over there? Do you think you can get to it without being seen?'

William looked out to where Chris was pointing at a dirty old piece of tarpaulin sticking out from behind some oil drums and planks of rotten wood to one side of the building.

'Yeah, I think so.'

'Good. When you've got the tarpaulin, wait for my signal. I'll knock him down with one of those oil drums and you throw the tarpaulin over him. Then we grab Manta and run as fast as we can. Got it?'

'Got it.'

'Right. Let's go.'

Keeping as close as he could to the wall of the building behind the debris, William made his way over to the tarpaulin, quietly tugged it free of one of the rotten wooden planks and waited for Chris's signal. He could see the tussle going on now between Amaranta and the Wicked Crow's henchman, and it clearly wasn't all going the goon's way.

'C'm'ere, you 'orrible kid,' the goon was shouting as he tried to keep hold on a struggling Amaranta with his burly arms.

'Lemme go, you nasty man!' Amaranta shrieked back at him at the top of her voice as she kicked and wriggled herself almost out of the man's grasp.

Out of the corner of his eye, William saw Chris get into position behind one of the larger oil drums; then the older boy's hand went up and William saw him suddenly tip the oil drum and launched it at the fat man in the suit.

The goon didn't see Chris or the drum coming. Taken by surprise, he toppled over almost immediately, howling in anger and pain as he fell backwards into one of the barbed wire tumbleweeds lying about nearby. Amaranta, also startled, would have fallen right on top of him, if Chris has not reached her in time to yank her away while William rushed up and threw the tarpaulin over the writhing henchman who was now shouting and cursing loudly at them.

'Kingfisher, c'mon!' Chris shouted, as he ushered Amaranta across the fairground site towards the dirt path leading to the riverbank. Without looking back at the struggling man, William ran after them as fast as he could, ignoring the scratches and pulls of prickly gorse and brambles as he clambered down the pathway to join the others.

As they pulled away in the boat, hidden from view beneath the brambles and silver birch trees lining the riverbank, they could hear the goon still shouting at them from the fairground site.

CHAPTER 24

The Falcon's Nest

I

T HE NEXT DAY, WILLIAM AND CHRIS found themselves back in Drunfarnam, waiting outside The Falcon's Nest bookshop for Amaranta to arrive. William had to admit that the two-storey building was an impressive affair: large windows filled with colourful displays of fascinating books in all shapes and sizes and, above the window, a large chestnut wood shop sign with the name THE FALCON'S NEST BOOKSHOP drawn on it in elegant, spindly letters. Beside the main entrance to the bookshop was another smaller blue-painted door bearing a brass plaque showing an engraved falcon above the words NIGHT BIRD SOCIETY. William couldn't help the thrill of excitement that ran through him, knowing as he did, what that sign really meant.

Still, he was anxious as to what Valcott O'Neill would say. Mr Wiglann had been furious when Amaranta told him what had happened in the Hannah fairground. Of course, being Mr Wiglann, he hadn't actually said very much, but he hadn't needed to – the thunderous look on his face had said it all. And the few terse words he had uttered were clear: 'Never. Do. It. Again. *Never*.'

Amaranta arrived in Byron Mullween's car, driven by Mr Wiglann and accompanied by Byron Mullween himself. Mr Wiglann shot fierce looks at the two boys as Amaranta clambered out and waved at the two men as the car pulled away.

'Mr Wiglann's still angry with us,' Chris sighed.

'Pretty much,' Amaranta said, 'but don't worry; he'll be all right soon. What did you tell Elsie and Bridget, Will?'

'Nothing,' William admitted. 'Mr O'Neill did it all for us. He telephoned Aunt Edna yesterday evening to ask if we could come in for an 'ornithology' lesson today. Elsie just rolled her eyes and she's, obviously, come along too, but to accompany Aunt Edna to do some shopping.'

Suddenly, the blue door opened and Mr O'Neill appeared.

'There you are, chaps and lass! And bang on time. But up you go,' he indicated towards the narrow stairs leading up from the blue door, 'the sooner we get settled, the sooner we get started.'

II

Valcott O'Neill's sitting room was a pleasant, light-filled room, pan-elled in light grey, with moulded ceiling cornices and huge floor-to-ceiling windows looking down on Drunfarnam town square and main street. The room also served as the club room for the Night Bird Society with tea tables and comfortable armchairs and sofas in brightly patterned chintz spread out around a large carved wooden fireplace, whose fire, William was sure, made the room extra cheery in winter.

To the casual observer, the walls of the room were covered in the kind of paintings, drawings and engravings of birds that you would expect in a birdwatching society club room. But for William, each painting was special: showing as they did, the twenty-four birds which made up the codenames for the twenty-four members of the Order – Knights and Squires alike. Corncrake, turnstone, chiffchaff, mallard – Abelard Greewoof's magpie and a watercolour of a blackbird with a bright look in its eye which, he had to admit, reminded him strongly of Amaranta. And the falcon was every-where: swooping through the plaster oak leaves and rose patterns of the cornices and the mouldings of the carved mantelpiece; a bronze version staring coolly at William from atop its stout wooden pedestal to the right side of the fireplace.

William turned his attention back to the conversation going on between the others who were all sitting in various armchairs drinking tea. To their surprise, Mr O'Neill hadn't told them off when they arrived; instead, he had handed around tea. Then sat himself down and asked them to tell them everything about their previous day's adventure in Hannah fairground all over again.

'I do wish you had come to me, or one of the other Knights, before you went near that accursed place,' Mr O'Neill was saying. 'You were lucky to escape unharmed. Anything could have happened now that it is property of the Wicked Crow.'

Madame Ophelia's words were playing in William's head. *They kept coiling up his body.* That's what she said. *All those incisions.* William shuddered as he imagined such a horrible sight. He now also realised, for the first time, just how close they had all come to being caught, and who knows what would have been come of them if that had been the case. Something else came into his mind.

'The man from the newspaper,' he squeaked. 'The man who died at the fairground, so they had to close it down – he was one of us?'

'Caplan, that's what his name was. Jim or Jerry something?' Chris said anxiously.

'Jerome,' Amaranta replied. 'The man's name was Jerome.'

'That's it, Jerome C. Caplan,' William was staring at Valcott O'Neill. 'He was a member of the Order, wasn't he?'

'Yes,' Mr O'Neill sighed. 'Jerome was one of us. Unfortunately, Aaron Seblean wasn't the first Brother we've lost to the Wicked Crow.'

'The Wicked Crow? I thought he had only just bought the fairground.' Amaranta asked nervously, the porcelain cup and saucer chinking in her trembling hands.

Mr O'Neill shifted uneasily in his armchair. 'Yes, well. The Wicked Crow starting taking interest in the fairground back then, probably because of what happened.'

'And, what did happen?' Amaranta insisted.

'We're not entirely sure, to be honest. It was all perfectly planned. Jerome was to follow Ignatius, which is what he did. Once they were in the Hannah fairground, Jerome followed Ignatius into Gallery Avernus, also known as The Cave of Horrors, a place where, in those times, snakes, mummified animals and deformed creatures were exhibited.' Mr O'Neill paused, a strange expression on his face. 'That's where he died. According to our confidant, the Wicked Crow pushed poor old Jerome into a pit with poisonous snakes.'

All three friends were now staring at Valcott O'Neill in shock. There were no words to describe such a despicable and evil act.

'That's just …' Amaranta mumbled, unable to finish the sentence.

'Horrible.' William interjected, at a loss for a better word. 'But, when you said "confidant", do you mean the Order's confidant? Who was it?'

'Madame Ophelia, she used to work at the fairground'

'Madam Ophelia? Madame Ophelia knows about the Order?' William felt disconcerted.

'What you have to understand, young 'uns, is that the Order can't do everything on its own. Often, we rely on brave people to help us out. People like Madame Ophelia, who put themselves in danger for our sakes. She doesn't know any details about the Order. But she knows what we stand for and that we are trying to prevent wicked creatures like Ignatius Nosmorum from gaining the upper hand.' Mr O'Neill explained. 'Of course, not all our, ahem, associates are as noble as dear Madame Ophelia. We have many friends in, er … low places, who come in very handy every now and again, shall we say?'

'*They* know about the Order?' Amaranta asked.

'No, of course not, lass. But the Wicked Crow's got a lot of enemies. The enemy of my enemy is my friend, as it were. Which is useful for us. *Very* useful.'

Chris had been very quiet and, from the look on his face, William could see that his friend was even more dumbfounded than Amaranta and himself.

'Wait a minute,' Chris broke his silence. 'How come nobody told me about this before? I've been part of the Order for a while now.' When he spoke, more than shocked, he sounded annoyed.

The bookshop owner gave a soft grin. 'Patience my dear friend, you have only been with us for over a year and there are still many things that you will have to learn over time.'

Amaranta's eyes were wide as the saucer in her hand. 'It's all so terribly interesting and exciting,' she breathed.

'Or just terrible,' Chris murmured and William felt that he wasn't entirely satisfied with the explanation of not being told about the matter before. Nevertheless, he didn't press it.

The sitting room fell into silence once more.

'Anyway,' Mr O'Neill continued, 'Gallery Avernus had always been an unpleasant place, but after that day it became even nastier. That is probably why Ignatius became so fond of it. And now that he is moving to Drunfarnam, finally decided to purchase the abandoned fairground and make it into his headquarters.'

'And a huge bird cage …' Chris added. William shuddered as he remembered all those malicious birds chasing them.

'That dreadful grey beast, we triggered it. Didn't we?' Amaranta sounded upset.

'Ignatius has it there to protect his property. It's been trained to set off the alarm if anyone who isn't supposed to trespasses' William said.

'Could they do that, though?' Chris asked. 'Train a crow like that?'

Amaranta nodded. 'Yes. Uncle Ernest says crows are hugely intelligent, so it's more than possible. He says,' and here she looked down at her feet, 'that's why we need to stay away from them – the human and animal varieties.'

'And the redoubtable Mr Wiglann is perfectly correct. Silly of you young 'uns to put yourselves in such danger.' Valcott O'Neill was looking at them all over the tops of his round wire-framed glasses and William felt his cheeks go red, knowing this probably was the nearest the affable bookseller would get to scolding them.

'Maybe that bird is there to protect something in particular, something in those cabinets.' William was not embarrassed anymore, but exited.

'Ohh,' Amaranta cried. 'The birds might have been trained to protect the bookshelves, the ones we didn't get to check.'

'The *Book of the Knights Templar Errant* could be there!' Chris said enthusiastically.

Valcott O'Neill chuckled. 'I'm happy to see your eagerness, but we're fairly sure it's not there.'

'How?' all three friends chorused in unison.

'The Wicked Crow as much as told Woodpecker the other day that he doesn't have the book! What a lark, eh?' he replied.

'On Tuesday last, in the library?' William asked. 'What did he say?'

'Yes. He got all bull-headed again because Woodpecker wouldn't let him into the rare books section. It's locked, you see, and you have to make an appointment. He didn't have one and when he went to make it, Woodpecker told him he'd need a letter from a university to show he was a scholar or researcher before he'd be granted access. Our nasty friend played true to form and worked himself up into a rage. The main point of his rant being that the last time he was in Drunfarnam library his own book was stolen from him by the librarian and never returned.'

'What did Woodpecker say to that?' Chris asked.

'So, he looks the Wicked Crow straight in the eye, explains that poor Mr Seblean is dead and not available to answer that wicked accusation, but if Mr Nosmorum has any problem with that, he's happy to give him the number of the library's legal advisers so that the gentleman can put his complaint to them.' Mr O'Neill let out a loud guffaw.

William and the others were grinning too at the thought of Brady Grayling getting the better of the Wicked Crow. Part of William was sorry they hadn't stayed in the library to watch the fun, but the other part acknowledged he was happier when he wasn't anywhere near the evil man.

'That's good news,' he said. 'At least no one else has to go into that awful crow chamber to check it out. Again.'

'Yes,' Valcott O'Neill said. 'Silver lining and all that.' He looked over at Amaranta. 'But you can understand why Flycatcher is so upset about your little escapade yesterday?'

Amaranta nodded sheepishly. 'I guess,' she said. 'I'd better apologise.'

'Wouldn't hurt, if truth be told, lass. And don't do it again. That's the most important thing.'

'I won't. Ever. I promise.'

III

After the 'lesson' had ended, Mr O'Neill led the three friends down the hidden staircase which led from his apartment into the book-shop itself. Amaranta, with Mr O'Neill's help, scanned the shelves for a purchase she wanted to make, leaving William and Chris free to browse in the shop themselves.

Chris glanced at his wristwatch. 'It's late, Will,' he said. 'Your aunt and Elsie will be waiting for us. We'd better get a move on.'

'Ooh, and there's Uncle Ernest come to collect me,' Amaranta squealed, as she peered out through the large shop window at the busy Main Street beyond. She shook Valcott O'Neill's hand. 'Thank you for a most superb lesson in ornithology,' she said, with a mischievous twinkle in her eye, making the bookseller chuckle.

'Thanks, Mr O'Neill,' William and Chris echoed, the bell on the bookshop door tinkling as the three friends left the shop and stepped out into the street again.

It was just past midday on market day and Drunfarnam market square and Main Street were busy with shoppers and workers hurrying off to lunch.

Mr Wiglann was parked further down the road from the bookshop and, after hugging both boys in turn, Amaranta ran off down the street towards the car, clutching the parcel of books she had bought in The Falcon's Nest.

William wasn't sure exactly what happened next, but, just before Amaranta reached the car, she let out a piercing scream.

'Ah, no! Let me go! Leave them alone – they're mine!'

William set off down the street, moving as quickly as he could through bemused passers-by, Chris following close behind. As he neared the car, he could see Mr Wiglann was out of the car and making his way towards Amaranta, who was grappling with a tall, lanky youth tugging hard on her parcel of books. Before Mr Wiglann could reach him, the thief yanked the books out of Amaranta's hands and set off running in the opposite direction.

William watched as the youth turned back briefly, and with a leering grin, made a threatening gesture towards Amaranta. It was his undoing: because he didn't notice the tall, dark-haired man in a dark cloak who was hurtling towards him at speed until the man bowled into him, sending him flying to the ground and the parcel of books hurtling into the air. The thief looked up in surprise, then realising the danger he was in, clambered quickly to his feet and scarpered off through the market place.

Byron Mullween picked up the books the thief had dropped and made his way back to where Amaranta was standing with William, Mr Wiglann and Chris.

'Are you all right, Miss Bonclane?' he asked.

'Yes, thank you, Mr Mullween. And thanks for getting my books back.'

William caught a shiny bright look in Bryon Mullween's eyes that intrigued him, as if Byron was going to say something else. Whatever it was, he didn't say it. Instead, he nodded at Mr Wiglann.

'Let's get Miss Bonclane back to the safety of Ravenwood, shall we, Mr Wiglann?' Ernest grunted and made his way to the driver's side of the car.

'Are you sure you're all right, Manta?' William whispered as Byron opened the passenger door and waited for Amaranta to get in.

'Yes,' she whispered back, 'I'm fine. But, Will, that man, he had a tattoo— a crow's head with red eyes. He was one of *them*.'

William watched as the car pulled away heading in the direction of Avenfore. He felt relief that Amaranta was safe, followed by an ice-cold chill down his spine. Maybe it was all a terrible coincidence, but a voice inside him said it was not. And he couldn't think of anything more sinister than that the thief was one of Ignatius Nosmorum's men and the idea that the Wicked Crow had now somehow set his sights on Amaranta.

CHAPTER 25

Picnic at Ravenwood

I

ATURDAY MORNING DAWNED DULL AND GLOOMY and William stretched out in bed and yawned lazily. Downstairs the telephone rang, and he heard Aunt Edna trot into the hallway to answer it.

Her initial 'Hello' was followed by lots of hums and aahs and finally by a cheery, 'Oh, that sounds lovely, Elwood, dear. I'm sure the children will be delighted. Tell Mary I'll bake some cake and scones for them to take with them.'

Interested, William sat up in bed. What on earth were the Dreephys planning? But after a few more hums and haws from Aunt Edna and a promise to pass on a message to Walter, William had to admit that he would need to get up and dressed if he wanted to find out what was going on.

Aunt Edna was already up to her elbows in flour and sugar in preparation for baking by the time William entered the kitchen. Elsie was eating breakfast.

'Picnic at Ravenwood,' she explained excitedly through a mouthful of bread and jam. 'Byron Mullween's invited us.'

'Oh,' said William, 'I thought you didn't like Ravenwood or Mr Mullween?'

Elsie shrugged. 'Manta says he's not too bad, so I guess he mustn't be. Besides, I'm curious and I've never been there. Mum's been, but it's probably all changed now.'

'Nope. I suspect it hasn't changed since it was built. But that's what makes it so great, I think.'

'Yes, it's a fine place,' Aunt Edna chipped in. 'All those lovely spacious rooms and paintings and furniture.' She lowered her voice conspiratorially. 'Rather glum, though. It's such a shame …'

'What's such a shame, Mum?' Elsie asked.

But Aunt Edna had returned to her baking ingredients. 'Now, shall I do cheese scones or plain scones? Which do you prefer, darlings?'

'Both!'

Aunt Edna laughed. 'You are a hard taskmaster, Elsie Harckwell.'

'And your scones are the best, Mrs Harckwell,' Elsie replied. 'Don't you think, Will?'

'Absolutely, the best, Aunt Edna.' But he wished Elsie hadn't made it so easy for Aunt Edna to change the subject. He'd also have liked to know what such a shame was.

'Oh, Will that reminds me,' Aunt Edna said, 'your uncle promised Elwood some special oil for the clocks. Would you mind popping over to the shop and picking it up before you go?'

William spread a double helping of homemade raspberry jam on his soda bread. 'Sure, Aunt Edna,' he said. 'Will do.'

II

A fine misty rain was falling as William made his way towards the village square and Uncle Walter's shop. His uncle packaged up the can of oil Mr Dreephy wanted, then sat down in the back room and began to write out what seemed to William to be a huge list of instructions for its use. To keep himself amused, William wandered back into the shop to see what new items his uncle had picked up for sale.

He was admiring a set of brightly painted lead soldiers – two opposing battalions in the Napoleonic wars, with a miniature Napoleon on horseback in command – when the front door bell tinkled and he turned to see Veronica Aguevals enter the shop.

'Well, hello, young Howbbler,' the librarian cooed. 'Just the young man I was looking for.'

As always when he met this woman, William could feel the hairs on the back of his neck prickling as she spoke. He never understood why everything she said to him, no matter how simple, somehow sounded like a threat.

He smiled as best he could. 'Hello, Miss Aguevals, Uncle Walter's in the backroom. I can get him, if you wish.'

She didn't answer but crossed instead to join him at the display case.

'Early nineteenth century. French. Probably made before Waterloo. Quite a treasure, really. Your uncle has an excellent eye for quality, I must say. Do you like them?'

Her question took William by surprise.

'Uh … yes. Yes, I do, Miss Aguevals.' He could smell her perfume – something astringent and sweet, followed by a hint of something darker, like the smell of damp earth. In contrast, he thought of the calm lavender and violet smell of his mother's perfume or the warm scent of vanilla and raspberry that seemed to surround Aunt Edna.

'As discerning as your uncle, then, young man,' Veronica continued. 'I must say, you continually surprise me. In a good way, of course.'

William started. She was staring at him, her head inclined to one side and he had a sudden flash of memory – the old grey crow in the crow chamber and the way it had crouched on its perch and stared at him and Chris. The image vanished from his mind as suddenly as it appeared and William stammered a reply.

'Uh … thanks, Miss Aguevals. Are you sure I shouldn't get Uncle Walter for you?'

'No. I don't need him.' Her tone was emphatic. 'I have something for you, William Howbbler.' With that, she placed her hand-bag – a neat black patent leather bag with a golden clasp in the shape of an 'H' – on a side table and opened it, another waft of her odd perfume escaping as she did so. She drew out a bundle of crisp white envelopes and began to flick through them. Finally, she handed two to William – one addressed to MISS ELSIE HARCKWELL AND MASTER WILLIAM HOWBBLER and the other addressed to MISS BRIDGET DURFFAN AND MASTER CHRISTOPHER DURFFAN.

'Invitations,' Miss Aguevals explained. 'To my nephews' birthday party on Thursday of this week. I thought it would be appropriate to celebrate the occasion of their turning fifteen. No expense has been spared; their parents have been more than generous. We've even hired the village hall and arranged for a popular dance band to play. I'm sure all you young people will thoroughly enjoy that.'

A gamut of thoughts ran through William's head: from shame the triplets didn't act their age to the fifteenth birthday party from hell, but that said, the dance band sounded good.

'Uh, thanks, Miss Aguevals. It's, eh … very good of you to invite us.'

The woman smiled at him – at least he thought it was a smile, but it could as easily have been a grimace.

'The girl who helped you with your wonderful play for the Falcon Fair competition – the pretty one with dark hair that's staying at Ravenwood Castle – what is her name?'

'I … eh, I-I-I …'

Miss Aguevals tutted loudly. 'Oh, really, young Howbbler; you are good friends with her; it can't be all that difficult.' Then, as if she had read his mind, 'I have an invitation for her also, but I need to write in her name.' As she said this she opened one of the white envelopes, drew out a gilt-edged piece of paper, pulled an expensive-looking fountain pen out of her handbag, and stood poised to write.

'Uh, A-A-Amaranta. Her name's Amaranta.'

'Amaranta what?'

William reddened. Why did talking to the librarian always feel like an interrogation more than a conversation?

'Uh ... Bonclane. Amaranta Bonclane.'

Miss Aguevals nodded. 'Bonclane,' she repeated as she began to write Amaranta's name on the invitation in sharp, precise handwriting. 'Amaranta Bonclane. A pretty name' – she was writing the name on the envelope now – 'for a very pretty girl.'

To his annoyance, William blushed. He hated the thought of Veronica Aguevals manipulating him – or laughing at him. One was as bad as the other.

'And she's a relative of Mr Wiglann's, I believe? The caretaker?'

This conversation was making him more uncomfortable by the minute. But Veronica Aguevals was clearly waiting for an answer.

'Yes, Amaranta is Mr Wiglann's niece. Her parents are in Scotland.'

'Ah, separated from her parents, just like our three dear boys. And yourself, of course.'

William wanted to laugh out loud at the thought that he and Amaranta were anything like her 'three dear boys', but he bit his lip and said nothing.

'And is Miss Bonclane staying long at ... Ravenwood Castle?' Miss Aguevals asked.

There was something in the way she said 'Ravenwood Castle' that made William curious and wary at the same time.

'No,' he heard himself say, 'Amaranta won't be here long; she's only here for the summer.' He had no idea why he had lied, but somehow it just didn't seem right to tell this woman anything more about Amaranta and he suddenly wanted this whole conversation to be over.

'Ah, there you are, Will. Wondered where you'd got to.'

William breathed a sigh of relief as Uncle Walter entered the shop from the backroom. 'And, Miss Aguevals, good day to you also,' Uncle Walter continued. 'You're here about the library clock, I presume?'

He handed William the clock oil package and his written instructions.

'Tell Elwood Dreephy to go easy on that oil. Clocks are delicate creatures – no use just slapping the stuff on. He'll do more damage than good that way.'

William nodded, although he was sure there was no way on earth he was going to tell Mr Dreephy anything – he reckoned it wouldn't go down too well.

'Are you going to Ravenwood Castle, William?'

Veronica Aguevals was staring at him curiously again in that birdlike fashion of hers.

'Yes, Miss Aguevals. This afternoon, in fact.'

'Then perhaps you would be so kind as to give this to Miss Bonclane?' She smiled again – the same strained, tight smile as before – and handed him the invitation with Amaranta's name on it. 'It would save me the journey. And, please, do give dear Amaranta my regards.'

III

Raindrops splashed onto William's head and shoulders as he made his way back up Fern Lane, so he hurried along, anxious to get back to the house before the weather got any worse.

He crossed the road and was about to pass by a tall overgrown bush in the front garden of his aunt's house, when he heard a strange noise.

'Psssst!'

William stopped, not sure if he had actually heard something or was imagining it. But there it was again, and it seemed to be coming from behind the bush.

'Psssssst! William!'

It knew his name?

'William, over here!'

William looked over the dry-stone wall of the garden. To his astonishment, Jack Aguevals was crouched behind the bush and beckoning at William to join him.

'C'm'here,' Jack hissed. 'Please, I need to talk to you. I want … to ask you a favour. Please.'

A large raindrop plopped down on Jack's forehead from the bush above him and trickled slowly down his nose. William felt a sudden urge to laugh, but the doleful look on the boy's face stopped him.

'What are you doing hiding behind this bush?' William demanded.

'I-I just don't want *them* to see me. Look, I'm really sorry about what happened in the forest … I couldn't do anything to stop them. They never listen to me.' Jack said timidly.

William didn't need to ask who 'them' or 'they' were. And it occurred to him that it took courage to stand up to your bullying brothers, especially if you were a triplet. That didn't mean William trusted him, but something told him the youngest Aguevals wasn't as generally ill-intentioned as his siblings. All the same, he threw a quick glance about to make sure Tom and Pat were nowhere in sight and that this wasn't all part of some annoying trick or trap on their part.

'Well, they're not here. So what do you want?'

Jack stood up, shaking more plump raindrops from the bush onto his head and face, and blinking as one of them hit him directly in the eye.

'I-I-I … Miss Aguevals … I mean, my aunt … she …'

William almost found himself tutting like Veronica had done to him only a few minutes before, but he saw the struggle on the other boy's face and held his tongue.

'Our birthday party, next Thursday?' Jack spluttered. 'Will you all go?'

William squirmed inside. 'Eh, I don't know. I'd have to ask the others.'

'That's what I thought you'd say,' Jack replied sadly. 'But you won't come, will you? None of you will. You'll find some excuse not to turn up. Tom and Pat won't care, but …'

Now William was uncomfortable again. Jack Aguevals had a pathetic look on his face as he spoke and William realised he actually felt sorry for the older boy.

'I know what people – what you all think of us,' Jack continued. 'The thing is, Pat and Tom don't care. They don't want people to like them …' the teenager paused for a moment, then let out a long sigh. 'But I'm not like my brothers. I do want friends. And I'd love it if you and Elsie and Chris and Amaranta and, uh … Bridget could come to the party. Well, especially Bridget,' he muttered. 'If you know what I mean.'

William didn't and shook his head.

Jack stared at him in astonishment. 'But you must … in the play and all … I mean, she's the prettiest and sweetest girl in the village. Surely …?' Then his face lit up. 'Of course, you and Amaranta, how dumb of me!'

'W-What do you mean, me and Amaranta?' William stammered.

Jack had an infuriatingly silly grin on his face. 'Oh, I forgot,' he said, 'you're just a kid.'

'I'm not!' said William irately, after all he was just a year younger. Clearly, giving Jack Aguevals the time of day had been a mistake. 'And there's nothing going on between Amaranta and me!'

Almost as soon as William had said it, he realised it probably wasn't true. He did care about Amaranta. But he was sure not in the way Jack meant. After all, he didn't want to kiss her or anything – did he?

Jack tapped his shoulder sympathetically. 'You see,' he said, 'we're in the same boat. I knew you'd understand.'

'I-I-I …' William's mind was racing: Amaranta and him? Jack and Bridget? What on earth was going on?

In true Aguevals style, Jack was clearly determined to take advantage of his confusion.

'So, promise me you'll all come to the party on Thursday? Aunt Veronica's arranged a dance band and all. Dad's paying for everything, cos he and Mum can't make it over. Work or something. Again. But the party'll be great fun, I know it. So, please. What do you say?'

William looked uncertainly back at Jack.

There was a look of desperation on his face. 'Please, this is my one chance to talk to Bridget. If she wants to, of course. Talk to me, I mean. That's all I want – the chance to talk to her. But if she doesn't come to the party, then—?'

'I'm sorry, I can't.' William was surprised at his own obstinacy. 'I mean, they won't come just because I say so.'

William was already backing away towards his aunt's house. As he entered the house, he heard Jack Aguevals call plaintively from the street: 'Please, Will. Please come to my party.'

IV

The weather cleared up late morning and by the time Aunt Edna drove William, Elsie and the two Durffans to Ravenwood Castle, the sun was shining hot and bright in a cloudless blue July sky.

Amaranta was waiting to greet them on the front steps of the mansion, looking very pretty with her dark hair tied up in a long ponytail. William was relieved to see she looked happy and excited as Aunt Edna's van pulled to a halt and they all piled out into the driveway.

Amaranta quickly ushered them all inside for an official tour of the Castle – Aunt Edna included. William dallied behind.

'I have a package for Mr Dreephy from Uncle Walter,' he called out. 'I'll deliver it first and catch up with you later.'

'That's fine, Will.' Amaranta beamed at him from the first-floor landing. 'We'll be in the library or the music room. You know where they are.'

William nodded. He did know. Or at least he thought he did. After delivering the package to Mr Dreephy, who grunted grumpily when he mentioned Uncle Walter's list of instructions, William returned to the first-floor landing, only to realise he really wasn't sure which way to go. He tried to remember which way the others had taken, but, in the end, he decided to go left.

It didn't take him long to realise he'd made a mistake. He didn't recognise the corridor he was wandering along and he reckoned it must be part of the private family side of the house because its walls were covered with a jumble of family portraits and photographs. Now that he thought about it, the library was back the other way. He turned, about to retrace his steps, when he heard a noise coming from one of the rooms up ahead. William hesitated. But then the noise came again clearer than ever and William's gut urged him not to ignore it.

He crept silently in the direction of the sound which was coming from a room at the end of the corridor. The door of the room was slightly ajar and, peering around it, William was surprised at what he saw. The room was a small parlour and reminded him of the music room where he had first met Amaranta, but, unlike the music room, the colours and furniture here appeared dusty and faded, as though they were only memories of what they had once been. Byron Mullween was standing, very still, in the middle of the room, facing something William could not yet see, and, to his astonishment, the man was crying.

'My darling Lucia, what am I to do?' Byron sobbed softly looking up.

The sorrow and hurt in the man's voice sent a chill down William's spine. As he began to weep again his head in his hands, William discreetly manoeuvred himself to one side of the doorway so that he could get a better view of what Byron had been looking at. He had to put his hand over his mouth to stop himself gasping out loud.

On the wall of the room facing the chair, partly hidden by the door, was a large, ebony-framed oil painting showing a beautiful young woman. She had black hair, green eyes and a dazzling smile – if William hadn't known better, he would have thought that it was a picture of Amaranta. But what struck him so forcefully was the family crest in the background of the painting: the red, grey and black shield, the lightning staff with its crow's head and two flanking grey crows – an exact replica of what he had seen on the back of the carved Gothic throne in the Wicked Crow's crow chamber.

Intent on getting a better look at the portrait, William nudged himself a little more forward. As he did so, the door creaked loudly, and Byron looked around warily.

'Who's there?' he called out. 'Ernest, is that you?'

William didn't wait for Byron to investigate further. His mind racing with confusion, he scurried back down the corridor towards the main staircase as quietly as he could.

V

William caught up with the others in the library.

'There you are, Will,' Amaranta said, 'Mrs Dreephy's set us up in the garden, I think. Shall we go down and eat?'

'Isn't it a blessing the weather has picked up for you?' said Aunt Edna.

Aunt Edna was right. The sun was shining gloriously as the five friends made their way out onto the lawn, where Mr Dreephy had set up a trestle table and chairs for them. It was adorned with a large vase of fresh wildflowers and covered in a feast that made William's mouth water: sandwiches of all varieties, cocktail sausages, bowls of red shivering jelly and jugs of custard and thick cream to be slabbered onto Aunt Edna's sweet plain scones over homemade jam, and followed by a slice of her famous frosted chocolate cake.

'This looks incredible.' Bridget gasped.

Amaranta grinned. 'I'm so glad you like it.'

They sat down to eat, the others laughing and chatting happily. William's mind was in turmoil, but there was no way he could talk to any of them about what he had seen in the study. Well, Chris, perhaps, later. But not Amaranta. He couldn't bring himself to tell her. Not yet, anyhow. If necessary, he'd wait until he had a chance to talk to Abelard Greewoof who was still away on his symposium trip.

'Penny for them, Will.' Elsie was staring at him curiously. 'You're very quiet,' she continued. 'Are you all right?'

'Yes. Yes, I'm fine thanks,' William said. 'Although' – he searched in the pocket of his cardigan hanging on the back of his chair – 'I do have these.' He pulled out the three envelopes Veronica had given them and handed them around.

'What are they?' Chris asked.

'Invitations,' William explained. 'To the Aguevals triplets' fifteenth birthday party in the village hall next Thursday.'

'You have got to be joking,' Elsie said, throwing the envelope she'd taken from William hastily onto the table. 'They invited us to their birthday party? After the way they behave, do they seriously expect us to go?'

'Well, strictly speaking, their aunt invited us,' William said.

'Oh, that makes all the difference,' replied Elsie scornfully, 'don't you think, Bridget?'

Bridget was staring at the invitation addressed to her and Chris. She looked up, flustered as she realised Elsie was talking to her. 'Eh, yes, I mean … well, maybe we … oh, I don't know … perhaps not. I don't …'

'Well,' Elsie said triumphantly. 'That settles it! We're not going.'

Bridget opened her mouth as if to speak, but then shut it again and stared miserably, first at her friend and then down at the elegant gilt-embossed invitation in her hand.

Amaranta piped up. 'A dance band, though, Els. It does sound good.'

'Not worth putting up with the Aguevals triplets for.'

Amaranta seemed a little disappointed. 'I'm sure you're right,' she said. 'And if you and Bridget aren't going, then I won't either.'

The rest of the afternoon passed in a summery haze. The five friends swam and went rowing on the lake, chased each other through the gardens and generally had so much fun that even Bridget cheered up as the evening wore on.

There was no sign of Byron himself for the entire day and, with Bridget and Elsie around, William didn't get a chance to talk to Amaranta alone. Finally, as the evening turned to dusk, he caught a moment with her as they sat at the trestle table while Bridget, Chris and Elsie chatted down by the jetty.

'So,' William said, keeping his voice low so the others wouldn't hear him, 'are you all right after yesterday?'

'Yes, thanks,' she whispered back. 'I'm fine now.'

She stood and struck a match to light tea lights along the table, her face bright in the warm glow of its tiny flame. 'It was a bit of a shock, though,' she continued. 'Especially seeing that tattoo.'

The mention of the crow tattoo immediately made William think of the portrait of the woman in the study, but he pushed the thought away. Now was not the time or the place.

'You're sure it was a crow?'

'Absolutely!' Amaranta sounded a bit offended at his question. 'I knew immediately what it was. The goon at the fairground site who tried to grab me had the exact same one, in the same place. I saw it when I pulled at his collar.'

'I just meant it all happened so quickly,' William reassured her. 'Did he say or do anything else to you?'

'What do you mean "do" anything?' Amaranta asked.

'Nothing,' William said. 'I just wondered,' he added, glad that Amaranta hadn't seen the thief make a threatening gesture towards her. At least she wouldn't fret over that. However, he would have to let Mr Wiglann or Abelard Greewoof know as soon as possible.

The worry was back on Amaranta's face and William searched for a way to change the subject.

'Any news on the parent front?' he asked and then kicked himself. Out of the frying pan into the fire! He really shouldn't have mentioned it. Especially now, this afternoon. When he had found out, well, something he didn't yet know himself.

'The Dreephys don't know anything, do they?' he asked hopefully.

'Well, if they do, they aren't telling me,' Amaranta said with another soft sigh.

'I'm sorry,' William said.

'It's okay. It's just I feel people are keeping secrets from me and I hate that. I hate secrets and being lied to. It's the absolutely worse thing!'

She lowered her voice again as she saw Bridget walking back to the trestle table from the jetty.

'But someone must know something, Will,' she whispered. 'And I will find out.'

William felt a pang of guilt as she spoke. He had a sinking feeling he was one of those people who knew things and Amaranta wouldn't be pleased if she found out. But it strengthened his resolve to speak to Abelard Greewoof as soon as he had a chance. The teacher would know what to do.

'Hi there.' Bridget had reached the table and sat down next to Amaranta. 'Look,' she said. She pointed to where Chris and Elsie were sitting together at the far end of the jetty, silhouetted against the backdrop of the lake as the first stars appeared in the twilight sky. They looked so peaceful and happy: Chris's arm wrapped tenderly around Elsie's waist, and Elsie's head resting on his shoulder.

'Don't they look sweet?' Bridget murmured. There was a slight catch in her voice that William recognised. He'd heard it three times today already: sadness. Jack, Byron and now Bridget. What on earth was going on to make everyone so unhappy?

Then a thought occurred to him and he nudged Amaranta. 'Manta,' he whispered. 'I need you to do something for me.'

She drew closer to him, linking her arm in his. 'What, Will?'

She smelled of strawberries and cinnamon and caramel ice cream and she was so close now that William could have almost … He breathed in and then blurted everything out in a hurry.

'I-I …I need you to help me persuade Elsie so we can all go to the Aguevals' birthday party.'

CHAPTER 26

An Unexpected Problem

|

WILLIAM WAS UP AND OUT FIRST thing the next morning. He scoffed down a hurried breakfast and left the house even before Elsie, who was normally up long before him, had stirred, and set off on his bicycle along the Hollypoint road towards Abelard Greewoof's house. William was anxious to talk to the Latin master, and now that Gregor Watengroe was somewhere far away, it was safe for him to go off on his own.

Reaching the house, he was disappointed to see there was no smoke coming from the chimney stack, but as he approached the front door, he could hear singing coming from the back garden. He made his way around the house in the direction of the singing, but couldn't see Abelard Greewoof anywhere, until, suddenly the teacher's head appeared from between two beds of tall purple foxgloves.

'Well, hello, there, Kingfisher,' he said. 'You're quite the early bird today.'

'Hello, Mr Greewoof,' William said. 'It's good to see you. It seems like you were away for ages.'

Abelard Greewoof chuckled. 'Only a week, Will, but when you've had as many adventures as you, Turnstone and Blackbird appear to have had, then even a week can seem like a long time.'

William laughed. That's exactly what he had thought himself.

'So, how do you like it?' said Abelard.

'What?' William asked.

'My herb garden, of course.' Abelard gestured around it and William had to admit it was a wonderful sight: beds of herbs he recognised – sage, thyme, parsley and chives – and many he didn't.

There was lavender and odd beds of tall nettles. Beside them, a patch of lawn almost invisible under a carpet of dandelions, clover and tiny daisies. Already, bees were buzzing around the flowers and the scent of leaves and flowers and freshly dug earth filled the crisp morning air.

'Eh, it's lovely, Mr Greewoof,' William replied. 'Do you need any help with the weeding?' He pointed towards the nettles and then wondered why Mr Greewoof chortled heartily.

'My dear Will,' the Latin master explained, 'they're not weeds; they're essential herbs with valuable medicinal purposes. Just like this chap here.' He gestured with the plant he was holding in his hand, which had bright green, fern-like leaves and delicate pink flower heads. 'Do you know what this is?'

'No, Mr Greewoof, I've no idea.'

'Valerian, Will, that's what it is. Excellent plant – and beautiful, too. From the Latin *valere*, meaning to be strong and healthy. It's been used as pain relief and an aid to sleep since ancient Greek and Roman times, don't you know?'

'No, I didn't know.'

'And that,' Mr Greewoof continued, pointing towards a bed of ravishing yellow-and-white flowers which ran like a stream throughout the garden and which William had mistaken for daisies, 'is camomile, good for calming anxiety and poor digestion. As is mint.' He pointed over to a number of large pots set up against the thin bark of a weeping willow tree. 'But we have to keep our greedy little mint friend in pots, otherwise it will try to take over and run everything else out of the garden.'

'What are those called? Over there?' William pointed to bushes of larger daisy-like flowers with dazzling white petals and large yellow centres.

'They're ox-eye daisies. If you like them, pick a few.'

William suddenly had a vision of himself presenting a bunch to Amaranta. But it was gone in an instant.

'Thanks, Mr Greewoof, I'm sure, eh … Aunt Edna will love them.' He caught Mr Greewoof looking at him curiously and felt his cheeks redden. 'But I came here to ask you something. In private. About … about Amaranta.'

'Yes, I thought it might be that,' Mr Greewoof said. 'But I must warn you, Will, before you ask, that I can't tell you what you want to know.'

'But it's important, Mr Greewoof,' William insisted, and he told him about Byron and the picture he had seen in the faded study at Ravenwood.

'So you see, Mr Greewoof, it has to be Amaranta's mother. And she's connected somehow to Byron Mullween, who seems to have been in love with her. Even more than that, she's connected to the Wicked Crow. She has to be with a family crest like that! And Amaranta needs to know. She needs to be told. Don't you agree?'

Abelard Greewoof didn't answer. Instead, he carefully dug out a hole in the bed of earth in front of him, planted the valerian flower, pressed the dark crumbling soil around it and poured water around the roots from a nearby watering can.

'Mr Greewoof, please. Please tell me what you know about Amaranta's parents. She's really upset about this and she needs to know. I know you know something about it and it's not fair that she's not being told.'

Abelard Greewoof walked over to the back porch and sat in one of the rocking chairs before he spoke. 'I'm sorry, Will,' he said at last. 'I understand how you feel, but I can't tell you what you want to know.'

'But why not?'

'Because it is not my story to tell, young Kingfisher,' Mr Greewoof explained. 'Besides, I gave an oath that I would not do so. And I cannot betray a trust. You, of all people, should understand that.'

'Not even to help Amaranta?'

The Latin master hesitated, but then shook his head.

'No, Will, I can't. Not even to help Amaranta.'

'That's so not fair, Mr Greewoof. And I … I don't understand how' – frustration was bubbling up inside William – 'how if Byron Mullween is connected to a woman who's connected to the Wicked Crow, how do we know that he's not the spy we've been looking for?'

'No!' Abelard Greewoof stood up, his voice sharper than William had ever heard it before. 'Byron Mullween is a flawed and unhappy man, I will grant you that. But he is not a traitor. As I have said before, I have given my word and cannot tell you what you want to know. I would ask that you please leave it be. I would also ask you not to say anything to Amaranta. I can't explain why, but it might put her in great danger.'

William stared at the older man sullenly. 'You're too late, Mr Greewoof,' he said. 'Amaranta's already in danger.'

The teacher frowned. 'Why do you think that, Will?'

'Because I saw what that thief did when he stole her books. She didn't see it, of course, but I did. He did this …' William drew his hand across his throat in a cutting motion.

Abelard looked taken aback. 'When did this happen?

'On Friday, in Drunfarnam. The thief who stole her books outside The Falcon's Nest bookshop.'

Mr Greewoof was staring at him solemnly. 'I didn't know about this,' he said at last. 'And I'm sorry I was sharp with you, but this is a complicated situation and I must ask for your patience a little while longer. I will do what I can, but, in the meantime, please say nothing to Amaranta about what you saw? Will you do that for me?'

William nodded.

CHAPTER 27

The Bad Harvest Showband

AUGUST

I

To William's relief, Amaranta kept her word and somehow managed to persuade Elsie to change her mind about them all going to the Aguevals triplets' fifteenth birthday party. Although, as the party was the talk of Avenfore, and the Arinduff twins announced they were *definitely* going, he guessed Elsie had needed less persuading than she pretended she did. But he was grateful for Amaranta's help all the same.

Thursday evening, Elsie and William made their way along Fern Lane heading for the village hall.

'I can't believe Manta talked me into this,' Elsie murmured as they walked along.

'Well, you look very nice, if you don't mind me saying so.' He wasn't joking. Elsie's floral-patterned summer dress with its full skirt and her hair lacquered into a stylish updo made her look very grown-up.

Elsie was laughing. 'If that's an attempt to wriggle your way out of trouble, then you're lucky I'm in a good mood. Besides, who'd want to miss the live showband? Not to mention the look on the triplets' faces when I give them the most boring birthday present in the universe – two books on geography or economics or something and one on birdwatching.'

She grinned at William slyly, but he ignored her. And she was probably right. The books sounded deadly boring, even to him. William smirked at the thought of the look on the Aguevals' faces.

'There, I knew you'd appreciate the joke,' Elsie said. 'Oh, and by the way, you don't look so bad yourself.'

'Wait'll you see Chris,' William said grinning at Elsie, who had a silly smile on her face.

The Arinduff twins joined them at the top of Fern Lane in, what appeared to William, to be a cloud of fuchsia-pink and lilac tulle. The Durffans arrived shortly afterwards, Chris, taller than ever in his dark tuxedo and Bridget looking radiant in pale blue.

Ernest Wiglann dropped Amaranta off just as the others arrived at the village hall and William found himself gawping. Dressed in emerald green, with her long dark hair pulled back into a neat bun and fastened with a beautiful silver comb in the shape of a bird, she looked like a film star.

William's stomach gave a flip as she ran over to them. 'You look really … eh, good.'

'Thanks, you too. The tux suits you. Actually' – she indicated towards the others – 'I think we all look pretty amazing tonight, to be honest.'

'True,' William agreed. 'We do scrub up pretty well.'

'Manta, Will!' Elsie was calling them. 'Over here! We're having our picture taken.'

'Ooh, yes!' Amaranta grabbed William's arm and pulled him over to the others. They chatted and laughed as the photographer huddled them together for the photograph, Amaranta on the edge of the group, still linking William's arm.

Veronica Aguevals greeted them at the door of the hall. She was dressed in a black evening dress not unlike Amaranta's and looked elegant.

'How wonderful to see all you young people here tonight,' she announced as she shook hands with each of them. 'And you must be Miss Bonclane.' She was holding Amaranta's hand, preventing her from following Elsie and the others into the hall. 'We've not yet been properly introduced. Delighted to make your acquaintance.'

'Thank you, Miss Aguevals,' Amaranta replied.

'So glad you can be with us, even if it's just for a short time.'

Amaranta looked puzzled. 'Eh, I …'

'Oh, excuse me, dear,' Veronica put her hand on Amaranta's arm. 'I must go and talk to the photographer briefly.' William turned to look behind him. The photographer did indeed seem to be beckoning to Miss Aguevals. The librarian tutted impatiently. 'Silly man, he always has so many questions. You'd never think taking photographs was so taxing on the brain, would you?'

'Eh, that's no problem, Miss Aguevals,' she said, throwing William a bewildered look. Being every bit as mystified as she was, he shrugged.

'You have had *your* photograph taken, haven't you?' The librarian's tone was sharper than before. She moved close in to Amaranta, nudging William out of the way.

Amaranta nodded and the woman smiled. 'Of course, you have, my dear; such a pretty girl too. You can order copies, you know, to send to your parents.'

'Eh, thank you, that's a great idea,' Amaranta said. 'I'm sure they would be delighted.'

William felt a stab of guilt. He didn't want the secret Mr Greewoof and others were keeping about her mother – whatever that turned out to be – to take away Amaranta's happiness. But his gut feeling – and his friend's reaction to the librarian's suggestion – told him it wouldn't be that simple.

'Wonderful,' the librarian continued. 'I hope you enjoy the party.' She moved away from them, stopping only to call back to Amaranta. 'And do come and see me in the library some day before you go, dear. We can have a great chat about all sort of things.'

'What on earth was all that about?' Amaranta asked once she and William were alone.

'I've no idea,' William said as he watched the elegant woman in deep conversation with the photographer, who seemed to be jotting something down in the notebook he carried.

II

William hadn't been in the village hall since the Falcon Fair play competition, but it looked completely different this evening. The hall was filled with party-goers in their finest outfits. There were balloons and streamers everywhere. Hanging from the rafters in the centre of the hall, a large mirrored glitter ball reflected dancing patterns of light from the strings of multi-coloured lanterns strung up all around the room. The band's instruments were already set up on the stage and a large banner overhead proclaimed:

HAPPY FIFTEENTH BIRTHDAY TO TOM, PAT AND JACK.

Along the wall opposite the entrance was an enormous buffet table covered with the greatest assortment of food William had ever seen. And in the middle of it all, the birthday cake: three large tiers covered in chocolate and vanilla icing, with the name of one of the triplets piped onto each tier.

'Incredible,' he said to Amaranta as they stared at the spread in awe. 'And I thought our picnic the other day was a feast ...'

They joined the others who were already queueing by the buffet table. William looked about curiously.

'So where are the triplets?' he asked.

'No idea,' Chris said. 'Haven't seen them so far.'

Elsie curled her lip in disdain. 'Perhaps they've decided to do us all a favour and not turn up to their own party,' she said, making Gladis Arinduff snort with laughter.

Bridget giggled too. 'Hopefully they'll behave themselves for the evening,' she said.

Elsie tutted. 'Sometimes you're far too nice, Bridge.'

William turned to see the band members take their place by their instruments and Veronica Aguevals clicking her way in her black dress and shiny patent high-heeled shoes towards a spotlight at the centre of the stage.

'And now, boys and girls,' Veronica said in a voice which somehow managed to simultaneously cut over and quell the noise of the crowd of teenagers in front of her. 'I want to thank you all for being here tonight to help my nephews celebrate the occasion of their fifteenth birthday. We thank you all for coming,' Veronica Aguevals was saying. 'And now' – behind her a drum roll sounded and Arline Arinduff stifled a giggle – 'the birthday boys you have all been waiting for: Tom, Pat and Jack Aguevals!'

The triplets ran onto the stage to a final crash of cymbals and polite applause from their guests. William nearly burst out laughing when he saw them. All three had slicked back their hair into high-rolled rockabilly quiffs and were wearing crazy coloured tuxedo jackets teamed with black trousers and a pair of the most sharply pointed black winkle picker boots William had ever seen. However, despite the outlandish outfits, the three brothers were looking impressively handsome.

To everyone's amusement, the triplets lined up, clicked their fingers and, as the band struck up a boisterous version of the popular hit 'Blue Suede Shoes', they bopped, twisted and jitterbugged in time to the music. They ended with a flamboyant bow and everyone applauded, apart from Elsie, who stood arms folded, watching with a fierce frown.

'Enjoy the party, everyone!' Tom Aguevals shouted as the showband singer took the microphone and began to belt out an energetic version of 'Rock around the Clock'. Tom and Pat leaped down into the auditorium from the front of the stage, sending a few guests at the front scurrying away in alarm. Jack followed them but took the long way around by the side steps and eagerly made his way over towards William and Elsie's group.

'You came,' he said with a wide smile on his face as he shook hands with each of them in turn. 'Thank you. I'm so glad you came to the party.'

He reached Bridget as he finished talking but didn't shake her hand. Instead, he just stared at her for a moment or two. 'Really, really glad,' he muttered and then blushed bright red. Bridget blushed too, clearly puzzled and embarrassed as to why Jack hadn't shaken her hand also.

William heard Chris groan behind him. 'Oh, no. They're coming our way.'

Sure enough, Tom and Pat Aguevals were now bounding towards the group with more than usual savage looks on their faces. They reminded him of vultures on the hunt for carrion.

'Well, there we are.' Tom Aguevals reached them first. 'You turned up then, Elsie Harckwell. Afraid to be left out of the cool kids' scene, were we?'

Elsie rolled her eyes. 'Afraid to miss you making an eejit of yourself, more like. Hope you like your present, by the way.' Arline Arinduff giggled, and Tom threw her a filthy look.

'It's my party and you can't be rude to me, Elsie Harckwell.' He stared at her viciously. 'You know what the penalty for that is? You're going to have to dance with me.'

William's heart sank. He knew his cousin well enough to know that this could only end badly.

Elsie snorted loudly. 'Seriously? I wouldn't dance with you if you were the last man on earth, Tom Aguevals. As you well know. Even if it is your birthday.'

A small 'Oh' escaped from the Arinduff twins and even Chris looked uncomfortable.

Tom Aguevals glared at Elsie, but then a malicious sneer crept across his face. 'Suits, me, Els,' he said. 'Not sure I want to be seen out with girls who like nerds.'

'Or girls who *are* nerds,' said Pat Aguevals, who then guffawed loudly at his own joke.

'Hey …' Jack Aguevals stepped in, but Tom pushed him roughly out of the way.

'How about you, gorgeous?' he said to Amaranta, 'You're not really one of this lot, are you? You're one of us. I can tell.'

To his astonishment, Amaranta laughed and linked William's arm.

'Sorry, birthday boy,' she said, 'you'll have to count me out. I'm with these nerds.'

Pat Aguevals gave another laugh and Tom glared at him. 'Well,' he said, with a particularly ferocious note in his voice, 'I guess it'll have to be fat Bridget, then. C'mon, Bridge, chop, chop!'

At that very moment, the first few bars of 'Heartbreak Hotel' started up and Bridget – the hurt on her face plain to see – let slip a strangled cry so acutely painful that it seemed to cut through each and every one of them around her, including the Aguevals. Then, as the others watched in stunned silence, she set off running through the crowded hall heading for the main door.

'Y-Y-You …' Jack Aguevals glowered at his brother with clenched fists. William had never seen the youngest triplet so angry ever before.

But it was Elsie who now found her voice. 'You are an evil, evil person, Tom Aguevals,' she screeched at him. 'I will get you back, Tom Aguevals. I will get you back for this.'

She would have launched herself at him had not Chris, with the help of Arline Arinduff, held her back. Now she was shouting at them. 'Let me go, let me go! Let me at him!'

'Will, for goodness' sake, help me, please. Do something!' Chris hissed.

'I'll go after Bridget,' Amaranta whispered to him, and as William placed himself strategically between his furious cousin and Tom Aguevals, he saw her slip out the front door of the hall, closely followed by Jack Aguevals.

Elsie was now shrieking at him. 'Get out of my way, Will!'

'No, Els,' he said, 'you've got to calm down.' The truth was he had no problem with Elsie hurting Tom; he just wanted to be sure it didn't happen the other way around. 'Bridget will be all right. Manta's looking after her.'

That seemed to stop Elsie in her tracks. 'Manta? No, it should be me. I'm her best friend. I should be the one looking after her.' All the fight gushed out of Elsie and William saw that she was now close to tears.

'You're right, Els,' he said. 'Why don't you go outside and see how Bridget's doing? Leave this to us.'

'Oh, yeah?' William turned to see Tom Aguevals drawing himself up – he was clearly spoiling for another fight. But his posturing was short-lived. The sharp voice of his aunt made everyone jump.

'What is going on here, may I ask?'

'Eh, nothing, Aunt Vonnie.' Pat Aguevals looked down at his feet anxiously as Veronica Aguevals approached them.

'Don't be an idiot, Pat,' Veronica snapped. 'I have eyes and ears, you know. A young woman has just left the building in tears. And I don't suppose it would be too wild a guess to ask if you or your brother here had anything to do with it? Would it?'

Pat shook his head sheepishly and darted a glance at Tom, who glowered at him.

'Thomas.' Veronica Aguevals glared at the eldest triplet. 'Did I or did I not say, that there was to be no upsetting of any young persons during the party?'

Tom Aguevals stared at his aunt sullenly but said nothing.

'Well?' Miss Aguevals' eyebrow was so arched it was almost in her hairline. 'Indeed, did I or did I not say, that being on your best behaviour was a condition of the party? Is that not so?'

Tom nodded, this time less sure of himself.

'Welllll?'

'Yes,' Tom mumbled furiously, 'best behaviour or no party.'

'And?'

Tom threw a vicious look at Elsie. 'It was all her fault, Aunt Vonnie,' he retorted. 'She was rude to me. And it's my birthday.'

Miss Aguevals face clouded angrily. 'Are you fifteen or five, Thomas Aguevals?' she hissed. 'What have I always told you? We must be disciplined. If we are to succeed, we must not let our tempers or our desires run away with us. We've talked about this – many times. Haven't we?'

Her tone was so harsh even Tom looked alarmed and William had the unsettling feeling that there was something going on in this conversation that he wasn't fully picking up.

Veronica herself seemed to have realised that she perhaps had gone a little too far even in the circumstances. She grimaced – or smiled, depending on how you saw it, William thought – and glowered at both Pat and Tom.

'This evening was supposed to be a wonderful evening for all your guests,' she said at last, 'that is what your parents wanted; what I wanted ... what *all* your family wanted.' Here again, William could sense those dark undertones in her voice and he was surer than ever that Veronica was warning her nephew about something other than being rude to party guests. But what that something could be, William had no idea.

'This is most disappointing, altogether,' Veronica continued. 'I will not have unhappy guests at my party.'

Pat Aguevals looked about to argue about whose party it was, but Miss Aguevals silenced him with a look. 'You know what to do. Pat.

Tom. Now!' The 'now' rang out like a shot, and Gladis Arinduff squeaked in fright.

William could see the conflict – the struggle – in Tom Aguevals' face. Then, to everyone's surprise, he turned to Elsie and muttered something in a low voice.

'I don't think Miss Harckwell can hear you, Thomas,' his aunt insisted. 'Speak louder, dear.' She said the last word as though it were something nasty or stupid and William almost began to feel sorry for Tom Aguevals. Almost.

Tom glared sullenly at his aunt, but he did as he was told.

'I'm sorry,' he said. 'I didn't mean to upset you or fa— I mean, Bridget.'

'Yeah, me too. Eh, sorry, I mean.' Pat Aguevals was staring anxiously as other guests began to notice William's group in the corner and wonder what was going on. As if on cue, the band launched into loud and raucous version of 'Jailhouse Rock', which William thought was particularly apt in the circumstances.

His cousin was clearly not in a forgiving mood.

'I should think you're sorry,' Elsie snapped at Tom Aguevals. 'You're a nasty, unkind boy and I will never forgive you for what you said to Bridget no matter how many insincere apologies you throw at me.' She turned to Veronica Aguevals, who was surveying her with a glacial stare. 'Now if you'll excuse me, I have a broken-hearted friend to comfort.'

Breaking free of Chris's grasp, Elsie stomped across the hall to the front door. As she left, she threw one last furious glare in William's direction.

'I was right not to want to come to this silly party,' he heard her say. 'You should never have made me.'

III

William, Chris and the Arinduffs stood in embarrassed silence as Veronica Aguevals escorted her nephews away from them and then clicked her way backstage and out of sight.

'Will the others be coming back?' Gladis Arinduff asked tentatively.

Chris looked over at William.

'I dunno,' William said. 'Elsie was in such a bad mood, I reckon not.'

'Oh, that's a shame,' Arline Arinduff said. 'Understandable,' she added, 'but still a shame, don't you think?'

'Not the best party I've ever been to,' Chris muttered, and William began to feel annoyed. It wasn't like he had actually forced any of them to come. Well, not really.

'Ooh, there's Els!' Arline Arinduff was pointing towards the front door. Elsie was, indeed, walking back into the hall, head held high, and, from the look on her face, she was in fighting humour. Tom Aguevals glared at her from a distance, but he made no move to come near her.

'Is Bridget all right?' Gladis Arinduff asked.

Elsie glared at her. 'Of course, she's not all right. She's very upset. Wouldn't you be?'

Gladis reddened. 'You're right, Els. It's all terrible, really,' she mumbled.

'Where's Bridget now?' Chris asked.

'Outside with Amaranta,' Elsie explained. 'I've come in to collect our things and then we're leaving.' She picked up a small handbag William recognised as Bridget's and two cardigans. 'Now, where's my own bag gone?' she asked, looking about. 'Oh, there it is!'

As Elsie reached for her handbag, two loud screams ripped through the hall, one after the other, from somewhere outside the main door.

'Amaranta!' William cried.

Just then Bridget burst through the main door of the hall in a terrible state. 'Help, help!' she shrieked. 'The man's got Amaranta! He's trying to tak—'

William didn't wait for the rest of the sentence. He rushed out of the hall and into the carpark and looked about him. Another scream rang out, followed by 'Help! Help!', and William realised the noise was coming from the corner of the carpark at the side of the hall nearest to the park wall. Racing around the corner, he saw three people ahead of him locked in a scuffle beside a car: Amaranta, a man he recognised as the photographer from earlier and – Jack Aguevals.

Seeing him, Jack called out. 'Hey, William, call the police. This bloke's trying to kidnap Amar – oooof!'

Amaranta screamed as the photographer landed a heavy blow on Jack's chest which winded him and sent him staggering back into a row of shrubs and bushes behind him.

Spurred on by fear and anger, William raced towards them and hurled himself at the photographer, knocking them both off balance and onto the ground. The man snarled as he and William wrestled for a moment. Then William felt a sharp blow to his head and everything went black.

CHAPTER 28

Two Notes

I

WHEN WILLIAM CAME TO, EVERYTHING AROUND him was quiet. Too quiet. He sat up in terror.

'Amaranta!' he cried. 'Where's Amaranta?'

'Will, it's all right, she's safe and well.' Abelard Greewoof's face was hazy, but his voice was calm and soothing.

'Mr Greewoof, you're here?'

Puzzled, William tried to focus, but his eyes didn't seem to want to do as he asked and his head hurt more than he'd ever experienced before.

'Yes,' Mr Greewoof was saying, 'Mrs Dreephy telephoned me when they heard what happened. You've been out for quite some time. We were worried, weren't we, Edna, dear?'

The blurry vision of the Latin master moved aside for a moment to be replaced by an equally blurry vision of Aunt Edna.

'Oh, yes, Abelard,' she said. 'We were so worried, Will, darling. I mean, what would I tell your dear parents? Oh, my—' She stopped as a large sob escaped her.

Abelard Greewoof patted her shoulder reassuringly. 'There, there, Edna, don't be upset. He's going to be fine. Aren't you, Will?'

William tried to nod, but his head throbbed so much, he gave up.

'I'm grand, Aunt Edna,' he croaked. He looked around the unfamiliar room and realised he had no idea where he was.

'Where is this?' he asked.

'Drunfarnam hospital,' Mr Greewoof replied.

'The doctor said it would be best,' Aunt Edna sniffed. 'He said they needed to keep you under observation' – her voice went all teary again – 'if – when you woke u—'

'There, there,' Mr Greewoof said again, patting Aunt Edna's hand. 'Tell you what, why don't you telephone Elsie and Walter and let them know the good news.'

'Yes, you're right, Abelard,' she said. 'I'll go let Elsie and Walter know. They're so worried about it all.'

'Tell Els I said sorry, Aunt Edna,' William said.

'Sorry, dear?' Aunt Edna sounded puzzled. 'What would you have to be sorry for? After you being so brave and everything?'

'Just something small,' William explained, 'Elsie will know.'

'Of course, dear. If it makes you feel better.' Aunt Edna bent down and gave him a peck on his cheek.

'Thanks, Aunt Edna,' William replied. 'See you in a few minutes.'

As soon as she was gone, William turned to the teacher. 'What happened, Mr Greewoof?'

Abelard Greewoof stared at him solemnly. 'What happened, Will, was that you and Jack got there in the nick of time.'

'Jack?' William was struggling to remember.

Mr Greewoof smiled. 'Yes, Jack Aguevals, would you believe it? If you two hadn't tackled the chap, then who knows?'

A shiver ran down William's spine at the thought.

'But how … why … what did the photographer want with Amaranta?'

'He told the police, he was just trying to rob her. Then you and Jack came along and he panicked. He didn't mean to hurt you, of course; he was defending himself.'

'And they believed that?'

'Of course, why wouldn't they? It makes sense to them. However, they weren't impressed with him attacking a young girl for money. I have no doubt he'll spend the next few years in jail, I'm glad to say.'

It was good to think the attacker would get his come-uppance, but something was niggling him about the man's story.

'But that's not the real reason, is it?'

Mr Greewoof hesitated.

'Please, Mr Greewoof, I need to know,' William urged. 'Why did the man attack Amaranta? Is it related to the other incidents?'

The Latin master sighed. 'All we know for certain is that the man involved—'

'The photographer, you mean?'

'Yes, the photographer – was working for Ignatius Nosmorum.'

'But why are they targeting Manta?' he asked, trying to work it out in his own throbbing head. He sat up as a thought occurred to him. 'Is it something to do with the woman in the portrait I saw in Byron Mullween's study?'

Abelard Greewoof didn't answer for a moment. Then he reached into his pocket and pulled out a slip of paper which he handed to William.

'Can you read this, Will, or does your head hurt too much?'

William took the paper and stared at it. His vision was still blurry, but he could just about make out the writing on the paper. He gasped at what he read there:

MEET ME IN THE YARD BY THE PARK WALL, 8.30 PM, IF YOU WANT TO KNOW SOMETHING ABOUT YOUR PARENTS. COME ALONE!!!

'But who knows about Amaranta's parents, Mr Greewoof? Other than you and Mr Wiglann and Byron Mullween?'

'That, my dear, Will, is the mystery we have to solve. Solve that and—'

'We know who the spy is!'

Mr Greewoof grinned. 'I'm glad to see a little concussion hasn't affected your brainpower, young Howbbler. But, yes, on a serious note, you are exactly right. If we can figure out who sent this note, we probably have our spy.'

William leaned forward eagerly, ignoring the pain and dizziness in his head.

'Are there any clues in this?' he asked.

'Not that we know of,' Mr Greewoof replied. 'The paper appears to be normal writing paper – you can see the watermark here – every person in Avenfore probably has this brand of writing paper. And the writing's in block capitals, so we can't match it up with any hand-writing samples – not yet, at least. And it wasn't posted – someone slipped it into Amaranta's handbag at the birthday party.'

'The photographer?'

Mr Greewoof shook his head. 'Amaranta says no. She says she was never near enough to him for him to give her the note until he attacked her.'

William nodded. His memory of the evening was all mixed up, but he knew Amaranta was right – there was no way the photographer himself could have given her the note. So who else could have slipped it into her handbag?

There was something buzzing in William's head – other than the concussion, he thought – but he couldn't quite figure out what it was. Something familiar, something he had seen or heard or smelled or tasted before. But the pain in his head was making everything fuzzy, he couldn't get his thoughts straight and trying was making his head hurt even more.

He leaned back again against the pillow.

'How is Amaranta taking all of this?' he asked quietly.

'Not well, I'm afraid. It's upset her greatly.'

Of course, it has, thought William. And the mystery about her parents only makes things worse. Whatever else happened, someone had to tell Amaranta about the woman in the portrait. Now more than ever, he was convinced it was important that she know.

'Mr Greewoof, promise me you'll tell Amaranta about her parents,' he said at last.

For once, Abelard Greewoof looked uncomfortable. 'As I said, William, it's not that simple.'

II

Amaranta, Elsie and Bridget came to visit him. Luckily, Elsie appeared to have forgiven him for making them go to the party, and, for once, it was Bridget who did all the talking. And what she talked about mostly was Jack Aguevals.

'He's so brave, don't you think?' she gushed. 'Rushing in like that to save you and Manta without thinking of himself.' Behind her, Elsie rolled her eyes to heaven, but said nothing.

'Eh, I guess,' William replied.

'The way he threw himself at that horrible photographer' – Bridget's eyes widened in horror at the memory – 'just as he was about to punch you again –' A cough from Elsie silenced her. 'Oh, I'm sorry, I wasn't thinking. But Jack really was so brave, don't you think?'

She was beaming at William, so he agreed to keep her happy, although, truth be told his memory of that evening was still very hazy.

'And Will too,' Amaranta said. She looked pale, William thought, and definitely not her usual confident self.

Amaranta was staring at him, her large green eyes, sad and bright. 'I shall always be grateful to you both for saving me from that awful man. Goodness only knows …'

She started to cry and Elsie put a consoling arm around Amaranta. 'Here,' she said, pulling some pennies from her purse and handing them to Bridget, 'go telephone Ravenwood Castle and ask Mr Wiglann to collect Manta.'

'I know Bridget's right, Jack Aguevals was brave,' Elsie sighed. 'But there's only so many times I can hear it without wanting to scream, to be honest. And who'd have imagined it – Jack Aguevals, the hero?'

III

The following morning, he was delighted to see Aunt Edna and Uncle Walter enter the ward first thing. Aunt Edna was carrying some fresh clothes for him and William took this as a good sign that the doctor also felt he was on the mend.

Aunt Edna beamed at him. 'How are you this morning, Will, dear?'

'Looks fine and dandy to me, Edna,' Uncle Walter said before William could answer. 'Got the colour back in his cheeks, I think. None of that white, pasty-faced look he had a few days ago.'

'You're right, Walter, darling,' Aunt Edna said. 'He looks much better. And the doctor thinks so too. Here you go, sweetheart' – she handed the clothes to William – 'put those on and let's get you home.'

William didn't hesitate. He got dressed as quickly as he could – just in case the doctor or Aunt Edna changed their minds – and soon all three were sitting in Aunt Edna's van heading out of the hospital towards Drunfarnam.

To William's surprise, his aunt pulled up in Main Street, right outside The Falcon's Nest bookshop.

'I have some shopping to do, Will,' she explained, 'and your Uncle Walter has to see a man about the town clock. Elsie wanted to come and keep you company, but she promised Bridget she'd go to Drishlean today and she didn't want to back out. She said you'd understand, dear.'

William did. Elsie may have forgiven him for persuading them to go to the Aguevals triplets' birthday party, but she clearly hadn't forgiven herself for the way Bridget had been treated by Tom Aguevals that night.

'We didn't want to tire you out so soon after your release from hospital by dragging you around the shops or the town hall with us, Will, dear,' Aunt Edna explained, 'so we've arranged for you to stay with Mr O'Neill until we can collect you and bring you home.'

William thought that a chat with Valcott O'Neill in the Order's club room sounded like an excellent start to the day.

IV

He wasn't wrong. Mr O'Neill was in top form and told so many funny stories, William's headache began to return because he laughed so much. The bookseller must have noticed this, as his face became sombre and he left the room to make William another cup of tea.

'Strong, sweet tea's the best remedy for a headache,' he insisted. William thought the older man was probably mixing that up with a cure for shock, but he decided not to argue the point.

He took the chance to wander about the club room again, admiring the falcon carvings on the ceiling and the walls. He spent a few minutes staring down at the passers-by hurrying along Main Street, attending to their daily business. A flock of pigeons on the rooftop opposite the bookshop scattered suddenly into the skies, William searched curiously to see what had frightened them – a cat, probably. Then he saw it – a bluey-grey peregrine falcon perched on the dormer window of the building opposite. For a moment, it seemed to stare right at him, then with a harsh cry, it took flight and disappeared once again over the Drunfarnam rooftops.

William felt his stomach roil in excitement, and a little fear. It was the first time he'd seen a falcon in real life. At the same time, it unsettled him. In the same way, he was happy to be in the Order, but the incident with the photographer had shaken him, just as it had shaken Amaranta.

'Are you all right, dear boy?' Mr O'Neill's voice behind him was anxious and insistent.

'Yes, I'm fine, Mr O'Neill, thank you. I, eh, just felt a bit chilly standing by the window, that's all.'

'Well, come and sit down over here, lad. Do you want me to put the fire on?'

'No, thanks,' William said. 'I'm sure the hot tea will help.'

'Oh, yes, it should do. But concussion's a serious thing, young Howbbler, so if you feel any worse suddenly, do please let me know, won't you?'

'I will, Mr O'Neill.'

'Jolly good, so,' he said. 'And do call me Siskin. "Mr O'Neill" sounds so awfully formal, don't you think?'

'Oh, eh, I suppose … Siskin.'

'That's the spirit, young Kingfisher,' the bookseller said, cheerful once more.

William sipped the hot, sweet tea Mr O'Neill had prepared for him and began to feel better. His eyes wandered towards the high bookshelves at the end of the room, filled with rows of old leather-bound books in an assortment of dark red, black, brown and dark blue covers.

'I wonder what it looked like,' he said at last.

'What?' Mr O'Neill asked. 'What looked like?'

'The *Book of the Knights Templar Errant*,' William replied.

'Oh,' he said, but nothing else.

'Do you think we'll ever find it?'

The bookseller sighed. 'I don't know, Kingfisher. It seems a long shot at the moment, I have to say.'

William could hear Madame Ophelia's voice echoing again in his head.

'What you seek lies hidden in a very dark place. There are no windows … there is an opening … thrice covered.'

'Eh …?' Valcott O'Neill was staring at him worriedly again and William realised he had been talking out loud.

'Sorry, Mr—Siskin. It's something Madame Ophelia told me. I was just trying to figure out what she meant.'

'Not much, I should imagine. I wouldn't put much store into all that clairvoyance hocus-pocus. I fear you might be greatly disappointed if you do. Nobody in their right mind could believe that she sees things in that crystal ball.'

'You're probably right, but I was intrigued by it all the same. It's a pity poor Mr Seblean didn't leave any clues, but I expect he didn't have time.' Too busy running for his life, William thought bitterly.

'Poor Aaron,' Valcott O'Neill said sadly. 'His death was a great blow to us, young Kingfisher. But he was as efficient in death as he was in life. He did indeed leave us a note. Or, at least, we think he did.'

'Really? Oh, but that's right. Now I remember! Mr Greewoof said something about a note found in Mr Seblean's jacket pocket.'

'Well, more of a riddle, really,' Mr O'Neill continued. 'We didn't even know if it was about the Book or not. It could well have been something else Aaron was trying to tell us. Or perhaps it was a crossword clue he was working on?'

'Can I see it? I mean … would it be all right for me to look at it?'

The bookseller considered William for a moment and then said, 'I suppose so, young Kingfisher. Can't do any harm, can it?'

William could hardly contain his excitement as Valcott O'Neill left the room. He could hear the man open a locked door across from the club room and rummage about somewhere. Then he heard the door close and lock again and Mr O'Neill returned to the club room with an envelope in his hand. He sat down opposite William, drew out a slip of paper from the envelope and handed it to William.

'There you have it, Kingfisher,' he said, 'poor Aaron's last words. Unfortunately, none of us are any the wiser for them.'

William stared at the piece of paper in his hands. It was mottled pink on one side, white on the other, and torn at two corners as if it had been torn from something and then torn in half again.

The paper looked familiar. There was some writing etched deeply into the fabric of the paper on the white side of the paper with something sharp. The paper had later been covered in black wax crayon to make the writing stand out. The scrawled handwriting was difficult to read, but eventually William made out the words:

from the gates of hell to where the echoes of heaven can be heard when the vigilant monks are blinded.

'Have you any idea what it means?' he asked Valcott O'Neill.

'No,' he replied. 'Mr Seblean was a great man for riddles and cryptic crosswords.'

William had no idea what the riddle meant and it was making his head pound badly.

'Problem is, you see,' Mr O'Neill continued, 'we don't really know where he got to that evening. We know he escaped Drunfarnam. But we lost track of him. His jacket was found floating in the Inni not too far from the town. It was the only trace of poor Aaron that we found, I'm afraid. We never recovered … anything else.'

They sat in silence for a moment, William's head now full of Seblean's riddle.

'Would you mind if I copied it down?' he asked.

'No, of course, not, lad,' the bookseller replied, 'There's some paper over there in the writing desk. Help yourself.'

Uncle Walter arrived as he finished copying Aaron Seblean's riddle. William stuffed the copy into his trouser pocket and made his way downstairs where Aunt Edna was waiting. He said goodbye to Mr O'Neill who waved as Aunt Edna's van pulled off Main Street and headed towards Avenfore.

They were almost home and had just passed the turn for Ravenwood Castle, when Uncle Walter shouted stop so suddenly that Aunt Edna jumped and the van jolted to a halt.

'Oh, my goodness, Walter, how many times have I asked you not to do that, please?' Aunt Edna cried. 'Are you all right, Will, dear?

'Yes, Aunt Edna,' William reassured her.

Aunt Edna stared at her husband crossly. 'At this rate, poor William will be back in hospital before we get him home and us along with him. What is it, Walt?'

Uncle Walter checked his pocket watch and pointed to Ravenwood Castle. 'Appointment with Elwood Dreephy, Edna. Arranged it last week.'

'But that's tomorrow, isn't it?' Aunt Edna said, with more than a hint of exasperation in her voice.

Uncle Walter shook his head. 'No, definitely today.'

Aunt Edna clucked and tutted to herself. 'We have to get Will home, Walt, dear. And I have to collect the girls from Drishlean. And then there's dinn—'

'Fifteen minutes only, Edna; that's all I need. Els will wait, she'll be chatting with her friends anyway. And the boy's fine also.'

'Uncle Walter's right, Aunt Edna,' William piped up. 'I'm fine and perhaps I could pop in to see Amaranta?'

Aunt Edna glanced around at him. 'Well, if you're sure, Will.'

'I'm sure.'

'Oh, very well, then,' Aunt Edna said as she reversed the van and turned off for Ravenwood, 'but next time, Walt, dear, please make sure to bellow stop *before* the turn, if at all possible.'

CHAPTER 29

Byron Mullween

I

W ILLIAM STOOD ALONE IN THE HALLWAY of Ravenwood Castle and looked about him. Aunt Edna had joined Mary Dreephy in the kitchen and Uncle Walter had trotted off to the library accompanied by Elwood Dreephy, who was muttering something about clock oil and complicated instructions as they went.

'Miss Bonclane's in the music room,' Mrs Dreephy explained to William before she left. 'You know the way there, don't you?'

'Yes, thanks, Mrs Dreephy,' William said, but he lingered in the hallway a while until the two women were out of earshot, enjoying the coolness of the space with its high vaulted oak ceiling and its sweeping staircases.

He grinned over at the Right Honourable Fergus Mullween who was glaring at him from his usual position within the ornate gilt picture frame hanging on the left-hand side of the lancet door. Even Fergus himself didn't seem quite so intimidating now that William knew the small doorway led to the castle's secret room for the Night Bird Society meetings and that Fergus had been a Knight of the Order like Mr Greewoof and his father. The painting of Lesciern also looked different and William moved closer to examine it in detail: the isle itself in the background, in the foreground, Ravenwood Castle and right up against the left-hand side of the frame, almost hidden entirely by the forest, the old Avenfore church – still intact before the fire which had destroyed it – and sporting a tiny perching falcon atop the cross bottony which formed the tip of a spire which, as far as William could recall, no longer existed.

Above him, a door opened suddenly and raised voices spilled out into the hallway. Someone was – or rather two people were – having an argument on the staircase landing above him. He recognised one of those voices immediately as Abelard Greewoof's. But there was an anger in the teacher's tone that William had never heard before, not even in relation to the Wicked Crow.

'I never had you as a fool, Byron,' Mr Greewoof was saying, 'but I'm telling you now that you are making a grave mistake with this business. There is only one way now and that is to tell the truth. The whole truth. As soon as possible.'

'Hush!' Byron Mullween's voice was as harsh as Mr Greewoof's. 'You are an old friend, and a good friend, Abelard, but you must let me do this my way.'

The two men were on the stairs now and William shrank back against the lancet door, embarrassed to be caught eavesdropping, even if it had been unintentional. But neither man seemed to notice he was there.

'There is too much at stake here,' Byron Mullween continued, 'I have lost so much already and I cannot risk losing everything a second time. You, of all people, should surely understand that?'

Mr Greewoof came to an abrupt halt at foot of the stairs. There was a ferocity about him as he turned back towards the younger man.

'But that's exactly what you will lose, Byron, if you don't tell the truth now. Everything. And this time, perhaps, for good. Is that what you want?'

Mr Mullween seemed to falter under the teacher's gaze.

'No,' he said at last. 'No, that's not what I want.'

'Then you know what to do, old friend,' Abelard Greewoof replied, 'and if you take my advice, you will do it quickly.'

The Latin master gave Byron no time to respond; instead, he strode across the hallway giving no sign that he was aware of William's presence and exited the castle, allowing the heavy front door to bang shut behind him.

William watched uncomfortably from his hiding place as Byron Mullween stood for a moment on the staircase, staring at the front door as if Mr Greewoof would somehow suddenly reappear again. When he didn't, the man turned to go back up the stairs and caught sight of William as he did so.

A rush of anger crossed his face and William felt a stab of fear. He didn't know Byron Mullween well and had no idea how the man would react to him overhearing his conversation with Mr Greewoof.

'You're here to see Amaranta?' Byron asked after what seemed to be an eternity.

'Yes, I was on my way to the music room—'

'She plays very well, don't you think?' There was a strange look on Byron's face as he said this: both happy and sad all at the same time.

'Yes, Mr Mullween,' William agreed. 'Amaranta plays beautifully. She's hugely talented.'

Byron smiled – a tight, anguished sort of smile that made William wince.

'Hugely talented, indeed. Just like—' He stopped himself. He was staring in William's direction, but it was as if he was looking at him, but not seeing him.

A thought began to form in William's head and he couldn't push it away. Something told him it was now or never.

'I think Mr Greewoof's right,' he blurted out.

'What do you mean?' Byron Mullween's reverie was gone.

'I think he's right that you need to tell Amaranta the truth.'

Byron Mullween didn't answer. He stared at William as though he had struck him, then turned away and bounded up the staircase.

II

Once the coast was clear, William made his way up the stairs and hurried in the direction of the music room.

The sad, sweet melody of what he recognised as a Chopin nocturne flooded towards him as he entered the room. Amaranta was seated at the piano, so engrossed in her music that it was as if she was wrapped in it, as if the sound itself vibrated through her whole body and out through her fingertips which seemed to barely touch the keys.

'Amaranta!'

She turned, the melancholy that had surrounded her gone in an instant. 'Will!' she cried. 'You're home!' She rushed towards him and threw her arms around his neck in delight. 'It's so good to see you! Are you feeling better?'

'Uh, yes, thanks. How about you? Are you all right too?'

Amaranta smiled. 'Yes, I'm fine now. Everyone's been so kind.' Something in her tone told William there was a 'but'.

'What is it, Manta?'

She took his hand and drew him over towards the window with a view out over the castle gardens and Lesciern Lake. They stood there in silence for a moment, William not entirely sure what he was supposed to be looking at.

'Will,' Amaranta said at last, 'I've been thinking ...' She hesitated, and he squeezed her hand gently in support.

'Uncle Earnest wants me to go back home … to Scotland. He thinks it might be safer for me. Until the term starts at St Clem's or perhaps … perhaps, for good.'

William's heart sank. Amaranta leave Avenfore for good? He couldn't even imagine such a horrible thing.

'But what about the Order?'

'Well, that's just it. Uncle Earnest thinks this is all his fault. He's the one who suggested me for the Order and now he feels it's a huge mistake and he's put me in danger.'

'Do you think that?'

A pale smile crept across Amaranta's face. 'Actually, I think I'm the one who's put everyone in danger,' she said quietly. 'But this last incident … at the triplets' party … I have to admit it shook me badly. So, there's part of me that wonders, if Uncle Earnest might not be right. Perhaps I should go home, for a few weeks, anyhow? What do you think?'

William stared at her. Amaranta's eyes were bright with sadness and his heart ached for her. All the anger he had felt at Mr Greewoof and Byron Mullween for not telling Manta about her past bubbled up inside him. This was the end result. Amaranta would leave Avenfore, and he would lose her.

Almost immediately a thought struck him. What had Byron Mullween said about losing everything? Now he understood how the man felt but … what was holding him back? But William wouldn't do that. He wouldn't be like Mr Mullween. Amaranta deserved the truth and he would tell her if he had to, even if it meant … He took her other hand in his, gulped and cleared his throat.

'Manta, there's someth—'

'There you are,' a voice said. William and Amaranta turned, hurriedly letting go of each other's hands to look over at Bryon Mullween who was standing in the doorway of the music room staring at them curiously.

'Your aunt is looking for you, William,' Byron said. 'It appears your uncle's business with Mr Dreephy is completed.'

'Uh, yes, well, I was just ….' William replied. He glanced over at Amaranta. 'See you tomorrow, then?'

'Miss Bonclane won't be available for the next few days, I'm afraid. Or, at least, I hope she won't be.'

William stared at the man in surprise. What on earth did he mean?

Amaranta seemed every bit as astonished as William. 'What do you mean, Mr Mullween? I wasn't planning on going anywhere.' Her cheeks went slightly pink and threw William a quick glance. 'At least, not just yet.'

Byron shifted uncomfortably in the doorway.

'I have to go to London tomorrow evening, Amaranta. On business. I thought you might like to accompany me.'

'To London?' Amaranta looked puzzled.

Something passed quickly across Byron Mullween's face; so quickly, William almost missed it, but it was there: fear. Then he caught William looking at him and drew himself up.

'Yes, London,' he repeated. 'I thought it might be a good diversion after the nasty shock you've had. We could do all the usual sightseeing things, of course. Madame Tussauds, the Tower of London, Buckingham Palace, all those sorts of places. You like the opera, I believe. I have tickets for Handel's *Julius Caesar in Egypt* at the Royal Opera House. I thought we could go together.'

Amaranta's eyes were as large as saucers. 'Oh my gosh, I … I … but, Uncle Earnest …'

'I've spoken with your uncle and your, er … parents and they have agreed,' Byron added hastily. 'So, if you would like to go …'

'Oh, Mr Mullween, thank you so much! I'd love to go!' Amaranta's eyes were shining with excitement as she turned to William. 'Imagine it, Will! Seeing all the sights of London. And going to the Royal Opera House to see an opera. It's a dream come true, don't you think?'

'Er, yes, I do. I mean, it sounds wonderful …' William hoped he sounded enthusiastic enough and that Amaranta wouldn't notice the disappointment he was suddenly feeling that she wouldn't be around to meet up in Avenfore in the coming week.

'That's settled then,' Byron Mullween said, his voice sounding much lighter and cheerier than it had done before. 'I'm delighted you'll be joining me, Amaranta, and I am sure we shall have an excellent trip. There's so much I'd like to show you …'

He paused and shot a meaningful glance over at William. 'And so much I have to tell you.'

CHAPTER 30

A Familiar Scent

I

T HE NEXT FEW DAYS PASSED BY slowly for William. He had Elsie to keep him company and they met up with Chris and Bridget every day, but William missed Amaranta – her laughter, her good humour and her enthusiasm to explore everything. Life, he had to admit, was certainly quieter without her, but also a lot duller.

Thursday of that week brought a surprise. Jack Aguevals joined the four friends in Malconary's for ice cream and cake – a treat insisted on by Aunt Edna.

'Mum's feeling guilty about you getting injured while she's looking after you,' Elsie had whispered at the breakfast table.

'She shouldn't,' William whispered back. 'It wasn't her fault.'

'Tell that to Mum. Or rather, don't bother, she won't listen. Anyway, Malconary's it is, at two o'clock. It's all arranged.'

'Shouldn't we wait until Manta is back?' William asked.

Elsie grimaced. 'Don't worry, Will. Mum's only getting started. It'll take a lot of treats before she feels better again.' She indicated over towards Aunt Edna who was busily weighing out flour and sugar in preparation for another batch of bread and cakes.

The Durffans and Jack were already seated at a window table when Elsie and William arrived in Malconary's that afternoon.

Jack stood up as they reached the table and shook hands with them both.

'It's great to see you again, Elsie. Thanks so much for the great present, by the way. I loved those books. Will, how are you feeling?'

'I'm, uh … much better thanks,' William replied.

'Bad business,' Jack Aguevals looked serious.

'Yes,' William agreed. 'Although, it could have been worse, but it wasn't thanks to you. So, thank you again.'

'Oh, it was nothing. Glad to help,' he said sitting back down. Then grinned happily as he saw Bridget beam at him from across the table. He waited until the waitress had taken their orders then asked, 'How's Amaranta doing? Is she all right?'

'She's fine, thanks. She's away at the moment.'

'In London,' Bridget added.

'With Byron Mullween,' Elsie said. 'Of all people.'

'I thought it was kind of him to invite her after the ... incident,' Bridget insisted.

'Yes, I'm sure the break away will do her good,' said Jack. He reddened again as Bridget threw him another bright smile.

'Yes, well, he's a very odd man,' Elsie said, 'but you're right; it was kind of him to invite her and I'm sure the change will help keep her mind off what happened. I'm so jealous, though. I'd love to go to London and see all the wonderful things there. The Tower of London, the Victoria and Albert Museum—'

'The British Museum,' Chris added. 'I'd love to see all those mummies.'

'The National History Museum,' said Elsie 'All those dinosaurs.'

'Oxford Street.' Bridget and Jack spoke together, then giggled at the coincidence, while William struggled to hide a smile.

'The National Gallery,' William said. 'And the British Library.'

'Yes, all those lovely, interesting places,' Elsie sighed as the waitress arrived with the tea and cakes they had selected. 'Someday, perhaps.'

'Definitely,' agreed Chris.

'The Royal Opera House,' said Bridget. 'That's where I'd like to go. I'd *sooo* love to see the ballet.'

'I've never been to the ballet,' Jack said. 'It's not the sort of thing Tom and Pat would be interested in, to be honest.'

'Where are they today?' Elsie asked.

'They're in Drunfarnam with our neighbour, Mrs Ellis,' Jack explained. 'Aunt Vonnie arranged it before she left. I just told Mrs Ellis, I wasn't feeling well and that I'd prefer to stay at h—'

'What do you mean "before she left"?' Elsie asked. 'Where's your aunt gone?'

'To London,' Jack said.

Something stirred at the back of William's mind – something urgent, desperate to get through. Something that had struck him before, but he hadn't been quite able to put his finger on it.

'Mrs Ellis always looks after us while Aunt Vonnie's away,' Jack continued. 'It doesn't happen very often,' he said defensively, 'only when there's a librarian conference on or something. Although, this one does appear to have been so sudden.' He turned to Bridget with a smile. 'And she's going to the Royal Opera House too. I heard her on the phone telling someone it was the best place to meet. I'll ask her if I can have the programme for you, if you like.'

Bridget beamed. 'Ooh, thank you, Jack,' she cooed. 'I'd love that.'

William's head was spinning. The something that had lurked at the back of his mind since Mr Greewoof had shown him the note slipped into Amaranta's bag had finally made its way through into his consciousness.

'When did your aunt leave for London?' he asked Jack.

'Uh… Tuesday, I think,' Jack said. 'But wh—?'

William stood up, his heart pounding.

'I'm sorry, everyone; I … I don't feel very well; if you don't mind, I think I'll go home.'

Elsie jumped up also, but William stopped her.

'No, it's all right, Els. Stay here with the others, I'll be fine after a short rest. Honest.'

'Well, if you're sure …' Elsie didn't look convinced, but to William's relief, she didn't insist either.

Once he reached Fern Lane, William broke into a run. He let himself into the house and listened for Aunt Edna. He could hear her bustling away down in the kitchen. His heart thumped so loudly in his ribcage that he thought Aunt Edna might hear it as he made his way over to the telephone in the hallway, picked up the receiver and dialled.

A voice at the other end answered on the fourth ring.

'Hello, Abelard Greewoof.'

'Magpie,' William whispered. 'It's Kingfisher here. I know who the Wicked Crow's spy in Avenfore is. And Blackbird is in danger. Real danger.'

II

'It was the scent, you see,' William explained to Mr Greewoof and Chris, who had joined them in the Latin master's living room following William's startling phone call.

'I met Veronica in Uncle Walter's shop,' William continued. 'The day she handed me the party invitations. She opened her bag and there was a smell of perfume. I didn't recognise it at the time, but I do now. It was patchouli – not as strong as the Wicked Crow's scent, but similar, perhaps a bit more … lemony. And it was the same scent that was on the note slipped into Amaranta's handbag on the night of the party. Now I think of it, it *had* to be Veronica Aguevals who gave her that note – probably while she was talking to Amaranta before we went into the party. Manta had that bag with her all the time and there was no one else around that it could be. And Veronica left suddenly for London on Tuesday, the day *after* Byron and Amaranta. It's all so clear now. I'm just annoyed with myself that I didn't figure it out before this.'

'You were concussed, for a start,' Chris said. 'Don't give yourself a hard time about it, Will; it's certainly not your fault.'

'Quite,' Abelard Greewoof agreed from the other end of the room, where he had been pacing up and down for some time. It helped him think, he explained. 'Let's just be grateful that we have discovered it in time to do something about it.' He shook his head in disbelief. 'Veronica Aguevals, of all people. Now how did we miss that?'

'Because she's good at hiding things,' William said.

'But how did Veronica know Aramanta is going to the opera?' Chris said.

'I don't know,' William replied. 'But she must have found out somehow.'

'I may be able to answer that,' Mr Greewoof said. 'I met Byron outside Avenfore library on the morning before they left for London. He was carrying a book on Handel's operas – for Amaranta, I would imagine. He may have inadvertently told Veronica exactly what she needed to know, including the fact that they were going to the opera.'

'Jack overheard her telling someone that "it was the best place to meet",' William said.

'Best place for what?' Chris looked puzzled. 'I mean, what is it they plan to do?'

'Finish what they tried to do at the Aguevals triplets' party,' Mr Greewoof replied.

'Kidnap Amaranta?!' Chris exclaimed.

'Yes, I'm afraid so.'

'But why go to London to do it? They could kidnap her anytime in Avenfore?'

William felt very guilty. 'I think that's my fault,' he said, turning a darker red as the others stared at him. 'In Uncle Walter's shop, Miss Aguevals was asking so many questions and I just didn't like it. So, I didn't tell her Amaranta was due to go to St Clem's. Instead, I told her Amaranta was only in Avenfore for the summer.'

'That would explain it, all right,' said Mr Greewoof solemnly, which didn't make William feel any better.

'Then this *is* all my fault,' he said sadly.

'Don't be silly, Will,' said Chris. 'Look at it this way – if you hadn't put them under pressure, Veronica would never have shown her hand and we'd never have figured out she was working for Ignatius Nosmorum.'

William wasn't convinced.

'Chris is right.' Abelard Greewoof moved to the sofa and placed a hand on William's shoulder. 'You've done very well.'

William felt some of the nerves in his stomach die down. 'Thanks, Mr Greewoof,' he said, 'I appreciate that.'

'My pleasure, young Kingfisher,' Mr Greewoof replied. 'But now to the real point of our meeting. What to do about this terrible business.' He flopped down on an armchair next to the fireplace and sighed.

'Can we contact Mr Mullween and Amaranta at their hotel?' William asked.

Mr Greewoof nodded. 'I have already tried to reach Byron. I telephoned him at the hotel, but he and Amaranta were out when I called. I left a message for him to call me back, but he hasn't done so as yet. I've also called Harry Smith in London and asked him to contact Byron to warn him of the danger. Hopefully, he will be able to do so, but for the moment, all we can do is wait.'

'I'm sure Mr Mullween will call you as soon as he can,' Chris said.

But William wasn't too sure. Byron and Mr Greewoof hadn't parted on good terms and, fearing another lecture from the Latin master, it is likely Byron would ignore the call. But Byron couldn't ignore Harry turning up on his doorstep, could he?

As if on cue, the telephone rang in the hallway and Mr Greewoof rushed to answer it. William and Chris sat in tense silence, listening as Mr Greewoof 'hummed' and 'yes'd' and 'aahed' in response to the caller on the other end of the line.

'Well, thanks, Harry,' he said eventually, 'that's all we can do for now. I shall be with you tomorrow evening in any event and we can take it from there.'

Mr Greewoof looked thoughtful as he came back into the sitting room. 'As you guessed boys that was Chiffchaff. Not good news, I'm afraid. Byron and Amaranta are not at the hotel and Harry is reluctant to leave an obvious warning message, in case it is intercepted. We can't be sure where Crow has his tentacles, even in the hotel. Knowing we are on to them may force them to do something even more reckless, which we want to avoid.'

'Is there any chance they've already done something?' Chris asked. 'I mean, if Mr Mullween and Amaranta have disappeared?'

'From what Chiffchaff can gather from the hotel staff, they were planning a trip to Oxford and Stratford-upon-Avon,' Mr Greewoof replied, 'so we can only assume that's where they are. Unfortunately, Byron arranged it all himself, so the hotel have no details of where they are staying and we have no way of contacting them. All we do know is that they are due back tomorrow in time to go to the Royal Opera House.'

'So what do we do?' William asked. 'What if they go straight to the opera and don't get Chiffchaff's message in time?'

'I've thought about that,' Mr Greewoof said. 'Harry Smith and I will be there at the opera to make sure nothing happens to them. If I catch the early morning boat, I should make it just in time before the opera starts. Speaking of which, I must now ask you two young gentlemen to leave so that I can arrange things for my journey.'

'I want to go with you,' William said.

The Latin master shook his head. 'No, Will,' he said, 'you've had more than enough excitement recently. Chiffchaff and I can deal with Nosmorum and his cronies. There is no need for you to put yourself in danger. Besides, I doubt your Aunt Edna would let you out of her sight after your last incident.'

'She would, if you persuaded her,' William said. 'I need to help make sure Amaranta is ok. I shouldn't have given so much information about her to Veronica in the first place. It's the only way I will ever feel better about it.'

Mr Greewoof shook his head again. 'I don't think …'

'What if we both went?' Chris said. 'Only you know what Veronica looks like, if Will and me went it would be easier, there's no way Veronica can get to Manta without one of us spotting her?'

'Please, Mr Greewoof. Let us help. For Amaranta's sake,' William pleaded.

'I …' for once, Abelard Greewoof was lost for words. Then he scratched his head vigorously and clapped his hands together. 'Well, that settles it,' he exclaimed. '"In for a penny, in for a pound", as the saying goes. The Night Bird Society has just decided to have an impromptu field trip to the British Natural History Museum to see their latest ornithological exhibition and you are both invited. There is, of course, one condition: that you do exactly what I ask you to do and stay out of harm's way. Once Veronica is located, Chiffchaff and I will deal with Nosmorum and his crew. Is that understood?'

CHAPTER 31

The Royal Opera House

I

ERSUADING AUNT EDNA TO LET HIM travel to London hadn't been as easy as William had supposed. It took a phone call from his father, Arnold, reassuring her that he too was attending the ornithology exhibition that swayed her in the end. Arnold Howbbler wasn't lying to his sister, as he explained to William during a hurried, whispered phone conversation.

'Magpie has told me all about it,' Arnold said. 'I'm on my way to London also, I shall meet you there as soon as I can.' He paused for a moment and when he spoke again, William could hear the anxiety in his father's voice.

'I'll be honest, Will,' he said, 'I don't like you being there in these dangerous circumstances, but you're right about being able to identify Veronica – that will be a big help. Promise me you'll do as Magpie says and stay out of trouble.'

'I promise, Dad,' William said, secretly glad his father would be there with them also.

If Aunt Edna was tough, Elsie was even tougher. She was clearly put out that she hadn't been invited to London also.

'I don't know what's going on, Will,' she said, glaring at him as he packed his suitcase. 'Why you need to bring your tuxedo to an ornithology exhibition, for a start.' William didn't know what to say. He should have known that Elsie would have noticed something like that.

'Uh, well … you never know,' he finally managed to stammer out. 'Have you never packed a posh frock, just in case?' He breathed a sigh of relief when Elsie didn't push the matter any further. But she looked unconvinced.

'There's something going on, William Howbbler,' she said at last. 'And when you get back from your "ornithology" trip, I intend to find out what it is. You have been warned.'

They set off the next morning before dawn. Chris's father, Edmund Durffan drove them all the way from Avenfore to Dun Laoghaire in time to catch the nine a.m. sailing for Holyhead in Wales. From there, they would take the train to Euston Station in London – a six-hour journey which would see them arrive in London with barely enough time to make their way to the Royal Opera House.

The sailing across the Irish Sea was quiet and calm. William spent as much time as possible up on deck watching the waves below him and enjoying the sea breeze blowing through his hair. The sea air made him hungry and he was glad of Aunt Edna's packed lunch, which, thankfully, was large enough to feed all three of them for two days. He wondered how his father was getting on; whether he had left Germany yet and when he would arrive in London. Despite all his worry about Amaranta, he was looking forward to seeing Arnold.

But Amaranta was on his mind all the time now. Not just because of the danger posed to her by Veronica and the Wicked Crow, but William also wondered if Byron had told her the truth about her parents. And what that truth was. He had any number of possibilities hammering through his brain at the moment, but his greatest worry was that Amaranta would take the news badly.

The train journey to Euston was long and dull. To while away the time, William read through the English translation of the opera that Mr Greewoof had brought along in case he was interested. He also studied some maps of London. When he finished that, and there were still hours to go, he sat at the window and watched the countryside chuff by until the suburbs of London came into view and, finally, the centre of the great city itself.

Leaving Euston Station, all three passed through the great arch fronting the station entrance and walked the short distance to Russell Square, Harry Smith lived in a three-storey Victorian terraced house on the south side of the square. William was relieved that it wasn't too far because by the looks of the dark grey clouds there was a storm brewing.

Harry was waiting for them, alone and already dressed in formal evening wear and ready to go out.

'You'll have to hurry, boys,' he told William and Chris, 'the opera starts in half an hour. I've ordered a cab for quarter to seven to get us there in time. So get your disguises on sharpish.'

'Disguises?' William asked.

'You don't want Amaranta and Byron to recognise you, do you? Or Aguevals the Spy, for that matter? I've left out some clear-glass glasses and other stuff you can use. Use the cream on your hair — that should darken it for starters.'

'Why do I get the feeling that you've done this before, Mr Smith?' William remarked.

Harry Smith laughed and pointed at Abelard, who was also grinning. 'Learned from the master, young Kingfisher. Now, off you go and sort yourselves out — cab'll be here in … oh, ten minutes.'

William and Chris donned their tuxedos, slicked back their hair, and rummaged through the theatrical box of tricks Harry had left out for them. William chose a wine cravat rather than a bow tie and a pair of round wire glasses with lenses so thick that, even though they were clear glass, he had to peer through them in such a way which made him look completely short-sighted and totally unlike himself. Chris chose a fake moustache, which made him look older and more grown-up than he was. He flattened out his moustache proudly. 'This moustache suits me don't you think?'

William laughed. 'If Elsie saw you like that she'd never look at you again.'

Chris looked displeased at this, but agreed with William: Elsie wouldn't be too impressed about it.

The bedroom they were changing in overlooked the street and, hearing the cab pull up outside the house, the boys raced downstairs into the hallway.

Abelard Greewoof was wearing a mid-length dark-blue brocade coat, richly embroidered, over a white evening shirt and black trousers. He was clean-shaven and William was fascinated by how different he looked without his beard and moustache. He looked like an eighteenth-century aristocrat, William thought, and, despite the eye-catching outfit, he figured he wouldn't recognise the Latin master himself if had seen him simply amongst the crowd at the opera house.

II

The taxi got them to the Royal Opera House in the nick of time, and dropped them off right at the entrance so they didn't get too wet. William heard Chris gasp behind him as they entered the opera box and stared out at the sumptuous auditorium in front of them – a dazzling confection of crimson velvet and golden curved tiers, illuminated by dozens of three-headed candelabra and covered by a magnificent pale blue-and-gold domed ceiling.

Harry Smith tapped his shoulder. 'We should be able to see most places from here,' he whispered. 'Except those directly above us and high up in the gods. But Magpie and I will check those out.' He handed William and Chris a pair of opera glasses each. 'You two stay here and see if you can spot Byron or Veronica. Byron likes his luxury, so I reckon they'll have a box or will be in the stalls, so keep an eye out.' William nodded, and the two older men left the box, leaving him and Chris alone.

Chris was already scanning the audience below them with his opera glasses.

'Anything?' William asked.

'Not yet.'

William had to take off his fake glasses to see through the binoculars. He surveyed the auditorium below. The stalls were filling up, people milling about as they took their seats. He had no idea how he would spot Amaranta in this crowd.

'Look!' Chris nudged his arm. 'Over there, five along, it's Manta and Mr Mullween.'

William looked over to where Chris was pointing and saw Amaranta and Byron enter one of the smaller boxes on the right-hand side of the stage. Amaranta was wearing the same party dress she had worn to the triplets' birthday party and looked every bit as beautiful as she had that night. More importantly, she looked happy and William wondered if Byron had plucked up courage yet to tell her what he knew about her parents. At that moment, Amaranta glanced over in their direction and William ducked down suddenly, afraid she would see him.

'What on earth are you doing?' Chris asked.

'Manta looked over at me,' William explained.

'Don't be silly,' Chris said. 'She's not expecting us, and you look totally different. Although,' he added, 'I'd put those fake glasses back on pretty quick, just in case. At least we know they're all right. Now all we have to do is to track down Veronica.'

'Eh, no we don't,' William said. 'Check out the box on the higher tier above Amaranta's.'

Chris did. 'You're joking me,' he said, 'they're sitting directly above her. What are the chances?'

'But it's good for us,' William said. 'The way the balcony curves, it makes it more difficult for Veronica to see who is sitting below her.'

The orchestra had now taken their places and were tuning up. As the auditorium lights began to dim for the performance, William looked over towards Veronica's seat and was shocked to see that the glint of opera glasses in the distance trained on their box. He quickly directed his gaze back to the stage. He told himself it was silly to be afraid. It was impossible for her to know they were there, let alone recognise them beneath their disguises. After a moment, he sneaked another look towards her box. Veronica was now running her glasses over the whole theatre and William realised that she must be trying to locate Amaranta.

He began to feel cheerful as the auditorium lights went out completely. The one place that was out of her angle of vision was the box directly below hers.

Mr Greewoof and Mr Smith appeared back in the opera box just as the orchestra launched into the overture. William and Chris pointed out where Amaranta and Veronica were sitting and Harry Smith grinned.

'Well done, you'll have to keep an eye on them from here and we will make sure they are safe during the intervals,' Mr Greewoof explained.

'You and Turnstone here need to stay put. Promise me you will do as I ask?' Mr Greewoof looked at the boys waiting for their answer.

'Promise,' Chris answered.

'William?'

'Promise,' William replied reluctantly. 'As long as Amaranta's all right, though.'

'Don't you worry, Kingfisher,' Harry Smith replied. 'She'll be fine. We'll make sure of that.' But despite Chiffchaff's confidence, William was uneasy.

'Is the Wicked Crow here? There's no sign of him with Veronica.'

The fact that Veronica was alone in the box didn't make William feel any better. Jack Aguevals had overheard his aunt arranging a meeting and he had no doubt that Ignatius Nosmorum would turn up at some stage. And William had no doubt that even if Veronica hadn't been able to spot Amaranta, the Wicked Crow would definitely figure out how to find her. With that thought, he begun to feel a lot less cheerful than before.

'No sign of him yet,' Abelard Greewoof said, 'but don't worry, we'll be on the lookout so we'll spot him as soon as he arrives.'

William wished he felt reassured by this, but he didn't. That said, there was nothing to be done for now other than to sit back and watch the opera – and Amaranta.

She was sitting right at the edge of the box staring excitedly at the stage as the heavy crimson velvet curtains pulled back to reveal the stage set for the first act.

Abelard Greewoof arrived again shortly before the end of the second act, there was still no sign of the Wicked Crow and the Latin master was starting to look worried. He even agreed to let William leave the box at the interval to help keep watch as his father hadn't arrived yet.

'But make sure you stay well out of sight,' he warned before he and Harry Smith slipped away again ahead of the crowd making their way towards the opera bar for interval refreshments.

III

Despite William's unease, the interval passed off without any incident. William had to duck out of sight twice to avoid being seen: the first time by Veronica, who was wandering about the bar area, clearly looking for Amaranta. The second time, he had to avoid Amaranta herself, who was chatting happily with Byron.

'She's definitely having a good time,' William explained to Chris, as he handed him one of the soft drinks Abelard Greewoof had bought for them at the bar.

'Well, that's something, at least,' Chris said. 'It's good news, after the shock of that party incident.' He looked over at William as he sat himself down at the front of the box. 'How're you doing?'

'Fine. I just wish we knew where Ignatius was.'

'I know,' William said. But the uneasy feeling in the pit of his stomach was getting stronger – as if something inside him knew something was going to happen – something bad. Thankfully though, they would soon have back up as Arnold was due to arrive at any minute: Harry and Abelard had gone to the entrance to greet him and explain the situation.

Across the way, Amaranta and Byron were taking their seats again. William glanced at the box one tier above; it was empty, but just as the orchestra returned to take their places in the orchestra pit, so did Veronica.

Not long after, William's fear was realised, a movement above him in Veronica's box caught his eye. She had turned away slightly, as if looking at someone or something behind her. Picking up his opera glasses, William trained them on the box. What he saw caused his heart to leap: a shadowy figure behind Veronica, tall, dark and sinister, sitting so still, he appeared to be lifeless. But unmistakable, nonetheless. The Wicked Crow was also at the opera.

William leaned over and nudged Chris.

'He's here,' he whispered as quietly as he could.

Chris frowned. 'How on earth did he get in without Chiffchaff or Magpie seeing him?'

'Maybe he was here all along,' William said. The Wicked Crow had a habit of appearing and disappearing as he liked.

'I expect you're right,' Chris whispered. 'At least, now we know where he is, so that's something.' Chris was trying to sound reassuring but William could tell that he was starting to worry also.

As Cleopatra bemoaned her fate, William glanced up at Veronica's box. To his horror, she wasn't there. Instead, the Wicked Crow was leaning over the edge of the box and staring down at the box below.

'They know,' William hissed to Chris. 'They know where Manta's sitting. Look!'

'Wait here, Kingfisher,' Chris said. 'I'll get Chiffchaff and Magpie; they'll be with your dad at the entrance.'

As Chris exited, William's attention was back on the box but the Wicked Crow was gone – he had left and was on the move.

Straight across from him, Amaranta and Bryon were still engrossed in the opera. William didn't think twice, he dashed out of the box and sprinted as fast as he could down the corridor. By the time Chris found the others it would be too late, it was best to go directly to the box. The only thing William could think of now was saving Amaranta, she was in imminent danger and time was of the essence.

William ran as fast as his legs would carry him, he could see Amaranta's box in the distance and, to his horror, the door was wide open. As he got closer he heard a muffled scream followed by Veronica Aguevals exiting the box. There was someone else with her, William saw, but it wasn't the Wicked Crow. He realised it was the goon from the Hannah fairground and he had Amaranta.

'Manta!' William shouted, he was out of breath but he couldn't stop, not now.

Veronica threw a poisonous glance over in William's direction. Behind her, the man placed his hand roughly over Amaranta's mouth and dragged her closer to the stairs.

William was nearly there, just a few more feet and he would be able to help his friend, but then, not knowing how, he tripped over and fell roughly to the floor. That was it, he would never catch up with them now. Looking up, Amaranta and her kidnappers were nowhere to be seen, instead, right in front of him, stood an evil looking figure. Ignatius Nosmorum was leaning on his crow's head cane smiling down at William – a smile so horrible, it made him shiver even to see it. 'William Howbbler, I presume?'

Another chill ran down William's spine but he jumped up at once. The man had a long pointed beard, a sharp nose and a cold, inscrutable, piercing gaze that struck fear into so many.

'Cousin Veronica has told me all about you, master Howbbler,' Ignatius Nosmorum continued, 'and Boyd had some few choice words to say about you and your friends following that incident at the fairground, I recall. Poor Boyd wasn't the same for days – getting tangled up in barbed wire is not a pleasant experience, don't you agree?'

The Wicked Crow smiled his horrible smile again. 'But there is a silver lining to every cloud. Boyd was so angry, he described everything in detail, including the girl he had seen, and I knew immediately that I had found something I had been looking for a very long time.'

Amaranta, William thought, *he's talking about Amaranta.*

The man inclined his head to one side, and William was immediately reminded of the old grey crow on the perch in Hannah fairground. Slowly, Ignatius Nosmorum stretched out his right arm towards William. His fingers were long and thick, and, on his middle finger, he wore a ring – a dark polished stone in a raised, ornate, silver-coloured setting. William couldn't help staring at it. In fact, he was having difficulty looking at anything else.

'I don't know why you are after Amaranta,' he stammered, 'but I won't let you take her.'

'Surely a smart lad like yourself will understand why I cannot leave her with a dangerous fool like Byron Mullween.'

'Byron Mullween would never hurt Amaranta,' William heard himself blurt out.

'Really? And why do you say that?' Ignatius was staring at him curiously.

'Because he's her father.'

The Wicked Crow inclined his head again and peered at William, his arm still outstretched, his ring glinting dangerously in the corridor lights.

'And who told you that, William Howbbler?' But he didn't let William answer. 'Yes, Byron Mullween is her father, but he is not worthy of that name. He killed her mother – my sister.'

'No!' In his mind's eye, William saw Byron in front of the woman's portrait in Ravenwood Castle and the pain in his voice when he spoke to her. 'He couldn't have,' he said. 'Byron loved her.'

Ignatius Nosmorum was inching nearer, his grey eyes still fixed on William, his hand with the large ring still outstretched. 'He destroyed my beloved Lucia,' he was saying, 'and for that I will destroy him. I will take away the one thing he loves, even if it has taken him this long to realise it. Besides, he has something else I want also ...'

The sound of his voice was making William feel sick. And he couldn't stop himself staring at the man's ring – it was as if it was pulling him towards it – hypnotising him.

That's it! The realisation hit William almost too late. Ignatius Nosmorum was so close now, he could almost touch him. And out of the corner of his eye, William saw the crow's head cane raised to strike.

A shriek rang out from the staircase, causing the Wicked Crow to glance over at it. It was only a momentary lapse of concentration, but it was all the time William needed. As the cane whistled down only inches from his head, he ducked under the man's arm and tried to make for the other staircase. He'd recognised that shriek – it was Veronica. But Ignatius Nosmorum was too quick. He lunged at William, grabbing him by the arm and holding him fast.

Struggling to free himself from the man's strong grasp, William could now hear a loud kerfuffle on the staircase landing below them. Shouts and voices he recognised: Veronica, the man called Boyd and Abelard Greewoof!

'Hold her, Chiffchaff,' Mr Greewoof roared, and this was followed by another shriek from Veronica.

Spurred on by what he heard, William lunged forward suddenly at Ignatius Nosmorum and pushed him as hard as he could. Taken by surprise, the man was thrown off balance and stumbled backwards, dropping his cane. He clutched at William, trying to break his fall, but William grabbed at his hand and yanked it away from him sharply. The Wicked Crow gave a cry of pain and jerked his hand back roughly. As he did so, William saw something round and shiny fly through the air and land on the floor beneath one of the flower displays that decorated the corridor.

Without thinking, William made straight for the ring and picked it up.

'No!' Ignatius Nosmorum shouted as he scrambled to his feet and looked about for his cane.

William tightened his grip on the ring, as he frantically tried to think what to do next.

'Give me the ring, boy.' Ignatius Nosmorum was once again advancing towards William, his eyes glowing with fury. 'Give it to me now, I say!'

As the man charged for him, his crow's head cane raised once again to strike, William dodged past him and ran towards the stairs. There was no sign of the others, where had they gone? There was no time to think, Ignatius was behind him, he had to hide.

IV

William found his way backstage and slipped into the Roman soldiers' dressing room. Ignatius would reach the area in barely a few minutes and William racked his brains to figure a way out. The room was brightly illuminated and full of costumes and all sorts of props.

William picked up one of the make-up mirrors and carefully pushed it through the crack in the door. To his consternation, Ignatius was systematically checking out all the dressing rooms and it wouldn't take him long to reach his one. His eyes fell on two trunks behind a dressing screen. The first was empty, but the second was full of Roman soldier costumes.

He was just buckling up his sandals when he heard Ignatius thrust open a door near the dressing room he was in. William tied a red cape over his shoulders quickly and walked out of the changing room as a complete Roman soldier. The costume and the helmet were a perfect disguise. He could indeed be taken for one of the cast from behind.

William was starting to feel relieved as he walked down the corridor looking for a way out, but then he made a mistake, he glanced back to see where Ignatius was. At the other end of the corridor the Wicked Crow was staring at him.

William set off as fast as he could – the costume was too big for him and it was hard to move quickly – through all the backstage machinery looking for the emergency exit. There it was at the far end, William started to run not daring to look back.

The moment he reached the exit he pushed down on the bar to open it. The door swung closed behind him. He looked around to see himself in a narrow lane at the back of the building. He got rid of the helmet and the cape as they hampered him when running. He also wanted to avoid drawing attention to himself, but the tunic and the sandals would do that anyway. The pouring rain had left the streets of London empty. Where was he to go now? Before he could decide, the door opened behind him.

CHAPTER 32

The Black Ring

I

WILLIAM RAN AND RAN UNDER THE pouring rain until his lungs were fit to burst and he could run no more. Panting hard, he stopped in a doorway to rest for a minute or so. He had no idea at all where he was, but that hardly bothered him. Looking down at the wet pavement he saw that the sandals on his aching feet were coming apart – they were stage props after all, and had not been designed for running in wet weather.

Having got his breath back, he peered cautiously around the corner of his hiding place, looking to see if he had been followed, but there was no sign of the Wicked Crow or anyone, for that matter. If he had managed to shake off Ignatius, he should get his bearings and figure out how to get back to the others without being spotted.

The question for William now was, which direction should he go in? William closed his eyes trying hard to visualize the maps of London he had been looking at on the train. It was impossible for him to remember anything, his mind was spinning: should he head back to Russell Square and wait for the others at Harry Smith's house? Or go back to the Royal Opera House?

He opened his fist and looked at the ring. The sight of it made him uneasy – the black polished stone on a large raised, wrought silver, filigree base had a swirl of grey running through it. Part of the natural stone, William thought. But it gave the impression the stone was moving, swirling and even looking at it now, William could feel its hypnotic power. Then, all of a sudden, he could hear Elsie's voice in his head. *'Stuff and nonsense, William, there's no such thing as magic hypnotic rings. People only have power over you if you let them.'*

William laughed. Even from over four hundred miles away, cousin Elsie and her matter-of-factness had come to his rescue. Whatever anyone else thought, the fact was that this ring clearly meant a lot to the Wicked Crow and, now, as the evening began to turn to dusk, William began to wonder if picking it up hadn't been the cleverest idea he'd ever had. It didn't make sense that the evil mastermind would give up so easily and a sixth sense told him that the Wicked Crow was out there, hunting him down.

A cold chill, that had nothing to do with him being dripping wet, ran through William and his heart began to thump loudly. The black ring felt cold against his palm, as if to remind him it was still there. He tucked it safely into his roman belt and slipped out of his hiding place. William was about to set off back the way he had come when he saw a tall figure appear in the middle of the street, coming towards him. Even from this distance, it was clear that the Wicked Crow had spotted William and was making straight for him. How had he found him? How could he have run for so long in such a large city and not shaken him off? William didn't hesitate on these questions. He turned on his heels and started running.

He ran along the empty streets for what he thought was ages. It was impossible for Ignatius to have followed him. William stopped at a lamppost and leant against it to catch his breath. A young couple huddled under an umbrella walked by. Seeing him leaning on the lamppost in such a state, they probably took him for a crazy person. They stared for a moment and then started laughing as they continued down the street. Once they had disappeared round the corner and their laughter had died away, the street fell eerily silent, except for the sound of the persistent rain.

Lost in London, dressed as a Roman soldier, soaked through and with a devilish ring he had stolen, pursued by a man who would cheerfully kill him: William didn't know whether to laugh or cry.

Seconds later William felt the blood drain from his face, he couldn't credit what he was seeing. The long sinister shadow of

Ignatius appeared once more at the far end of the street. William realised that it was useless to flee, but he ran anyway, veering right through an archway below a black-and-white-timber-framed house and into a narrow laneway. William was in such a haze, he tripped over some stonework jutting out at the narrowest part of the laneway before it spread out into a tree-lined courtyard.

He put out his hands to stop his fall and yelped when they hit something sharp. He picked it up: it was a small sharp dark stone, perhaps a piece of masonry which had fallen off the building beside him. He looked up at the building and gasped. Even in his state of panic, William recognised its circular nave. He'd read about this. It was Temple Church – the church built by the Knights Templar in the twelfth century. The same order of Knights who had fled to Avenfore to escape persecution by the French king some two hundred years later. The same order of Knights to which William now belonged. This thought gave him hope and, pocketing the stone, he ran on through the gardens surrounding the church and headed east, he remembered that the river was nearby.

II

William found the river at the same time the Wicked Crow found him.

'You can't escape me,' his pursuer cried.

William knew he couldn't outrun Ignatius much longer. He had to accept the fact that it was time to confront his enemy once and for all.

Looking ahead of him, he saw a bridge. Something in his head told him it was probably Blackfriars Bridge, but at this point in time, William didn't care which bridge it was. It would do as well as any other for the plan that had suddenly formed in his mind.

Summoning up his last reserves of strength, he put on a spurt towards the bridge. Ignatius seemed to guess his intentions and started to run faster too. William reached the stone viewing point in the middle of the bridge and leant over the ledge as he gasped to get his breath.

Ignatius appeared at the other end of the bridge and approached cautiously. Perhaps he was expecting a trick? But there was no trick. Just this.

Slowly, William stretched out his arm. The ring lay in his palm, its black stone gleaming in the lamplight above where William was standing.

'This is what you're after, isn't it?' he shouted at Ignatius.

'The ring is mine,' he said, his voice calm and steady, like an urgent breeze whispering on William's skin. 'Give it to me. Don't meddle with things, you don't understand, boy,' he hissed, his eyes black with rage. 'Hand it over now and it ends here. There will be no repercussions for you ...' his eyes glinted sharply in the lamplight, '... or your family, William Howbbler.'

Panic spread across William, his mind racing. What had he told Veronica about his family? His mother's name? His sister's name? How could he have been so stupid giving her all the information they needed to hurt him and his father. His father – his father would be looking for him, but goodness only knows how he would find him. Now his clever plan didn't seem quite so clever. But he had no choice: he had to go through with it.

It was then that Ignatius raise his cane. William heard it whistle through the air next to his shoulder and crack against the stone ledge of the viewing platform. The Wicked Crow cursed, and William took the chance to run again. But a second blow caught the back of his legs and he fell heavily to the hard ground.

Ignatius towered over him, a cruel smile appearing on his face now that he had William at his mercy. But William had one last chance.

'You want the ring?' he said, scrambling to his feet. 'Then have it.' With that he raised his arm, and swinging it as hard as he could, he threw it high into the sky and out over towards the river.

'Noooo!!' Ignatius raced towards the side of the bridge, and, with surprising agility and the help of his cane, levered himself up onto the railings next to the stone viewing point and reached up to catch the ring. He let out a shout of triumph as it flew into his hand, swiftly followed by a sharp cry of alarm as he lost his footing on the narrow railings and began to topple forwards. Then, arms and legs flailing in the air, the Wicked Crow let out one final terrifying shriek and plunged into the dark river below.

William rushed over to the railings and looked down into the murky waters of the Thames. There was no sign of Ignatius Nosmorum.

'You'll pay for this,' a cruel voice yelled from across the bridge. William looked up in fright to see a frenzied Veronica Aguevals. She stared fiercely at him, like a huge, angry bird, ready to pounce on its prey.

William stared at her in horror.

'You'll pay for this, William Howbbler,' she hissed, 'mark my words.'

'Will!'

William turned at the sound of the familiar voice behind him. Relief flooded over him as Arnold Howbbler came running along the pavement in his direction.

'It's all right, Dad. I'm all right, Dad,' he shouted.

Behind him, he heard something that sounded like a loud, harsh croak, but when he looked around, Veronica Aguevals was nowhere to be seen.

CHAPTER 33

Homecoming

I

THE JOURNEY BACK TO AVENFORE SEEMED longer than ever for William. His father had insisted that he, Chris and Abelard Greewoof catch the early train from Euston in time to board the afternoon Holyhead boat back to Dublin. There was no time for sightseeing or to find out how Amaranta was – Mr Greewoof reassured him that she was well, but she and Byron were travelling to be with Amaranta's family in Scotland. There was something about the way he said it that let William know that Byron had finally told Amaranta the truth about being her father. And much as William wanted to be with her and know she was okay, he also knew that being with her parents and sister was probably the best place for her to be right now.

The train journey from Euston was also one of explanations. Chris and Abelard Greewoof explained how, in the end, Amaranta had as good as saved herself. She'd escaped from Boyd by kicking him hard in the shins and running away.

'You'd think he'd have learned his lesson with Manta in the fairground,' Chris said with a grin. 'She gave him hell then, too.'

'Of course, they chased her, but by that time Chiffchaff, Bryon and I had found them.'

'Where *was* Byron when they took Amaranta from the box?' William asked, suddenly remembering they hadn't seen him when everything had gone down.

'Veronica used some sort of chloroform-based spray on him,' answered Mr Greewoof, 'but it was only strong enough to daze him for a few minutes. Enough time, of course, for her and Boyd to escape with Amaranta. Byron recovered quickly enough to chase after them. He caught up with them at the same time as Harry and I, and, fortunately, before they could link up with the Wicked Crow.'

'Which is, of course, where you come in,' Chris said.

William shivered as the memory of the Wicked Crow's final cry echoed in his mind once more.

'You're looking peaky, young Kingfisher' Mr Greewoof was looking at him anxiously. 'Shall we go up on deck and get some fresh air?'

William followed the teacher out of the lounge seating area and up onto the deck of the ship. Gulping in the fresh salty air made him feel better. He leant on the deck railings and looked out across the horizon where the grey of the sea met the blue of the sky.

'I-I … I was just thinking about Amaranta,' William said. 'I was wondering how she was.'

'After Byron's news, you mean?

'Yes. Did she take it well?'

Mr Greewoof sighed. 'By all accounts, no.'

'It's hardly surprising,' William blurted out. 'After all, who wants to find out they've been abandoned and lied to all their life?'

To his astonishment, the Latin master sighed again and shook his head sadly. 'No,' he said at last. 'We – I – should have been firmer with Byron, but I thought we were protecting Amaranta by keeping her past a secret. I made a mistake. I see now that you were right, Will. Amaranta had a right to know. I only hope she can forgive Byron – and myself – for not being truthful with her before now.'

Something the Wicked Crow had said came to the front of William's mind and he turned to the Latin master.

'What happened to Amaranta's mother, Mr Greewoof?' he asked. 'The Wicked Crow said some awful things.'

'Whatever the Wicked Crow told you was a lie,' Abelard Greewoof's voice was sharp, 'Byron Mullween loved Lucia Nosmorum, he would never hurt her. After all, he had already given up so much for her, including his family.'

'But why?'

'Fergus Mullween and the Wicked Crow's grandfather were sworn political enemies. The men hated each other, so when Byron and Lucia fell in love, both families tried to separate them. But they eloped and got married in London. They returned to Ireland towards the middle of the war, after Byron's grandfather died. They were happy at Ravenwood Castle for a few years. But a few weeks after Amaranta was born, Lucia became ill with pneumonia and died.'

'Byron was grief-stricken. He couldn't imagine life without Lucia. He was so deeply depressed he began to ignore his young daughter. She reminded him too much of her mother, he said. It was around that time too that Ignatius Nosmorum and his mother began to show up at Ravenwood trying to claim the child as theirs. Which was complete nonsense, of course. But with Byron behaving so strangely, we – his friends and the Order – became concerned for Amaranta's safety.'

'So you sent her to live with Mr Wiglann's sister in Scotland?'

'Yes. The Bonclanes are good people. We knew they would care for her as their own daughter. Besides, it was only supposed to be a temporary arrangement.'

'But …?'

'But Byron wouldn't have her back. He convinced himself if he did bring her back to Ravenwood, something terrible would happen to her – as had happened to her mother. We couldn't persuade him otherwise. So Amaranta stayed in Scotland with the Bonclanes where she was safe. And happy.' Mr Greewoof looked over at William suddenly. 'Was it really such a bad idea to leave her there, Will? Did we really do the wrong thing?'

William hesitated for a moment, the sea breeze cool on his face. 'No, I guess not,' he admitted at last. 'But it would have been nice for her to have known the truth.'

'I suppose so,' Mr Greewoof replied. 'But again, we were con-cerned for her safety. Afraid it would get out that she was Byron's daughter and that the Nosmorums would find her and try to take her away.'

'So, how does Veronica fit in with all this?' William asked. 'Ignatius Nosmorum called her his cousin. Is she?'

'Yes. But no one was aware of that – not even Byron. Harry Smith did some digging once we knew what to look for, and it appears Veronica's mother was a Nosmorum.'

'Blimey.'

Abelard Greewoof laughed – for the first time in days, William realised.

'Indeed, young Kingfisher.'

II

The Avenfore William returned to seemed like a different place to the Avenfore he had left. Amaranta had not yet returned to Ravenwood Castle and there were rumours – which made William's heart sink – that she wouldn't be returning at all.

Veronica Aguevals had vanished without trace. About three days after William had returned from London, the Aguevals triplets left for the States for what little remained of the school holidays, although Jack assured a miserable Bridget that they would be back as boarders at St Elm's when the new term started at the end of the month. In the meantime, he promised to write to her every day, which cheered Bridget up immensely.

William also had to square things with Elsie, who, true to her word, had insisted that he tell her what was really going on with the birdwatching club. In desperation, William turned to Mr Greewoof, and had to stifle a smile as he listened to the Latin master explain to his clever cousin that the birdwatching society had been founded to keep watch on certain types of rare birds which caused damage to other nesting birds; that membership was limited and the list was full, but that, as Elsie had now shown an interest in the society, he would keep her in mind the next time a membership place came available. And the exhibition had been cancelled last-minute. William had no idea if Elsie truly believed everything Abelard Greewoof told her, but she seemed happy enough with the idea that she was on a membership waiting list and stopped asking awkward questions. Although she still stared at William curiously every time the Night Bird Society was mentioned.

The call William had been waiting for came less than one week before school term began at St Elm's. An invitation from Byron Mullween for William to go to Ravenwood Castle.

Byron was waiting in the grand hallway in front of his grandfather's portrait when William arrived. He looked tired and was less flamboyantly dressed than usual, but he seemed younger and happier somehow. He smiled at William.

'Good of you to come, Mr Howbbler,' he said. 'Aramanta is upstairs in the music room. I shall leave you to talk alone.'

'Thank you, Mr Mullween.'

Byron Mullween's face was solemn.

'No, thank you, William,' he said. 'For everything.'

A haunting, plaintive melody floated across the music room as William entered it. Amaranta was at the piano, her fingers moving lightly over the keyboard as she played.

'That's beautiful,' William said. 'What is it?'

Amaranta flushed slightly. 'Thomas Tallis. "If ye love me."'

'Oh.' William was blushing too.

'So, how are you?' he asked after a short silence.

'I'm okay, I guess,' she said, but her tone was sad.

'Only okay?'

She nodded. There was another silence and, not knowing what else to do, William waited for Amaranta to continue. But she didn't.

'So how are your ... parents?' he said at last. 'Are they all right?'

Her face clouded over. She was close to tears.

'Yes. They're sad, of course, but they know I love them and they'll always be my parents. Byron – I still can't call him 'dad'. Amaranta's face was a picture of hurt and confusion. 'Sam Bonclane is my real dad. He and Mum have been there for me for the past fifteen years. And my sister … I can't just throw that all away all of a sudden, can I?' Her voice caught. 'It's just so confusing. You think you know who you are then, suddenly, out of nowhere, you turn out to be somebody completely different.'

All William wanted to do was to hug her. To make her pain go away. But something rooted him to the spot.

Her green eyes were fixed on him now. 'The thing is, Will, what if you don't want to be that new person? Or you don't like who that new person is? Or who they might be? Or what they might be part of?'

William walked to the piano and sat down beside Amaranta on the long piano stool. He took her hand gently in his own as he spoke.

'Who you are doesn't have to change,' he said, 'you can be who you want to be. And, if you don't mind me saying so, I think you've been doing a pretty excellent job so far. Somehow, I don't think that's going to change, no matter who your parents are.' He smiled at her.

Amaranta returned his smile. 'Thank you, William the Kingfisher,' she whispered. Then the intense gaze was back. 'Promise me, something,' she said.

'I promise.'

She laughed. 'You don't know what it is yet.'

'I still promise.'

'Really?'

'So, what is it?'

'No secrets,' she said at last. 'Promise me there'll be no secrets between us, Will. Only the truth.'

'I promise,' he said.

Then Amaranta, leaning forward, kissed him softly on the cheek, enveloping him in an exotic scent he couldn't place. No Veronica. No Wicked Crow. Just pure Amaranta.

William gulped.

III

He was still reeling when he arrived back in Fern Lane that evening. Amaranta's words – her kiss – had thrown him into turmoil. He had already broken his promise to her before he even made it. Because he did have a secret – not just from Amaranta, but from everyone.

He pulled out his copy of the *Chronicle of the Noble Order of the Alliance* from the bookshelf in his bedroom and unwrapped the something in a handkerchief hidden behind it. There, staring up at him, with its grey swirl through black stone, was Ignatius Nosmorum's ring. He had never intended keeping the ring. He was sure of that. Yet, here it was. And what lay instead at the bottom of the river Thames with the Wicked Crow was the small black piece of masonry he had picked up outside the Temple Church.

William moved to the window and stared down at the river Inni glinting through the dark trees in the half-moonlight below. Amaranta was right. There should be no secrets between them. He had promised her. But he had also seen the danger she had been in twice from the Wicked Crow and his cronies. Mr Greewoof's voice played in his head: '*Despite our best intentions, Kingfisher, life does not always go to plan.*' Yes, he knew he should tell someone about it, but he was the only one who even knew it existed. Surely, it would be safer, if only he knew about it? By the time the moon had disappeared behind a dark cloud, William had made up his mind. He would say nothing. Next chance he got, he would hide the ring, where no one would find it.

CHAPTER 34

The Vigilant Monks

I

TWO DAYS LATER WILLIAM FOUND HIMSELF at an impromptu meeting of the Night Bird Society in the club room above The Falcon's Nest bookshop with Chris and Amaranta. It was the first opportunity they had to talk about the adventures of the past weeks and to fill Amaranta in on how William had discovered Veronica Aguevals was the Wicked Crow's spy in Avenfore.

'I would never have believed it,' Chris said. 'I mean, I didn't like the woman, but even still … Who'd've guessed she was the Wicked Crow's cousin? Oh, sorry, Manta, I didn't mean …'

'I expect I'll have to get used to it,' Amaranta said glumly. 'And about Byron too.'

'He does seem keen to make it up to you,' William said.

Amaranta sighed. 'I know. It's a bit tiring, to be honest. Last night I got so frustrated I told him if he really wanted to impress me then he should stop shirking his responsibility and re-join the Order.'

'What did he say?'

'He said he wasn't sure if they'd have him back. I told him of course they would and to get Mr Greewoof to sort out any problems.'

William laughed at the thought of Byron being bossed about by his fourteen-year-old daughter. Although, he reckoned, after all that had happened, Byron wouldn't have it any other way.

'There is something odd, though,' Amaranta continued.

'About Bryon?' Chris asked.

Amaranta shook her head. 'No. About Veronica being the spy. Or should I say, there only being one spy in Avenfore.'

'What makes you think that?' William asked.

Amaranta shrugged. 'Nothing in particular, it's just intuition. So, do you think it's gone forever, then?'

'What is gone forever?' Chris asked.

'The Book of the Knights Templar Errant.'

'No.'

Chris and Amaranta looked at William in surprise.

'You seem very sure, Will,' Chris said.

'I have this feeling that there's something missing and, if we could just see it, we'd be able to figure out Mr Seblean's riddle and where the Book is.'

'Mr Seblean's riddle?'

'Er, yes, Mr O'Neill showed it to me last time I was here,' William explained.

'What did it say?'

'Something about some vigilant monks,' William said. 'I can't remember it off-hand.'

'We should ask Mr O'Neill to show it to us. Perhaps we can figure it out together?' Amaranta said.

'I doubt it,' Chris replied. 'If Mr Greewoof and Will's dad couldn't solve it—'

'There's no harm in us trying.' Amaranta was already half-way to the top of the stairs. 'I'll ask Mr O'Neill.'

A few minutes later, all three were staring at Aaron Seblean's last note.

from the gates of hell to where the echoes of heaven can be heard when the vigilant monks are blinded.

'This paper looks familiar,' Amaranta said.

William nodded. 'I thought that too, but I can't figure out where I've seen it before.'

'I can,' Chris said. 'It's the part of the flyleaf from a prayer book – like the ones you get in church.'

'Of course!' Amaranta said excitedly. 'So maybe the Book's hidden in a church?'

'Maybe.' Chris replied. 'But which church? There are two in Drunfarnam.'

William thought for a moment. 'What about the monks – is that a better clue?'

'Avenfore church has monks – on both sides of the organ, I saw them when Byron organized for me to practice there one day,' Amaranta said.

'But Aaron Seblean disappeared in Drunfarnam,' Chris said. 'His jacket was found floating in the Inni near Drunfarnam, so there's no reason to believe he was anywhere near Avenfore on the night he disappeared.'

'But maybe that's it!' Amaranta exclaimed, her eyes shining with excitement. 'Will, you've just said that there might be something we're missing. What if what we're missing is that Mr Seblean *didn't* hide the Book in Drunfarnam?'

'Manta's right.' William said. Every part of his being telling him that they were on to something very important. 'Everyone always assumes Mr Seblean disappeared while he was trying to make his way *out* of Drunfarnam with the Book. But what if he had already left, having hidden the book in Avenfore and was on his way back *to* Drunfarnam when the Wicked Crow found him?'

Chris gasped. 'That would mean the Book has been somewhere in Avenfore all along, but nobody thought to look for it there. But where?'

'Avenfore church!' Amaranta cried.

'You think it's that simple?' Chris looked dubious.

'Mr Seblean loved riddles and clues,' William explained. 'Even if the Book itself is not there, I'm sure there will be some clue that will tell us where to look for it.'

Amaranta jumped to her feet. 'So, what are we waiting for?'

II

The sacristan, Frederick Boarnys, let them into the church and unlocked the door to the choir loft.

'What's so special about the monks?' he wanted to know.

'I thought they were birds,' Chris murmured, glancing up at the monks high on their pedestals above them.

'So did I,' said William. 'I only realised they were monks the last time I was here.'

'Of course, they're monks,' Mr Boarnys said. 'Bound to be, aren't they? Now be careful up there,' he warned. 'I don't want any accidents.

'We'll be careful, Mr Boarnys,' Amaranta promised.

'Right, so,' the sacristan replied. 'I'll leave you to it. Let me know when you're finished.' Then he wandered off chuckling to himself as the three friends climbed the steep stairs to the choir loft.

'We should check for hidden panels in the organ casing.' Chris said.

They spent the next fifteen minutes searching the loft, but found nothing.

'I still think there's a clue here that we're missing,' William insisted. 'Maybe we should look more closely at the monks themselves, seeing as they are mentioned in Mr Seblean's riddle.'

William, who was staring up at the monks, said at last. 'Both are facing in the same direction that could mean something.'

'Where are they looking?' Amaranta asked excitedly.

Chris stood on tiptoes so he could examine the figures more closely. 'You're right, Will, they're looking to the left-hand side of the altar.'

'But where exactly do you think they are looking?' Amaranta asked.

'Over there,' Chris replied. 'To the urn with the relic of Saint Elm next to the altar.'

'It has to be a clue.' Amaranta said eagerly.

William walked back to the edge of the wooden balcony to get a better look of the altar. 'You're right Chris.'

'Oh my goodness,' Chis cried out loud. 'The Book – It's in our school!'

There was a brief silence before Amaranta spoke looking below. 'I don't think so, Chris. I think the Book is here, in this church…. right there.' Amaranta pointed to St Elm's urn.

'I think Amaranta is right.' said William. 'I reckon Mr Seblean came to Avenfore by boat, passing the fairground—'

'Gallery Avernus!'

'The gates of hell!' Chris and Amaranta spoke at the same time.

'Exactly,' William replied. 'The organ is the sound of heaven and the doors of the keyboard partially cover the monks sight once opened'.

'The vigilant monks are blinded!' Chris and Amaranta said enthusiastically.

As fast as they could, the three friends went down the steep stairs bumping into each other. When they reached the bottom, they stood looking at the urn for a few intense seconds.

William's heart gave a leap as Madame Ophelia's words echoed through his mind. *Thrice covered!*

William finally spoke. 'The Book must be inside the pedestal. Come on! Let's move it together.'

With great care, they inched the urn to one side. It moved easily despite its weight, but they were wary of moving it too far for fear of it tipping over.

'Gently, now.' Chris said.

There was a gap of about three inches. Large enough to shelter a book.

None of them dared to utter a sound, they just stared at the small dark opening. The three leaned over to look inside. Amaranta gasped and a soft 'Oh, my …' escaped from Chris as he kneeled down to peer into the narrow opening.

'There is something here,' he whispered.

Amaranta and William exchanged glances, but otherwise kept still as statues. Chris, holding his breath and careful not to push over the urn, reached inside the pedestal. William could hear his heart thumping fervently. Chris finally pulled out a rectangular parcel wrapped in cloth and tied with string. He looked up at the others and William just nodded unable to speak.

'Y-y-you do it.' Chris stammered nervously standing up and handing the parcel to William.

But before William untied the string and pulled back the protective waxed cloth, he already knew what they had discovered, what he was holding in his own two hands. A treasure missing from the Order for almost five centuries. The Order's most secret and valuable possession: the lost *Book of the Knights Templar Errant*.

CHAPTER 35

Endings and Beginnings

I

TOMORROW, THE LAST DAY OF AUGUST, William would start his first term at St Elm's. But before that he had something even more special to look forward to – a celebration banquet to be held at Ravenwood Castle that evening in honour of the recovery of the *Book of the Knights Templar Errant*.

News of the Book's discovery had spread quickly. Many of the Brothers had been too shocked to believe it was true at first. William thought back to four days earlier, when he Amaranta and Chris had rushed into Abelard Greewoof's house carrying their special treasure. The look on Mr Greewoof's face had turned from disbelief to astonishment and joy as he carefully leafed through the many pages filled with strange symbols and glyphs exactly like the cipher code parchment he had shown William all those weeks ago. One thing was clear: whatever secrets the Book held, they would take years to decipher.

But there was also a look of deep sadness in the Latin master's eyes as he closed the Book. 'Thank you, Aaron,' he murmured, 'we are in your debt.' Then he turned to William, Amaranta and Chris. 'And thank you to you three wonderful young people also,' he said, emotion choking his voice. 'The Order will be eternally grateful to you for what you have done.'

An Extraordinary General Meeting of the Night Bird Society was convened at Ravenwood Castle for that Sunday. Members travelled from all over Europe to be there.

'We've just discovered a rare species of bird; one we thought went extinct centuries ago,' was Arnold Howbbler's excuse to his sister and her family for his sudden presence in Avenfore. 'It's all very exciting, as you can imagine. And what's better' – he put his arm on William's shoulder proudly – 'Will here was one of the people to find it for us!' Aunt Edna applauded and even Uncle Walter looked impressed.

'I've no idea what you are really up to, Will Howbbler,' Elsie whispered as she hugged him, 'but whatever it is, congratulations! Your dad seems really proud.'

'Thanks, Els,' William replied. It was his one regret – that he couldn't tell his cousin the full truth.

And it wasn't just Arnold Howbbler who was proud. As William, Amaranta and Chris entered the banqueting hall at Ravenwood Castle that evening, a loud burst of applause and cries of 'Bravo' and 'well done!' rang out from all the Brothers in the room, including Byron Mullween, who had finally taken his place again at the Order's table.

As they sat for dinner, Abelard Greewoof tapped his glass for silence.

'Brothers and Sisters, we are here tonight to celebrate the return of the Order's most secret and beloved treasures – the *Book of Knights Templar Errant*. We are also here to give witness to and to show our gratitude to one of our Brothers who gave up everything to ensure that this treasure was returned to us. As a mark of respect and a tribute to the sacrifice made by Aaron Seblean to ensure that the Order's most precious treasure remained safe and out of the hands of the wicked man who sought to keep it for himself and use its secrets for evil purposes, we will tonight bury his jacket and the note we found in it on the Isle of Lesciern.'

At this there was another round of loud applause and more shouts of 'Bravo!'

'Ladies and gentleman, please raise your glasses,' Abelard Greewoof declared, 'in toast to our dearly departed Brother, Aaron Seblean, without whom this night would not have been possible.'

The company rose as one. 'Aaron Seblean!'

'And to our three intrepid Knights Postulants,' Mr Greewoof continued, 'who finally managed to figure out what poor Aaron was trying to tell us all along.'

'To our Knights Postulant!' rang out the cry around the table.

In the general melee after dinner, William made his way over to the package containing Aaron's jacket, which was now to be buried on Lesciern, and slipped his fingers into his trousers pocket. There, lurking darkly in a corner was the Wicked Crow's ring. His father had told him about the package and he had decided that it would make a fitting hiding place. Making sure no one was watching, he quickly stuffed it under the cloth covering the parcel, pushing it in so it wouldn't bulge or be noticed.

Then he walked away, happy that the cursed ring would soon be out of the way for good.

II

Autumn was already showing her true colours and dusk turned to darkness much earlier than the night in July when William and the others had last sailed across Dronfore Lake. There was no moon out this night and, as they crossed the lake, only the twinkling stars above and the sparks from the burning fire pit, leaping high into the sky over the island guided the boats as they glided over the water in darkness.

At the standing stone circle, there was a short ceremony as Abelard Greewoof, helped by Arnold Howbbler and Edmund Durffan, buried the package with Aaron Seblean's belongings. Then, the Brothers chanted the ancient oath:

'The flame that our ancestors ignited one day is the same one that we will ignite today. May this fire serve to remember and keep alive that which united them in the hope that our children and the children of our children will continue to serve this noble cause. So that good may never bow to evil, we ask God to give us strength to fight it.'

Harry Smith stepped forward carrying three long swords.

'Brothers and Sister' – he smiled over at Amaranta who grinned back at him – 'we have paid tribute to our fallen Brother, but it is now time to celebrate the living. This night has also been occasioned by three of our youngest members – our three Knights Postulant – who despite their youth have shown courage, resilience and wisdom beyond their years.'

A low murmur of agreement passed among the circle of Squires and Knights and, in the flickering light of the flames from the fire pit, William could see his father beaming at him proudly. Mr Greewoof and Byron Mullween were smiling too and even Ernest Wiglann nodded solemnly at him.

'We have honoured the past,' Chiffchaff continued, 'now it is time to honour the future. Christopher Durffan, Amaranta Mullween Bonclanc and William Howbbler, please step forward.'

Amaranta slipped her hand into William's and squeezed it. As they stepped forward together, William's heart throbbed with pride and happiness.

'Please kneel,' Harry Smith instructed.

All three knelt as bidden, and William wondered what on earth was going on.

'In recognition of your great contribution to the Order and your part in restoring the *Book of the Knights Templar Errant*, the brethren have unanimously elected that you should, all three, on this night be raised to full Knights of the Order of the Alliance – an honour never before bestowed on Knights Postulant of your age.'

William heard Chris gasp and Amaranta put her hands over her mouth as if to hold in her surprise. He himself felt dizzy with astonishment, hardly able to believe that this was happening.

But it was. As Harry Smith came towards him, William saw Brady Grayling break the circle to stand beside him, holding his lighted torch high over William's head.

Harry Smith was now in front of him and taking one of the swords, he lightly tapped William with it on each shoulder.

'Arise, Kingfisher, Knight of the Order of the Alliance.' As William stood up, Harry whispered to him. 'Hold the sword aloft, Will, when I give it to you.'

Then he cried out '*Aeterna vita iustis!*' and handed the sword to William, blade facing downwards.

Flames from the fire behind him leaped into the starlit sky as William held the sword aloft, and shouted, 'Eternal life to the just!'

In the firelight, he saw the smiling faces all around him and thought back over the past few months. All the scares and excitement, but also all the happy memories. It wasn't just that he was starting a new school tomorrow or the promise of seeing his mother and sister at Christmas. Or his friendship with Amaranta, Elsie and the others. Deep down inside him, he knew that his life had now changed forever. He had changed. He was now William the Kingfisher, with a whole new life ahead of him. A life he was very much looking forward to living.

ACKNOWLEDGMENT

A deep debt of gratitude to all those who have believed in me and supported me from the beginning. They have been an essential factor in the writing of this book. Special thanks are due to my wife Gerardine, and my daughter Clarissa, who have assisted me in editing the book. And to all my friends  *in Ireland who have helped me understand the wonderful folklore, history and traditions, they are very dear to me.*